The Battle for Gullywith

The Battle for Gullywith

SUSAN HILL

BLOOMSBURY

Bloomsbury Publishing, London, Berlin and New York

First published in Great Britain in 2008 by Bloomsbury Publishing Plc
36 Soho Square, London, W1D 3QY

This paperback edition published in 2009

A CIP catalogue record of this book is available from the British Library

ISBN 978 0 7475 9477 2

The paper this book is printed on is certified independently in accordance
with the rules of the FSC. It is ancient-forest friendly.
The printer holds chain of custody.

FSC
Mixed Sources
Product group from well-managed
forests and other controlled sources
Cert no. SGS - COC - 2061
www.fsc.org
© 1996 Forest Stewardship Council

Typeset by Dorchester Typesetting Group Ltd
Printed in Great Britain by Clays Ltd, St Ives Plc

1 3 5 7 9 10 8 6 4 2

www.bloomsbury.com
www.gullywith.com

For

Ethan Haruki and Martha Eleni Pack

CHAPTER ONE

Goodbye, Wigwell Avenue

Number 58 Wigwell Avenue was disappearing. Olly Brown looked out of the back window of the car as they moved away from it, further and further, until they were almost at the end where Wigwell Avenue joined North London Road.

Now he couldn't see the front door of their house. Now he couldn't see the gate. Now he couldn't see the roof. Now . . .

'That's it,' Pete Brown said. 'Goodbye, 58 Wigwell Avenue, and goodbye, London.'

'Yaay.' Helen Brown raised her arm.

'Bye-bye, bye-bye.'

Olly's baby sister, Lula, waved at the windows.

Olly went on looking as they left everything behind. Now the supermarket. Now the newsagent. Now the bus shelter. Now the library. Now the gates of the MLP, short for Muddy Little Park.

The car picked up speed and Olly turned round before he started to feel sick. But he kept his eyes closed and behind his eyes he saw Number 58 Wigwell Avenue, the house he had lived in for his whole life. It looked the same in the picture behind his eyes. But it wasn't. It would never be the same again. Their furniture had gone. Lula's finger paintings had been taken down from the kitchen walls, leaving tiny bits of Blu-Tack, and some fluff from what had been the space under his bed had rolled up against the skirting board. The old rabbit hutch and Lula's broken buggy were on the skip outside.

Number 58 Wigwell Avenue was empty. When Dad had banged the door shut for the last time, it had sounded weird and hollow.

Empty. It would be empty until the Reillys arrived.

'Bye-bye.' Lula was leaning over to poke Olly in the ear. 'Bye-bye.'

He couldn't go on pretending to be asleep for much longer but he knew that when he did open his eyes, something would have happened – something would have gone click and that would be that. Number 58 Wigwell Avenue would no longer be part of his life or of him, not even as a picture behind his eyes.

He opened them.

In the empty house called Gullywith, three hundred and nine miles away, things were the same as they had been for a very long time, except that a small window in the attic which had been slightly ajar was now closed, the door on the barn which had always swung open was now shut and padlocked, the old water trough which had been full of black rainwater topped with green slime was now empty, and a tap on the wall which had dripped since anyone could have remembered, if there had been anyone, did not drip any more.

Little things like that.

There was something else, too, something you could not quite put your finger on. The house seemed to be listening, and watching out and waiting. The empty kitchen waited. The staircase waited. The grey slates on the roof waited. And every so often the house made a slight sound, like the sound of a person who has been deeply asleep and is beginning to stir.

It was a grey, dull, still sort of day but, from time to time, a small, warning wind came from nowhere to blow through the rooms, in and out of each one by turns.

Then, a small stone scratched with peculiar marks appeared on the attic landing. It was still for a moment, and then it began to roll towards the staircase, and then to drop down, step by step, making a series of hard, purposeful, little sounds which echoed through the house. When it reached the first landing, it rolled again and descended the second staircase, the one with the treads that tipped to the left, and so on until it dropped down the last step on to the floor of the dark hall. The flags were uneven and broken in a couple of places, with deep cracks, but the stone rolled on across them as if it were rolling over silky smooth marble, until it reached the kitchen door, which was closed.

Almost all the doors in Gullywith had spaces beneath them to let the draughts in, but the kitchen door was pressed tight to the ground, too tight for water or a draught to get underneath.

The stone lay flat and still. It seemed to be gathering itself.

CHAPTER TWO

A Small Round Stone

Olly didn't know what he thought about Gullywith because he hadn't actually seen it. Mum and Dad had seen it, twice, and Lula had seen it because she couldn't be left behind, but when they had travelled up, first to view the farm and then to attend the auction, it had been term time and Olly had gone to stay with Jamie Coombes on the other side of Wigwell Avenue, at Number 115. He sometimes did. He liked it, and the fact that his parents had gone three hundred miles, first to look at a house and later to bid for it at an auction, had not made a very strong impact on his mind. If he thought about it at all, it was to assume firstly that it was just another of his mum's mad ideas, secondly that they wouldn't like the place and, when it seemed that they did, that they wouldn't succeed in buying it.

When they came back the first time, they had brought a DVD which the agents had made. 'For serious prospective purchasers,' Mum said. Olly had turned the thin plastic box over in his hand. Coopers, Arch and Dunne, Estate Agents.

Gullywith Farm was written on the label in green ink.

'Want me to put it on?'

'Can I look at it later?'

'Why don't you want to look at it now?'

Olly had not been able to say why he didn't, but he didn't. He needed a particular time to look at it and when that came he would know.

It came in the middle of the night.

Number 58 Wigwell Avenue was quiet and still, and the minute Olly woke he knew that it was because the right moment had come. He slid out of bed and crept very carefully down the stairs. He didn't need to put on any lights until he had got into the den, where the television was, and closed the door.

The quality of the DVD was not very good and it only lasted for eight minutes but it was enough. He saw everything. The lane leading down. The broken gate. The muddy track. The yard. The derelict cowsheds. The barn with the door swinging open. The empty chicken run.

In the background you could just make out the face of a steep hill.

The house had a wavy roof and looked as if it might collapse in on itself any minute. When the camera went inside, it was difficult to make out much. It was dim and spidery and empty and the stairs tipped to the left. The windows were scummed over with greenish dirt.

Olly watched the DVD twice right through and when he had finished and turned off the television, he sat thinking for a long time. He was pretty sure they would never actually move to Gullywith, just as they had never moved to Brighton or Norwich or the small and remote Scottish island . . .

He knew what he would feel about leaving Number 58 Wigwell Avenue if they ever did. This was home, it had always been home, everything he knew was here, he never wanted to leave it and if he had to he would miss it. He would not cry or throw a tantrum but he would feel lost inside, as if a bit of him had been cut out.

But what he would feel about another place, wherever it was, he had no idea and he didn't try to guess or imagine it. It wasn't going to happen anyway.

He put the DVD back into its sleeve, left it on the top of the television where he had found it and went quietly out into the hall, but as he did so he felt a sharp pain in the sole of his foot, which made him let out a yelp. Olly froze. The yell sounded blood-curdling through the whole house but, to his surprise, no one seemed to have heard it. The doors stayed closed and the lights stayed off. Olly hopped about, holding his foot. Then he bent down to see what he had dug into it.

On the hall floor was a small round stone. Olly picked it up. He did not notice the odd marks scratched on its surface. He went very cautiously back up the stairs to his bedroom, where he put the stone down on the table beside his bed and forgot all about it.

CHAPTER THREE

Safely into the Rucksack

The journey from London was long and boring and Olly had an odd sad feeling inside him, as if something heavy had settled on his heart. He decided that the best way of forgetting about 58 Wigwell Avenue, and everything he was leaving behind in London, was to make his thoughts dark as night every time they seemed to be going anywhere near those things. It was a good trick and after a while he could do it pretty well. He let his thoughts go to other places, like the beach in Dorset where they had been on holiday and found fossils or the gleaming white rink where they had seen *Aladdin on Ice*. For the rest of the time, he listened to a story-tape and played a bit with Lula. They stopped twice to eat and so that Dad could stretch his legs, and shortly after the second stop, Mum said, 'Look . . . can you see how the countryside has changed? Lots of hills and sheep and streams. Isn't it great?'

Olly looked out of the window. They had come off the motorway and he could see sloping green fields leading to steep, sharp-looking hills and, criss-crossing the fields, ribbons of uneven grey fences.

'The sheep could jump those.'

'Sheep don't jump,' said Dad.

'Yes they do! Haven't you ever seen them leaping about in the spring?'

'That's lambs, not sheep.'

'Anyway, they could jump those fences.'

'Walls. They're not fences. They're part of the land-scape here . . . dry stone walls. Why do you think they're called that, Olly?'

'Because they're not wet, I suppose.'

'No, because they lay the stones on top of each other very carefully without using any mortar to cement them together. The walls stay up because of the way they balance the stones.'

'Oh.'

'Dry stone walling is . . .' Dad's voice went on and on in the way it did when he started about something he thought Olly ought to find really, really interesting, but Olly had stopped listening. It wasn't that he found what Dad was saying boring, or not very boring. It was some-thing else. He had a strange sensation in his leg, under the pocket of his jeans, as if something were stinging him or burning. He wriggled about in his seat belt and got his hand in. Whatever it was stung his finger.

'I think there's a wasp in my pocket.'

'There can't be.'

'Don't be silly, Pete, of course there could be, wasps get into all sorts of places. Don't you remember the time Grandma had one inside the rim of her gardening hat? You'll have to stop. Poor Olly.'

Dad stopped a little way along the road and pulled up on to the wide grass verge.

The sheep were quite close and staring at them. 'Moo moo,' Lula said.

'Come on, let's see, turn out your pocket carefully. No, wait – I'll do it.'

'It's OK.' Olly didn't care for the thought of Mum digging in the pockets of his jeans by the side of a road. Anyone might go by and the anyone might think he had needed to wee and had to have his mum to help.

He put his hand in and probed about. Wasps were small and soft and furry but what his fingers touched was small and hard and smooth.

Olly took a stone out of his pocket.

'Not a wasp.'

'Oh, thank goodness for that – just a pebble digging into you. Come on, get back in the car, we've still got about sixty miles or so to go.'

Dad started the engine. Mum handed Lula a new book she had in the bag of playthings that came out one by one on a journey.

'Moo, moo,' Lula said, waving the book at the sheep.

Olly looked down at the stone in the palm of his hand. It had small, strange scratches on its surface but it was perfectly round and smooth and he couldn't see how it had made his leg sting and burn at all. But, to be on the safe side, he pulled his rucksack over, unbuckled the front pocket, and dropped the stone inside. That way, it couldn't hurt anyone.

CHAPTER FOUR

Rattling Noises

The stone stayed quietly in Olly's bag all night on the chair beside his bed at the Happy Traveller Inn, where they were staying that night because nothing would be ready at Gullywith. Olly lay looking at the moon through the thin curtains and listening to the hum from the pipes and boilers running up to the eleventh floor, where the room was. He felt as if he was nowhere, like a person dangling in space and out of touch with real time. Real time was either back in London and Number 58 Wigwell Avenue, or it was tomorrow and arriving for the first time at Gullywith, but it was not here in the Happy Traveller Inn. Here, time was a little separate bubble in which Olly had explored all the cupboards and drawers in his room, the lifts, the stairs, the front lobby, the lounge, the games room, the dining room and the doorway to the bar, had taken Lula for walks up and down the carpeted corridors and round and round the reception area, put a small spoonful of almost everything except beetroot from the salad bar on to his plate, eaten the whole of a lasagne and carrots, half a bowl of fruit salad and a quarter of an ice cream, drunk one whole glass of fizzy apple juice and played with the shower in Mum and Dad's bathroom until the head came off and he got into trouble.

The hotel was full of other people, none of whom he had ever seen before or would probably ever see again so that they were all in this out-of-real-life-and-time bubble together. Now, he watched the silvery beam of moon-light climb the curtain and let the bubble rock gently, with his bed rocking inside it.

He was not thinking about anything. It was safer that way. He felt happy in the bubble.

But just as the rocking was making him slide sideways down into a dream, he heard it. It was an odd sound, like the thin, high whirring whine of a tiny electric saw or an angry insect. Olly switched on the lamp. The noise stopped.

He lay down again and waited. Nothing happened. Then the hotel pipes made a loud watery noise. That was what it must have been, something in the plumbing. He put the lamp out and tried to think himself back into the bubble but, just when he was climbing inside and the rocking had begun very gently, there it was again, a mean, angry, hissing, whining sort of sound. This time, Olly didn't move. He waited. The moon had gone in now but his room was not quite dark because the light from the corridor shone under the door. The sound went on.

It was coming from somewhere on the other side of the room.

Olly wasn't scared. He was interested. But he was also

quite tired and the bubble had begun to rock again and after a few moments the sound and the rocking blended together and he felt himself falling down and down into a soft, warm, dark, velvety sleep.

But the sleep did not stay warm and velvety for long. It became a different, more uncomfortable and disturbing sleep, a sleep in which Olly was trying to walk along a path that at first was just hard and a bit uneven, but then became stony and after a time thick with shingle, pebbles in layers into which his legs sank with a crunching sound. It was very hard to walk. He had to pull his legs out one at a time with a great effort and the stones bruised his shins and dug into the soles of his feet. He could hear something through his sleep too, a sound like the thin, high, whirring whining but much louder, as if the sea were crashing on to the shingle, and then as if the shingle were being thrown against something hard and quite nearby.

Olly came awake with a bump. The windows of his room were rattling and something was hitting the glass hard, as if it were raining not rainwater but thousands of tiny mean little stones.

Olly pulled the covers up over his ears and closed his eyes hard. But the noise went on and it was a very long time before he got to sleep again.

CHAPTER FIVE

The Coldest House in the World

Olly sat on a low wall as far away from the house as he dared get. He hoped he was also out of sight, of the house, and of Mum and Dad in that order. It was just after eleven o'clock in the morning. When they had arrived, he had gone cautiously inside, taken one quick look into every room and then fled and now, beside a bent metal gate and an odd, small, narrow building with nettles growing out of it, he thought that if he never had to go back he would be happy.

A narrow track led from the broken gate across an open field. Beyond that rose a hill and the track seemed to climb up it, meandering between sheep to the summit and then disappearing over the top. Behind the hill the sky was ink-dark.

Gullywith Farmhouse smelled. Oliver could smell it still, even out here where the smell should have been of green grass and open air. And nettles. The smell was very old, very musty, very cold. Yes, Olly thought. Most of all, it was a cold smell, as if no warmth had been allowed to creep in and take its place for hundreds of years, as if there had never been a crackling fire or a roaring range or hot radiators, never been sunshine pouring in through the windows and warming the walls, never been a patch of it for a cat to lie in or doing its job of cooking the food and airing the clothes. It was the last week in July out here, not boiling hot, not swimming-in-the-sea weather, but quite warm enough for Olly to be comfortable in a T-shirt and shorts, but inside Gullywith he had shivered. In the rooms, it was deepest winter, dark winter where the sun never rose, not December winter, not Christmas winter.

He wriggled on the stone wall. Something unpleasant had happened. The cold from the house seemed to have got inside him. A small hard dark lump of it was there, trying to spread and radiate outwards not only through the rest of his body but through his mind and into his heart. It was a dreadful sensation and frightening. Olly jumped down quickly from the wall and began to run down the narrow track across the field, as if he could somehow shed the feeling like a snake could shed its skin. He ran towards the sunlight, which was chasing shadows down the hill one after another.

'Go where you like so long as it's not near water and you can see the house if you look back,' Dad had said. He had gone, not only to escape from the cold, empty rooms but in case Mum asked him to look after Lula. He loved Lula but there were times when he needed just himself.

The hill was much further away than it looked and the closer Olly got to it, the further away it seemed to recede. He stopped. The sun was still chasing the shadows. He could hear the sheep making their hollow, sad, plaintive sound.

The field was wide. The hedges were far away on either side.

This was not a good place.

And then he saw something. He looked hard. No. There was nothing. Just the sheep and the sun chasing the shadows.

Yes. There it was again. Something was moving, a small speck, moving down the hill. After a moment, it seemed to separate into two. Two small specks. Olly watched. When the shadows raced over, the specks disappeared into them but when the sun followed they reappeared.

Olly waited. After a moment, he sat down. The small specks became blobs as they grew steadily nearer, coming down the pale, narrow ribbon of track towards him, on and on. One moved steadily, but the other moved faster and now and then it dodged about a little, darting forwards then back like a yo-yo on a string.

In a little while, Olly saw that it was a dog and that the other blob had become a figure.

He stood up. He thought he should turn and run back. The figure and the dog were strange and he was in a new and unfamiliar place. But to go back meant the house. Mum and Dad would be taking things out of boxes and shifting furniture about in cold dark rooms.

Quite suddenly, he seemed to leap backwards very far, back to Number 58 Wigwell Avenue, and as he did so, he felt a sharp pain shafting through his heart, a pain which almost made him cry out, the pain of having left everything he had always known, and everywhere he had always been safe and happy, far behind.

He would have cried out, tears would have prickled his eyes, if he had not felt something warm and cool at the same time, on the side of his leg.

A black and white dog was standing beside him, licking his calf gently. Olly looked down. The dog had treacle-brown eyes and its lick seemed to be healing up the pain in his heart and the hollow feeling and melting the coldness that had been clinging to him from the house.

'He's not done that before. You must be all right.'

The dog was the first blob and the second had come right up beside him.

'You've come to Gullywith,' the girl said.

CHAPTER SIX

'You've come from London,' the girl said.

'How did you know?'

'Everybody knows. You'd have to be from some-where like London to come and live at Gullywith.'

'Why?'

'Because.'

'Where have you come from, then?'

'Peagarth.'

'What's that?'

'Where I come from.'

She was an annoying sort of girl, Olly decided. She'd hitched herself up on to the wall as if it belonged to her, the dog had settled down at her feet and they had looked as if they meant to stay there. Olly kicked at the bottom of the wall.

'You don't want to do that,' the girl said.

He stopped, not because of what she said but because kicking the wall had made his toe hurt quite badly.

'Told you.' She patted the wall beside her. Olly jumped up and sat there. He hadn't meant to. He had meant to walk off, but he found himself doing what the girl told him all the same.

'If you know where I come from, I suppose you know my name and everything.'

'No.'

'Ha.'

'What is it, then?'

He thought of not telling her, of keeping it to himself because it was none of her business, or of making up a weird untrue name but he just said, 'Olly Brown. What's yours?'

'KK.'

He laughed.

'That's Jinx.'

'Jinx's a good name for a dog but KK isn't a proper name for a person.'

She shrugged.

'What's it stand for?'

'Just KK. I'll tell you something. Gullywith's the coldest house in the world.'

'Have you been inside it?'

'Not me. No one goes there.'

'Don't be daft.'

'You'll see.'

'Well, loads of people have been there now and we're living in it. It is cold though.'

'Said so.'

'Only because nobody's lived there for a bit and the heating and the fires aren't going. Dad'll do that, then it's going to be good.'

'The chimney'll smoke.'

'My dad can sort that as well. He's good at chimneys.
And things.'

'You could come to my house if you wanted.'

'I'd have to ask.'

'Ask, then.'

'Is it far off?'

'Up the track.'

Olly looked towards the hill. The ink-black clouds
behind it were swelling and spreading but the hill was
still sunlit, etched against the darkness. The track had
gone so pale it looked white.

'It's going to rain.'

'So what?'

'You come to my house while I ask, then we can go to
your house later if it isn't raining.'

'You want me to come to Gullywith?'

She didn't sound afraid, she sounded as if he had made
a not-funny joke, or suggested that she go to the moon.

'Why not?'

She sat silent for a moment. She had straight brown
hair cut short and her stubby hands splayed out on the
stone wall like starfish.

She sat for a long time without speaking and Olly
realised that she was trying to work something out in her
head. He waited. The dog lay still, quiet, but not asleep,
as if it would leap up and start to bark or run in a split
second if it needed to.

He looked at the hill. The sun had gone and it seemed
to be merging into the ink-black clouds so that hill and
sky were blotting together.

Then KK said, 'All right. I don't always do what people think I'll do and I don't always listen to what they say, whatever it is, so I will come with you.'

'What do you mean? What did people say? What did they tell you?'

But she shook her head and jumped down from the wall. The dog sprang up and they both began to run so fast that Olly could hardly catch up. They headed for the house, and behind them, the storm clouds began to run too, gathering and rolling forwards across the fields like a giant black ball.

Gullywith Farm lay ahead, tumbledown and empty-looking.

Thunder cracked behind them, making the ground quake, and lightning snapped at their heels as they ran. Olly was out of breath but KK and Jinx seemed to streak over the ground.

That falling-down, broken-backed, ancient-looking place couldn't be home, Olly thought, even if he could see their car outside. It looked uninviting, unhappy, a place without light or laughter, not a place waiting to welcome him back but a place telling him to turn round, to go, go, go. Not wanted, it said. He looked behind him quickly but the black storm was almost on top of him now. He could feel it clawing at him, trying to drag him into itself, rumbling and roaring and occasionally cracking like a vivid electric whip.

He felt trapped between Gullywith and the storm clouds, pressed helplessly so that he could hardly breathe.

'Come on,' he heard KK shout. 'Run, Olly, run.' She had almost reached the yard leading to Gullywith, Jinx very close at her heels.

'Run!'

There was one terrible, vivid flash that lit up the world with a greenish-white light and a crack of thunder louder than Olly had ever heard, which seemed to lift him off his feet.

He felt himself hurtle forwards, borne up on a rush of air beneath him and at the same time there was a great rumbling sound, as if a mountain of stones was on the move, rolling and tumbling from a great height, tipping out of the sky towards them.

Olly, KK and Jinx flung themselves forwards and went hurtling through the door into Gullywith Farm as the thunder and lightning and the mountain of stones came crashing down.

CHAPTER SEVEN

A Small Peculiar Room

'Shut the door, shut the door for goodness sake,' Mum shouted. Olly slammed it hard against the surge of wind and rain as the storm broke all round them.

They were standing in the hall of Gullywith. KK looked round her slowly and carefully.

'Come on.'

The kitchen was a mess of half-opened boxes and crates with Mum in the middle of them and Lula asleep in the old travel cot. But two rings on the small electric stove were working and the kettle was on. Dad was bent over looking inside the old range with his bottom in the air.

'You want that riddling and banging out,' KK said.

Dad turned round. 'I do?'

'I could have a look. Mind, it hasn't been lit for about a hundred years, it'll be cold and the flues'll be blocked up. It's easy.'

'It is?'

KK went up to the range. There was an ancient black iron poker on the hearth beside it. She picked it up and began to bang the range and the pipes behind it. There were bumps and crashes as lumps of ancient, clotted soot fell down. 'You don't want to vacuum that up. You'll only clog it up. You'll have to brush it out.'

'Right.'

'You have got a brush and shovel?'

'Er . . . have we?'

KK sighed. 'OK, looks like we'd better go over the hill to ours and fetch some.'

Helen and Pete Brown were looking at KK. Olly was looking at KK. Lula was still asleep. Outside, the storm roared and prowled, shaking angrily at the windows and door trying to get inside.

KK did not seem to be a girl of around Olly's age and size. She seemed to have grown and taken charge, to be bossy and knowing and competent, and they seemed to be letting her.

'Well, I'll drive you, of course,' Pete Brown said. 'To – where was it? Or we could go and buy a broom and a shovel from the shop.'

'What shop? No, we've got old ones. Only best wait till it brightens up a bit.'

KK went to the window and peered out. The sky was still ink-black and churning.

'Where did you say you lived?'

'Only over the hill.'

'Right.'

'Peagarth.'

The kettle whistled suddenly, there was a tremendous clap of thunder, and Lula woke up crying. Jinx, who had stayed behind in the hall, started barking.

'Lordy,' KK said. Olly followed her. Jinx was standing looking at the front door and barking loudly at the dark water which was slithering under the crack and running over the flags.

It didn't take very long to block up the space with old newspapers which KK found in the scullery and folded deftly into rolls and it didn't take long for the rolls to be soaked through, but by the time they were leaking a bit the rain had eased and the wind had given up and stopped throwing itself at the door. KK had found the teapot and mugs, sugar and milk and made everyone a drink and then lifted Lula out of the cot and started to play hide-and-seek with her round the edge of a packing case. Helen Brown looked at her with wonder.

'Do you have a big family at home?'

'Six and me. It's clearing up. We'll go and get that stuff when we've drunk our tea,' KK said to Olly. He felt like Mum looked – as if KK had taken them over and they could do nothing about it, and weren't sure they wanted to.

Lula was laughing behind the packing case.

'I don't even know your name,' Helen Brown said.

'KK.'

'KK what?'

'Just KK.'

She set down her tea mug and went to the door, then glanced back at them all.

'Welcome to Gullywith,' she said.

Olly followed her.

They went round the whole house, KK going

carefully, as if she might stumble and fall, or as if everything was liable to go suddenly black. She put her hand on the wall now and again, and sometimes she stopped dead and waited, sniffing the air slightly, or listening. Jinx followed very close to her heels and occasionally he growled low in his throat. From the kitchen they heard Lula shouting out, 'KK, KK, KK.'

At the top of the first landing, KK looked round. 'Feel that.'

At first, Olly did not know what she meant, but then he realised that although the whole house was cold, they were standing in one patch that was far, far colder than anywhere else, freezing cold. They went into an empty room which smelled of mould. Out again. Into another. The sun fell in a couple of diamonds on the floorboards and there was a faint smell of something light and flowery. KK smiled. 'Fine,' she said. 'That's OK.'

She opened a cupboard door. There were broken shelves and the plaster on the wall behind was crumbling away. The smell here was horrible, dank and mealy.

KK shook her head. 'I don't like it,' she said.

They went up the second narrow flight of stairs and along the attic corridor.

Jinx stopped. Then he began to back a little, whimpering. KK looked at him carefully. 'He knows.'

'What?'

KK shook her head. Here and there, the wallpaper was peeling off to show holes in the plaster behind. KK put out her hand and touched it. The cold came off the walls like an icy breath in their faces.

The last room was at the back and here the cold hung about in patches like freezing fog. A small pool of water lay on the floor. Olly looked up but there was no hole in the ceiling.

He went to the window and looked out, across the yard and the field with the pale track, towards the hill down which KK and Jinx had first come. The sheep were scattered like scraps of paper and the sky was brilliant blue.

'Let's go out.' He turned round. The little, dingy room with its cold patches and its mildew smell, and weird-looking fungus growing here and there out of the walls was unpleasant and he wanted to be in the air and sunlight. He tried not to think about having to sleep at Gullywith or to wonder if it would ever be warm and comfortable and filled with their furniture and their happiness like Number 58 Wigwell Avenue. He turned his mind sharp left away from Wigwell Avenue. Better not to go there again.

KK was crouching down in a corner of the room near the window.

'What?' Olly went over to her. 'What is it?'

KK held out her hand. In the middle of it was a small stone. She pointed. Close to the floor was a tiny hole in the skirting board, as if a mouse had gnawed its way through, and in the entrance to the hole were a couple more stones. She picked them up. Olly looked. The stones were very cold and had the same, faint, odd scratch marks on them, like letters of a strange language.

'These are the same,' he said. 'Just like the first one.

They're all the same.'

And he told KK about the stone at Wigwell Avenue, the stone that had stung him through his pocket.

'I don't like it,' KK said again, standing up straight and looking at the hole. 'I don't like it at all.'

'What are they for? What do they mean?'

She frowned. 'Nothing good,' she said at last. 'Which is only to be expected.'

'What do you mean?'

'Gullywith of course.'

From the kitchen they heard Lula crying loudly.

'What should we do?'

'We can't do anything on our own. We need advice and there's only one place to find it. Come on.'

'Where? I thought we were going to get the brush and shovel from your house, I thought . . . KK.'

KK was going fast – along the corridor then running down the stairs.

'To see Nonny Dreever,' she said. 'Nobody else will know but Nonny always does. Come ON.'

But as they reached the last few stairs, Helen Brown came out of the kitchen carrying Lula.

'Don't go out, Olly, I need you here. There's something wrong with Lula.'

'What? What's happened?'

KK stopped dead.

'I don't know, she started to cry and make a funny choking noise. I wonder if she picked up something . . .' Helen Brown backed into the kitchen again, carrying Lula nearer to the window where it was light. Lula had been crying. But now her mouth was clamped tight shut and she was quite pale.

KK went up to her and as she did so, Lula smiled. KK put out her hand.

'Give it to me, Lula,' she said. 'Look, Jinx is waiting to lick you better. Give it to me.'

Lula's face wrinkled up with her stubborn expression for a second, but then Jinx came nearer and held up his paw. Olly thought he might stop breathing. He loved Lula. What if she had eaten some old bad food or some mouse bait, something that might make her really ill? What if . . .

But Lula was putting her hand to her mouth and then she was spitting something into it and holding out the hand for KK to see.

In the pink, curled-up palm, and still wet from being inside her mouth, lay a small dark angry-looking stone.

CHAPTER EIGHT

Nonny Dreever

'Run,' KK said.

Olly knew why without having to ask. If they didn't run fast until they were out of earshot, Mum and Dad would stop them with a lot of be carefuls and when will you be backs and mind how yous. He had never been free like this in Wigwell Avenue because London was dangerous and he had grown up knowing it.

They were a long way down the track and running towards the hill with KK out in front, before he had to stop to ease the stitch in his side and get his breath. One or two sheep looked up briefly, stared hard and then went on grazing. KK had turned and come back. Jinx lay down.

'Look.'

Olly looked. Behind them, Gullywith was in shadow and the windows gleamed strangely.

'Did you know the people who lived there before?'

'Nobody did. I told you. Not for a hundred years. Or about that. Nobody would ever have lived there again if you hadn't come.'

'But it's a perfectly good house,' Olly said, which was

exactly what he had heard his mother say that morning.

'No,' KK said. 'Whatever it is, it isn't that. Anyway, you're there now so we've got to try and make the best of it. Come on.'

Jinx jumped up. Olly noticed that although he was some kind of sheepdog, the sheep took no notice of him whatsoever. He might have been completely invisible.

'Is it very far?'

KK looked scornful. 'Too far for London legs, then?'

'No. I just asked.'

'Huh.'

She went ahead again, up the track as it got steeper and steeper.

It seemed hours before they got towards the top and the path became bumpier and harder to climb. There were white chalky rocks sticking out from the green grass and Olly realised that they had left the last sheep some way behind them on the lower slopes. Jinx was running ahead now. It was growing windier and the clouds seemed as if he could have reached up and touched them.

Then KK disappeared.

Olly stopped and looked round him in panic. Green hills. White chalky rocks. Wind. Sky. And him.

'KK,' he shouted, but his voice was whisked up by the wind and away.

He looked back but the clouds had gathered in and were shrouding the fields behind. Gullywith had vanished too.

'Oi!' KK was beside him again, emerging through the mist. 'You don't want to get me out of sight up here.'

'I wasn't, I . . .'

'You need to stay close.'

He stayed close, and they pushed together through the white cobwebby clouds, climbing the last few steep metres and then dropping suddenly on to the other side and out into bright sunlight.

'It does that.'

Olly looked down. They were on top of one hill and for miles ahead others rose higher and higher, one behind the other, grey and violet and indigo, but in between there was a wide open landscape of green fields and trees, fences, a church tower, and tiny cows and sheep looking as if they had come from a toy farm. There were roads. There was a thin silver line of river.

'Over that peak is Withern Mere. You can't see from here.'

'Is that where we're going?'

'Not today. Nonny Dreever's is that way.' KK pointed but the sun was in their eyes. 'By Wakes Wood.'

'Should we get the broom and shovel first?'

'No,' KK said, 'this is a whole lot more important.' And she set off down the other side of the steep hill.

Olly had not liked his legs being called London legs, but it was true that he was not used to so much walking, and he had no idea how far they had to go or how long it would take and KK marched just ahead of him all the time without saying anything. Once they were down to the lower slopes of the hill, they turned left along a narrow track that led towards some woodland, but instead of going into it they skirted the edge and Olly had difficulty keeping his feet because the path was thick and tussocky with grass and bordered a ditch. He kept his eyes to the ground in case he missed his footing, so that it was only when KK stopped that he realised they had come to a small wooden gate.

'And I just hope he's here,' KK said.

'Won't he be at work?'

KK just laughed and pushed open the gate. Jinx raced ahead of them to what looked like a low wooden shed with a small stepladder propped at the front, leading to a half-door. The top half was open and hooked back. From inside there came an odd noise, a bit like sawing and a bit like humming.

'Good,' KK said, making for the steps. 'He is in. Come on.'

Olly hesitated, then slowly followed her.

He was about to meet Nonny Dreever.

CHAPTER NINE

The House on Stilts

Olly stared. And then he stared again. And went on staring. He stared in amazement and wonder and he also stared in a certain amount of disbelief. If he had been a boy in a story, he would have rubbed his eyes.

In fact, it was his eyes that were the problem because it was taking a few minutes for them to adjust to the dimness of the room. When they did, he went on staring because there was so much, so very very much, to stare at. He thought that if he stood there staring for a week he would not possibly have seen everything.

The first thing he worked out was that Nonny Dreever's house was on stilts. That was why there was a stepladder up to the front door – or rather, just the door, because there didn't seem to be a back one. The long low wooden room was built on four wooden piles with space beneath. Olly remembered seeing pictures of houses like that on a television programme about a country where the houses were built on water, though they had been much higher. Nonny Dreever's house seemed to be less than a metre off the ground.

KK was down at the far end of the one long room next

to a man who was perched on a high stool in front of a bench that ran along the wall.

KK said, 'Come in, Olly, nothing'll bite you.'

Olly was not so sure. There seemed to be plenty that might if it chose, though, apart from some dogs, he was unsure what animals did bite people and what did not.

A small black iron stove stood in one corner. It was lit and glowing gently and lying on the rug in front of it was a deer. Its eyes were closed but Olly had the feeling that it was not asleep. On the bench beside KK and the man was a large cockerel with a gleaming eye, a scarlet comb and a big tail spread like a fan. Not far from the deer was a white goose with an orange beak. Olly had heard about geese and their beaks, but for now it was taking no notice of him.

The owl was. It was perched on a shelf high up in one corner of the room and it had its tawny yellow eyes fixed on him without blinking. Once, its head swivelled almost completely round and back again, as if its neck was on a spindle, but somehow it managed to keep its eyes on Olly while it did so.

There were other things too, so many other things, some of them living, some not, that Olly's head seemed to spin round like the owl's.

Then the man said, 'Come on in, Oliver Mackenzie Brown.'

'How do you know my name?'

Nonny Dreever chuckled. 'And shut the bottom half of the door.'

He did as he was told.

'Good, now come here and let's take a look at you. It's a while since I saw a boy from London.'

Olly went slowly across the room until he was a pace or two away from the bench but he made sure he was on the same side as KK and away from the goose, even though the dog Jinx had curled up next to it and gone to sleep, which the deer, in its turn, did not seem to have noticed.

To look at, Nonny Dreever was one of those people who might have been a young man or a middling one, or even one who was old – it was impossible to tell, and you couldn't quite tell from the way he spoke either.

He had red hair, red as berries, red as cherry leaves in autumn, red as the carpet in Olly's grandmother's front room, and the red hair was long, down to his shoulders, and wavy. The other thing Olly noticed was that he had large eyes which were an ordinary brown except for a tiny chip of gleaming gold in each one. He wore several large rings on his fingers and sitting on the back of his right hand was a frog. The frog blinked a slow blink.

Nonny Dreever looked at Olly steadily without speaking for some time. KK stood quietly and Olly saw that she was holding a grey rabbit, whose silky ears she was stroking in a gentle rhythm. Olly let himself be looked at and somehow felt perfectly comfortable. The room was quiet. But it was full of watching eyes.

Then Nonny Dreever said, 'You'd better tell me what's been going on.'

They told him, once they had been given a glass of Nonny's own-brewed lemonade, which made Olly's cheeks pucker in and go dry when he first tasted it. His eyes were getting used to the room. It was a bit like a caravan and a bit like a narrowboat. There was a bunk bed let into the wall at one end, a table, an armchair and a small, squashed-in couch with coloured rugs spread over it. The shelves and every nook and cranny were crammed with things – china mugs, tin plates, jugs, kettles, pans, brass animals, paper boats, wooden toys, books, jars of pens and brushes, angels made of glass, dogs made of plaster, pictures, postcards, pots of glue, packets of tea and porridge oats. There was also a black and white cat, both of which sat so still Olly could not make up his mind whether they were alive or not until, like the owl and the frog, they blinked their eyes. Eyes were everywhere. Especially Nonny Dreever's eyes, with their tiny, gleaming gold chips.

KK had brought several stones out of her pocket and Nonny Dreever was holding them in his hand. Now and then he tipped them into the other. Then he rolled them about gently. Then he held them up to his ear one by one and listened to each of them as if it were a shell. All the time he did so, Olly watched his face. The expression kept changing, as if the sun and shadows were chasing over it as they did over the hill.

They waited a long time and KK seemed to be quite aware that this was usual. She sat stroking the rabbit and her eyes seemed to half close. Olly's eyes were used to the room now and every time he glanced round he spotted more and more – jointed wooden dolls, a carved and painted merry-go-round, a basket of shells, another of pine cones, and then, close to him, a large, greenish-grey stone. He had not noticed it before. It had markings, too, like the squares of a chessboard. They were quite unlike the scratchings on the stones he had been finding, but he wondered if they had come from the same place or had ever had anything to do with each other.

He bent to examine the markings more closely and, as he did so, he thought he saw the stone move. No. Stones did not move. He waited. Nonny Dreever was still sitting, hunched slightly in his chair, his hand tightly closed now. Olly looked from him to the stone. The air in the room was warm and dim and quite sleepy-making. KK seemed to be asleep.

The stone moved again. It grew legs and a neck and a head and began to amble forwards.

The stone was a tortoise.

'Withern,' Nonny Dreever said. KK opened her eyes. 'That's where you'll find out more. Withern shore.' He opened his palm. They all looked at the stone lying quietly in the centre. 'Go there. Take this with you. That's where it belongs and where it needs to be. Only thing is, whether it will stay there.'

'If we put it there, it'll have to,' KK said. 'Stones don't move.'

Olly looked down. The tortoise had shuffled off out of sight under a bench.

'Of course they move,' Nonny Dreever said. 'How do you think this one got to Gullywith. How did it get into Oliver Brown's pocket? How did the others get to be beside the mousehole? Stones move. These have probably been moving about for years. But maybe – ' He shook his head.

'Are there more of them?'

'Like this? Probably. The markings will help them know one another. They belong together.'

'Why don't they just stay at . . . at this Withern place where they belong, then?'

'Because they've something they need to be doing. Maybe they're not happy with how things are. Not for me to say. I'm just telling you where I think they've come from. When they took themselves to Gullywith – who knows? Maybe last week, maybe thousands of years ago.'

'I don't understand any of this,' Olly said grumpily. 'They're just stones.'

'Nothing,' Nonny Dreever said, unfolding his long legs and getting up out of his chair, 'nothing is "just" anything, especially not here.' He held out his hand. 'Take them, Oliver Mackenzie Brown, and put them back where they once came from. See if they'll settle.'

Olly took the stone cautiously, afraid of it now. But it lay innocently in his hand. Yes, just a stone, after all.

'Be careful,' Nonny said as they went down the wooden steps. Olly thought he meant be careful not to trip, but there was something more serious than a Mum sort of 'be careful' in Nonny's voice.

Olly turned round. 'Do you think the stones are dangerous, Mr Dreever?'

'I'd say they were angry stones and angry things are to be watched out for. That's what I'd say.'

'I want to throw it away. I don't like carrying it.'

'Carry it back to Withern as soon as you can and you won't be bothered more.'

'People like to go back to their own homes.'

'And where's your home, Oliver Brown?'

Olly stood still in the sun. He couldn't answer. Gullywith wasn't home yet, and he couldn't see how it ever would be, but Number 58 Wigwell Avenue was not home now either.

'I don't know,' he said. 'It feels as if I haven't got one at all.'

He didn't go because he wanted to ask something and he didn't ask because he was anxious not to seem rude but he knew that if he didn't ask it would bother him for the rest of the day and even in the night he might wake up being bothered.

'Mr Dreever?'

'That's me.'

'I wondered . . .'

'I know. I generally do when people are wondering.'

'It's just . . . in your house there are so many things and they're so interesting and I don't think anybody could discover even a half of the things you've got.'

'A half? They couldn't discover a hundredth.'

'No. I expect not. But in the corner . . . was there a Christmas tree?'

'Well of course there was a Christmas tree!'

'But . . . it's July.'

'What difference does that make? There's always a Christmas tree. What's the point of having it for one Christmas and taking it all down and putting it away and then flash-bang you're getting it out and putting it all up again? Why not leave it where it is and save yourself the trouble?'

'Because Christmas trees drop all their needles and then they die.'

'Mine doesn't.'

'Oh. It didn't look like a plastic one.'

'It's not.'

Nonny Dreever looked at Olly and Olly looked at the ground and neither of them spoke for several moments. KK was halfway down the path, waiting.

'Well,' Olly said at last. 'Thank you very much for the lemonade and . . . goodbye.'

'Don't you want your present?'

'What present?'

'Your Christmas present of course. What good's a Christmas tree without presents underneath?'

'KK –'

'She had hers long since but you haven't. You'd best go back in and get it.'

Olly went back into the room and his eyes had to get used to the dimness again, but he made his way down to the far end, where he had first thought he had seen the Christmas tree. It was standing on a block of wood, decorated with baubles and tinsel and with an angel on top and there was a set of fairy lights, ready to be switched on when it was really Christmas, he supposed. He touched the tree. It was definitely real, real and fresh and it smelled of green pine needles, like a tree that had only just been cut.

Underneath the tree there were presents, wrapped in bright red and green Christmas paper dotted with gold and silver stars. A present? A Christmas present? Why would there be one for him? It was the most amazing surprise and Olly looked at them all, not knowing exactly what to do. You couldn't just take a present. You had to be given one. How would he know which one to take? They were all different sizes and shapes.

He stood staring down at them, feeling foolish.

'Well, take it,' Nonny Dreever said from the doorway. 'Time you were getting back.'

'I . . . I don't know which one to take.'

'Can't you read, then?'

'Of course I can read,' Olly said. 'I am ten years old.'

'Then read the labels. The one with your name on will be the one for you, won't it?'

Olly bent down. Each present had a label tied to it neatly but only one of the labels had anything written on it. He picked up the very small parcel. *Oliver Mackenzie Brown*, he read. The writing was strange, curly and very fine, in violet-coloured ink.

'Thank you,' Olly said. The parcel was oddly heavy. 'When should I open it?'

'Whenever you want to. Now . . . skedaddle. I've got important things to do.'

Olly skedaddled, out of the room, down the wooden steps and up the narrow path, to where KK and Jinx were still patiently waiting.

CHAPTER TEN

A Small Brass Tortoise

Things were rather different at Gullywith by the time Olly got back. KK had made him go straight home because they had been so long at Nonny Dreever's, while she went to fetch the shovel by herself. When Olly asked if they wouldn't be worried about her too, she gave him a pitying look.

Firstly, as he came down the hill he could see smoke rising from Gullywith's chimneys, which must mean they had managed to light the kitchen range. And when he got inside, there was a better smell somehow, as if the damp and darkness had retreated a bit back into the walls and people were settling in. There was even a fire in the grate in the big room at the front – a bit black and withered-looking, and burning rather sulkily, but still, it was a fire and it cheered things up.

A lot of the boxes and packing cases were piled up in the yard at the back and the table and chairs were set out in the middle of the kitchen. They didn't look right though, Olly thought. They were much too small in the big space and they looked as if they belonged in a town kitchen. Which they had.

'Your bedroom's up in the attic,' Helen Brown said. 'I thought you'd like to be up near the clouds and out of the way and you've got a great view of the hill.

'And I'm glad you found a friend but what's her real name? Did you go to her house? Where does she live? What are they . . .'

Olly fled. Mum's questions followed him as he ran up the stairs like a long tail that got thinner and thinner and fainter and fainter until he couldn't hear them any more.

The woodsmoke had curled up the stairs too and was hanging about the landings and along the corridor, wispy and sweet smelling.

Outside the door of the attic room that was now his room, Olly stopped. He knew what he must not do, not now, not ever. He must not look at his things, the bed, the chest, the chair, the blue painted trunk, and remember how they had been at Number 58 Wigwell Avenue. He mustn't try and put them back the old way or think how different they looked. They would be different because everything was different and there wasn't anything he could do about it.

He opened the door.

The first thing he saw was the hill rising up ahead, clear as clear out of the window. It was a dark violet-blue against the sky and the track was pale as bone. In front of it was the wide field he had crossed with KK. No one was there now. The sheep were little white blobs, heads bent, grazing.

The sight of the hill made Olly feel good. It seemed to lodge in his heart, already something he knew and loved.

He felt as if the hill was looking out for him.

His room was much bigger than he had expected and his bed looked very small up against the wall but his rag rug was down beside it and the trunk was safe at the end of it. His toys and books and clothes were still in packing cases piled up and there were no shelves at all to put them on but he thought Dad would get some put up eventually. They had found his lamp and plugged it in too, the old one he had had when he was three, with giraffes going round and round the edge. He had been really keen on giraffes then and Mum had stencilled them on his lampshade. Olly switched it on. It worked. The giraffes glowed soft tawny brown and gold against the pale shade. He felt better still. The dull evening made the room fairly dark but with the lamp on it was fine. Olly sat on his bed. It felt the same. It was the same. His bed. He bounced on it a bit and it still had the same nice soft spring to it.

Things were improving and they improved even more when he remembered that he not yet opened the Christmas present from under Nonny Dreever's tree. He took it out of his pocket. He turned it over and over. It was small and heavy. It felt like a stone.

He unwrapped it quickly and took out a small, cold, hard, shiny object. It was heavy because it was made of solid brass.

His present was a brass tortoise with gleaming eyes. Olly held it in his hand. It felt friendly. He put it down beside the lamp and tucked the wrapping paper and label away in the drawer. Then he bounced on his bed again.

His bed. The tortoise watched him. His tortoise. His bed. His bed in Gullywith.

'Gullywith,' Olly said out loud.

There was a bang, the lamp went out and the room was plunged into darkness.

CHAPTER ELEVEN

Fiddleup

The next morning Olly woke with the sun shining on to his face. Mum was opening the curtains and from his bed he could see the hill bright and clear and with the sheep like cotton-wool balls to match the clouds. In the kitchen, Dad was frying bacon and eggs on the range, Lula was banging her spoon merrily on the table and the back door was open to let the morning in.

'Right, Olly Brown, get a good breakfast inside you. We're off to Fiddleup.'

Olly would be going to school at Fiddleup, the market town twelve miles away. The name made him laugh.

'I promised Mum I'd find a proper electrician to come and sort us out. I'd better not do what I did last night ever again.'

They had been in darkness until after eleven, with Mum standing under the ancient fuse boxes with a torch while Dad tried and failed to get the lights back on.

'And other things.' He made a face at Olly. 'Mum's given me a list.'

'Do I have to come?'

'Yes.'

'Can we have ice cream in a café?'

'If there is a café.'

'Of course there's a café,' Mum said, putting a cut-up egg in a dish in front of Lula. 'We went there when we first came here. Don't you remember? The Cuckoo or the Magpie or something like that.'

Olly tipped the ketchup bottle upside down and squeezed it. Nothing happened.

'KK might come over again.'

'If she does, I'll be pleased to see her. Got her feet on the ground and her head screwed on the right way, that girl.'

Olly laughed, imagining both things. As he did so, the ketchup came lurching out in a huge glob on to his plate.

'Oliver!'

Through the open back door, from far away on the hill, Olly could hear the sheep baaing to one another.

'Cows,' Lula said.

Fiddleup was set on a hill. The streets ran steeply down to the market square at the bottom and, further on down below that, to the river. Olly's legs ached by the time they had climbed up and down trying to find an electrical shop and organised a man to come out to sort their wiring and bought most of the things on Mum's list. The sun was warm, the town was filling up and Olly mentioned the café, a cold drink and the ice cream several times before Dad took any notice.

'Right . . . let's look up here. This seems familiar. I think maybe that café was on the left.'

But it wasn't. They climbed the next few steep streets. No café.

'There's got to be a café down in the square, then. Maybe the one we went to has closed.'

'No it hasn't – look.'

The Bluebird Café was bang opposite them. It had cakes displayed in the window, tables behind, and a swinging ice-cream sign.

'Dad . . .'

'Great,' Dad said. 'But just before we go in, I wouldn't mind having a look in that second-hand bookshop next door. There's a 1950s Triumph Roadster manual I've been trying to track down . . .'

Olly groaned. Dad was always trying to track down old manuals for vintage cars and once he started rummaging through the shelves of an old bookshop they could be stuck there for hours. Olly saw his ice cream receding over the horizon.

'Five minutes,' Dad said. 'Well – ten minutes, tops.'

They crossed the street and pushed open the door of the small shop. The bell jingled. They always did in old book-shops, Olly thought. He'd been in plenty of them with Dad. Whenever they were on holiday, in Wales or Jersey, Cornwall or the Isle of Wight or the Isle of Skye, Dad managed to find an old bookshop which might, just might, have the manual of the 1950s Triumph Roadster or the 1930s Austin 7 or the 1953 Jaguar, that he had been trying to track down.

The shop smelled exactly the same as every other old

bookshop they had ever been into, musty and dry and leathery. There was a high counter in one corner, and on the counter top was a small handbell. *Please Ring for Attention*, it said on the notice propped up beside it.

Dad stood looking round, trying to see the Transport shelves. No one seemed to be behind the counter.

'Ah ha!' Pete Brown said, and dived round behind one of the bookcases into a corner. Olly sighed. If Dad had found Transport, they could be there for quite some time. He went round into the next bay. Biography. History. Antiquities. Classics. Olly ran his finger along the shelves. Ice creams formed beautiful pictures in his mind, buttery yellow, strawberry pink, deep soothing chocolate . . .

Poetry. Drama. Natural History. *The Battle for Gullywith*.

Olly stared. He closed his eyes quickly, opened them, and stared again.

The book was sandwiched tightly between one about skylarks and another called *Hedgerows and Their History*. They both had paper dust jackets – but this did not. It was bound in very dark blue or possibly green cloth and the small writing of the title down the spine was in dull gold but, somehow, a gold that gleamed and dazzled in the darkness. *The Battle for Gullywith*.

Olly bent his head more closely to the shelf of books but when he did so that one seemed to shrink back between the others. The gold of the title lettering still gleamed out though.

Just then, Olly heard the sound of a door opening

somewhere at the back of the shop, and then Dad's voice. He pressed himself to the bookcases. He did not want them to find him yet. He wanted to examine the book. His heart was beating very fast.

'. . . automobiles,' the shopkeeper said, in an old man's voice, quite frail and quavery.

Dad started to talk.

The Battle for Gullywith. The book seemed to have slid forward again so that it was once more level with the one about skylarks on its left and the one about hedgerows on its right. Olly stretched out his hand. As he did so, the bell jingled as the shop door opened. But there was something else. It had been a beautiful July day, sunny and warm and still, but as the door opened a gust of wind roared through it and swirled round the shop. The door slammed shut, the bell jingled fiercely, and a book hurtled out of the shelves and fell on to Olly's foot. It was as if a huge and very heavy brick had landed there, hurting his toes a great deal, so that he shouted out.

'Ouch!'

'Olly? What are you doing?'

Dad's face appeared round the end of the bay of books. 'Be careful with books. Don't pull them out and drop them – you can cause a lot of damage.'

'I wasn't, I didn't, it was the wind, it made the door bang and it made the book fall out of the shelf on to my toes. It really hurt.'

'What on earth are you talking about? You're far too old to tell stories to try and get yourself out of trouble, Olly.'

'I was not! I told you, the wind made the door bang.'

'What wind? It's a beautiful summer's day, there isn't a breath of wind.'

'Yes there was, it blew the door shut and –'

'The door shut because someone came in, that's all.'

'And it made the book fall on to my toe.'

'Oliver . . .'

Oliver looked down. The book on the floor beside his foot had a dust jacket on with a drawing coloured green and white and brown. *Hedgerows and Their History*.

'That's funny . . .'

'Now what?'

Olly bent and picked the book up. 'It wasn't that book that fell on my toe, it was another one. It was . . .'

He put the hedgerows one back on the shelf but something wasn't the same. It fitted neatly next to the book about skylarks and there was no room for any other book between. The one called *The Battle for Gullywith* had gone.

'Ah . . . Yes, I thought I had it. Would this be the Triumph Roadster manual?'

Pete Brown disappeared.

Olly took out the hedgerows book, slipped his hand into the space and felt around. *The Battle for Gullywith* had obviously got pushed to the back.

There was nothing. He took out the book about skylarks and felt again. He felt as far as he could on either side but there was just a space and then the shelf back. No book.

Maybe it was still on the floor. Maybe he had pushed it under one of the bookcases when his foot had been hurting.

He knelt down.

Nothing. There were no books on the floor. No books

hidden behind the others on the shelf. And no space between hedgerows and skylarks.

The book called *The Battle for Gullywith* had vanished.

'Olly . . . come ON. Do you want that ice cream or not?'

Dad was standing at the end of the bay, holding a book-shaped package. He had a big grin on his face.

'Got it! Isn't that amazing? Been looking for this for donkey's years. Are you coming or what?'

Olly looked at the ground. Then at the bookshelf. Then at Dad. Then back to the bookshelf again. It was still not there.

He followed Dad out. He needed to think.

When they had come into the shop, the door had been closed – he remembered hearing the bell jingle. Someone else had come in and made it jingle too, but each time, they had closed the door behind them. He was quite certain. He remembered the jingling.

Now though, the door was propped open. Olly pulled at it but it was wedged by a large doorstop. The doorstop looked like a big stone but had markings on the surface, in a grid of little squares, and it was shaped like a tortoise.

Please close the door, the sign read. The writing seemed strangely familiar.

Olly nudged at the doorstopper tortoise with his toe and the door came free.

But as he closed it, he glanced down.

The tortoise had two small bright beady eyes with a golden gleam in their centres and as Olly looked, one of the eyes winked at him.

CHAPTER TWELVE

A Moonlight Visitor

In the Bluebird Café, Dad sat looking at his manual of the 1952 Triumph Roadster and Olly sat thinking about the book he had seen. The book he had absolutely definitely seen. They both ate ice creams, which were probably the best Olly had ever tasted, and because Dad was in such a mega-good mood about finding the book, they had three scoops each, chocolate, raspberry and butterscotch. The chocolate had tiny chips of real milk chocolate, the raspberry had soft pieces of real fruit, and the butterscotch had little chewy chunks of golden sweet toffee which gleamed out of the shining, creamy ice.

'I wonder what Mum's going to say about another car book.'

'Oh, she won't mind,' Pete Brown said cheerfully. 'Everything's come up roses now. She loves the house, she's getting it all straight and it won't be long before I get the work done on her studio. The sun's shining. She won't mind one more little book. Let's get some of those buns for tea. She'll like those.'

But when they arrived back at Gullywith there were other

things to think about. As they drove into the yard, Mum came out of the front door, carrying Lula. They both looked hot and dirty, Lula was howling and Mum's face was like thunder.

'The electricity has gone again and the range went out but before it did, it started to belch horrible-smelling black smoke and I can't get any water out of any of the taps. Why were you so long?'

'Moke,' Lula wailed, 'moke, moke.'

The smoke and smell seemed to have eeled their way not only into every room but every crack and crevice.

'Why were you so long?' Mum kept on saying. 'And what's that? Oh, Pete, honestly, don't tell me you've bought a book, and when's the electrician coming?'

'Er . . . Friday afternoon. Don't worry, I'll fix the range. It'll just be a bit of soot like yesterday, I'll riddle it out.'

'Friday afternoon? We can't wait until Friday afternoon, this is Tuesday, you'll have to ring him, honestly, Pete, why . . . Olly, where are you going? Here, have Lula a minute.'

Lula was hot and sticky and smelled of dirty nappy. Her nose was running too.

'Did KK come?'

'Who? Oh, that girl, no she didn't.'

'More's the pity,' Dad said. 'She seemed to know how to deal with ranges. Maybe she knows about electricity as well.'

'Of course she won't, she's a child. Olly, take Lula outside a minute, only hold on to her, you know what she's like.'

Outside, Lula pulled away from Olly's hand and slipped

over on a patch of dirt and after that the rest of the day went on in the same, dirty and miserable way.

Dad spent several hours struggling with the range but every time he thought he had cleaned out every last scrap of soot and rubbish, and lit it, the smoke belched out. He had forgotten to take the phone number of the electrician too, so he had to drive back into Fiddleup to try and get him to come out urgently.

'Olly, go round the house, see if there are any candles.'

'Why would there be any candles?'

'Well, it's the sort of thing people leave, isn't it? Just look, don't argue, Oliver.'

Why would people have left candles in a house a hundred years ago, Olly thought, thumping up the stairs, and even if they had, what use would they be by now? None. They'd be damp or worn out or just old. Something.

He went from room to room and of course there were no candles. He'd known perfectly well there wouldn't be.

He got to the very end room down the corridor, the little dismal room that smelled of damp and had cold patches and at first, he thought he wouldn't go in. He hadn't liked this room and nor had KK. But then he heard his mother shouting from far below, probably telling him to go on looking.

He pushed open the door slowly and went in.

The room was the same. It smelled the same, damp and mouldy, and it had the same cold patches when he moved around in it.

But two things were different. The hole in the corner of

the skirting board was bigger now, and coming out of it was a trail of small stones, the stones with strange markings on them, and the trail led across the room almost to the door, where it ended in a little heap. They had not been like that the last time Olly had been in here. There had been two or three beside the hole, that was all.

Now there were twenty or thirty, making a definite line towards the door.

Olly looked round quickly. Nothing else. He bent down and hesitated, then very quickly, scooped up one of the stones and put it into his pocket.

It was late before he got to bed. Dad had come back from Fiddleup with candles, torches and a promise from the electrician that he would be there the next day. He had banged the range a lot just as KK had showed them, but although a lot of dust and debris had come down the pipe, it still wouldn't light. They had eaten cold meat and salad and the buns they had brought earlier and just before Olly went up to bed Dad had put four candles in old bottles and set them on the table. The flickering light threw tawny shadows on to the walls and glimmered in reflection in the windows.

'Cosy,' Mum said.

Olly felt as if the whole room was wavy.

'Come on, you're only fit for bed.'

He stumbled up the stairs, his legs heavy and woolly with sleep. His room was very dark.

'I'll leave the torch here. You can switch it on if you're worried,' Mum said.

'I'm not Lula,' Olly said. 'I'm ten. I don't mind it being dark. I like the dark.'

Besides, once he had been lying on his back for a while with his eyes open, Olly realised that it was not as dark as it had seemed because the moon had risen and was shining softly on the wall. Somewhere outside an owl hooted. He had always thought owls were spooky, but after he had seen the owl in Nonny Dreever's house somehow he had felt differently about them and now the hooting sounded comfortable and friendly.

For the first time, he began to feel that Gullywith might be home.

He woke out of a soft, warm, woolly dream with a start. Something had rattled against the window. Olly sat up in bed. The moon had slipped off the wall and his room was dark. The sharp rattle on the glass came again.

Olly reached out his hand for the torch on his bedside table but what he felt wasn't torch-shaped, it was flat and square with edges.

He knew he hadn't left a book there. All his books were still packed in the boxes.

He felt around for the torch and switched it on. At the same time, there was a louder, angrier rattle on the windowpane, as if someone was throwing handfuls of stones at the glass.

Olly got out of bed.

Outside, standing on the grass in the moonlight, stood KK.

CHAPTER THIRTEEN

Withern Mere

Olly had never been so pleased to see anyone in his life. He pulled on his jeans and T-shirt and went downstairs carrying his shoes so as not to make any sound.

It was very warm outside, like a summer's day rather than the middle of the night and the moon made everything look silky and silver. He started to tell her about the bookshop and the book that had vanished but KK interrupted him.

'We've got to go now,' she said. 'There isn't much time. Nonny Dreever sent a message. He said he'd heard it, and that we had to hurry up and get the stones back. We have to go to Withern Mere tonight.'

'But how can we carry a load of the stones? There are a lot more. They came out of that hole in the wall and more fell down the flue at the back of the range. We'd need a barrow.'

'No. We'll just take a few . . . the rest will follow.'

'How far is it?'

KK shrugged. 'Over the hill and on a bit.'

'I ought to tell Mum and Dad.'

'You can't, they'd say no, and anyway there isn't time. How many stones do you have?'

Olly felt in his pocket and touched the stone he had picked up from the floor of the back room earlier. It felt icy cold.

'Only one.'

'I've got two. They were on the path. I threw some at the window as well . . . there are masses out here now, we have to get them back.'

Olly looked down at the ground and saw that the whole front yard was stony now, far more than it had been that afternoon, and as he looked, he saw that the stones were moving very slightly, stirring and simmering within themselves. They looked angry.

The stone in his pocket was so icy cold now that it seemed to be burning.

'OK.'

Jinx, who had been lying low and pressed to the ground in the shadows, got up and ran off across the yard towards the track. The moonlight made the white patches on his back gleam.

They followed him, walking steadily and without speaking, and the stone in Olly's pocket burned cold through it and on to his leg. Once across the track and up on to the hill among the quiet, moonlit sheep who stared at them in wonder, they slowed down and Olly told KK about the bookshop and the book that had vanished.

'And just when you were trying to wake me up, I felt a book on the table by my bed, only then you threw some more stones and I didn't get to look at it properly.'

'It was probably the same one,' KK said, making books that vanished and reappeared in another place sound like the most unremarkable things in the world. 'I don't like any of this. It's all part of the same thing.'

'Yes, but what thing?'

'The stones of course.'

Olly felt his head whirl. Vanishing books. Moving stones. Walking up the white track in the moonlight, he felt as if it were a million years since he had been Olly Brown of 58 Wigwell Avenue, London.

When they got to the top of the hill Jinx ran to the left, where another track led off towards a thin belt of woodland. Olly was not afraid and not surprised to find himself walking through the country in the middle of the night with a girl and a dog. It seemed normal. It also seemed urgent that they get to Withern Mere.

He had no watch but they seemed to have been walking for a very long time when, suddenly, Jinx stopped and lay down, like a sheepdog waiting to round up a flock.

KK whistled a low, soft whistle. Jinx growled and began to run in small circles.

They were on the edge of the wood.

Then Olly looked round. Behind them, stretching as far as he could see in the direction they had just come was a line of stones, gleaming ominously, a dull gunmetal grey, and the stones were moving.

'They're following us,' KK said.

'Do you think that means they're leaving Gullywith?'

'Probably.'

Jinx growled again.

'He doesn't like them.'

The stones were moving but Olly did not see how. They were stones. They had no feet and neither were they rolling. They just moved, steadily and purposefully and silently, towards them.

'Come on,' KK said.

Jinx ran round in a circle a couple more times but then streaked off into the wood. The path went through a clearing and was easy to follow. Now and then, they heard a rustle or a stirring of the undergrowth. Once they heard an owl hoot, and the moment they did so, Olly felt better, as if they were being looked after. Once, he thought that he saw eyes looking out at him, gleaming a thin topaz-gold gleam. A couple of times, he was certain that there were more eyes, hidden in the hollows of tree trunks. But the owl hooted each time and he didn't worry. Jinx pattered steadily ahead through the soft piles of dead leaves. Behind them, just a few metres behind, but moving steadily all the time, came the stones.

'How much further is it?'

'Through here, over the next hill. That's called Withern Hill. It leads down to Withern Mere. It's pretty steep, you'll have to be careful.'

KK was right. From the top of the hill, Olly looked down and the drop seemed to him as sheer as a cliff, but he saw that Jinx picked his way easily and that there were tussocks of grass, clumps of briars and brambles and big boulders, all of which broke up the steepness of the descent and gave them handholds, and the path itself wound round and round as it went down, so that it was easier to scramble down than Olly had expected. He was so busy watching where he put his hands and feet, and making sure that he didn't slip, that at first he didn't notice that the air around them had grown colder and seemed to be clammy, like cobwebs on his skin. They were climbing down into a long billow of grey fog which shrouded them when they reached the flat so that he and KK could barely see one another. There was a queer muffled silence closing them in. Jinx had come close to them and was pressing against KK's legs, whimpering.

'We have to be really careful. The water isn't far ahead.'

'Go anywhere you like as long as you can still see the house and you're not near water,' Pete Brown had said, that first morning Olly had gone out to explore around Gullywith. What would he say now?

But as they stood there, the night began to give way to a thin, sour dawn and from somewhere above them a bird or two began to sing in a tentative way. The fog was growing thinner and then, as the light came through, became more of a mist, a vapour with holes which grew larger, and began to evaporate.

The sun had not risen and the morning was quite grey and cold too, but as they watched, they could see the water ahead with the last shreds of mist wreathing over its surface.

'Withern Mere,' KK said.

It was enormous, a great flat stretch of water that spread away from them as far as they could see. It was still and steely grey and forbidding. The way down to it was at first over rough grass but that gave way to shingle. The whole shore of the mere was like a stony beach. Olly looked round. The line of stones that had been following them had stopped and had formed itself into horizontal battle lines, five or six deep. There were hundreds, perhaps thousands of stones, and as he looked more came up behind and fell into line. They were still only small, grey stones. He knew that he could have trodden all over them, but there was something so menacing and attentive about their silence and stillness in the straight even lines that they were as frightening as an army.

'Look!'

'I know,' KK said. 'I don't like it. We need to get rid of our stones as fast as we can before anything happens.'

'What are we going to do?'

'Throw them as far as we can into the mere. When they drop into the water, the others will want to follow. This is where they came from. This is their home. They won't stay with us.'

Olly took his stone from his pocket. It had grown colder, a smooth knob of burning ice in his hand, trying to stick to his skin. KK had two smaller ones.

'Come on, right to the edge.'

They began to walk slowly forward, but as he did so, Olly looked down and saw that there was a stirring in the shingle under their feet and just ahead of them. Not every stone had the faint scratched markings on its surface but those that did were moving, mumbling and turning and churning slightly, like a volcano that was shifting in its sleep, uncoiling itself and beginning to wake.

He looked round. The battle lines of stones were marching silently forwards but when he stopped they stopped. They were quite close to him now.

'Hurry up,' KK said.

She was near to the edge of the water. Olly went after her, over the moving, shifting shingle. KK raised her hand. 'When I say "throw" we both throw together. Throw as hard as you can. They have to go right in, where the water's deep.'

'Be careful, don't fall in, KK.'

All round them now the marked stones were stirring and turning. The mist was still lying just above the far water like gauzy ribbons. Olly shivered. It was very cold here and the cold came off the mere.

'Now!'

They lifted their arms and threw. KK's stones separated and flew high, then began to tumble towards the water but Olly's did something peculiar. It spun in the air, round and round like a top, then lurched back towards him like a boomerang.

KK's stones hit the water hard and sank. At once, there was a tremendous gurgling and a small, fierce whirlpool appeared and began to swirl round faster and faster where the stones had gone in. At the same time, Olly's stone was heading through the air back to the shore. Beneath his feet, he could feel the shingle shift dangerously.

'I think it's going to suck us down,' KK said. 'Quick, get round the other way.'

But as they tried to run they felt the stones drop down here and there into holes and Olly and KK had to leap and jump out of the way in case they sank.

Nearer the water the ground was wet but firmer. The whirlpool in the middle of the mere was drawing more and more of the water into itself and the hole it was making was spreading out further and further.

Jinx began to bark furiously.

The mere now had a great hole in its centre and the hole was dark and churning round furiously.

'Oliver, look.'

It was the fact that KK called him Oliver that made the whole thing both strange and terrifying. KK was pointing to the hole in the middle of the mere.

Something was rising very very slowly out of the middle of the whirlpool. Olly clutched at KK's arm. Everything was stock still – the two of them, Jinx, and all of the stones, which seemed to be standing to attention. Those that formed the shingle at their feet had ceased to move and were frozen still where they lay.

The figure that emerged was pale grey, as grey as clouds, as ash, as mist. It had a pointed crown, long stiffly waved hair that did not shine or move like living hair, and a similar long white beard with waves that were set and stiff too. One arm was raised up and as it emerged little by little, towering out of the whirlpool, its garment came into view, a tunic with long, stiff sleeves, tied with a rope belt round the waist. The face was expressionless, set and stiff and as grey as all the rest. Only the eyes gleamed.

Olly felt amazed and scared and excited all at once. Who was this? Why was he here and what was he going to do?

They stared, frozen to the spot.

'A stone man,' KK whispered.

'It's a king. A stone king.'

The stone king was huge now, towering out of the vortex of water.

'It can't harm us if it's made of stone. If we just turn round and ignore it, then it might disappear back into the mere,' said KK.

'We'd have to try and climb fast back up the hill.'

'Right. Turn round. Pretend it isn't there. It can't leave the water.'

'How do you know that?'

'Because it's rooted deep down. Withern Mere used to be Withern Quarry thousands of years ago, before it flooded, and the Stone King belonged there.'

Olly wondered if she was making up a story to reassure him.

'Move!'

It was when he tried to lift up his foot to do as KK said, and move, that Olly realised he felt strange, heavy and cold, and that he could not lift his leg or his foot off the ground. He looked at KK. She had gone very pale. He could see that she was trying desperately to lift up her own feet.

'Olly.'

'I know. I know.'

Instinctively, they both looked at Jinx but the dog was able to move, and now he was on his feet and barking furiously, the hackles on his neck raised, and his bark seemed louder than the bark of any dog Olly had ever heard. It broke through the stillness and echoed round and seemed to race up the hill and over the other side.

'Go, Jinx, go.'

Jinx began to streak fast across the shore, over the shingle stones. Olly wondered if the dog could fetch help before he and KK had turned completely to stone and how he would make anyone understand where they were or what was happening. KK's skin was ashen grey and her lips were set and stiff. He felt as if his own eyebrows were set in cement and his ears felt numb.

He was too cold and still to feel frightened and his thoughts seemed to be slowing down, as if he were drifting to sleep and everything was becoming hazy and muddled.

He saw KK's eyes looking at him in desperation, willing him to stay awake.

And then, from the hill behind, came a noise. It was if something were creaking and cracking open, like a very old door that needed oil on its hinges. Olly could only move his eyes now, but he could see the base of the hill behind, where it joined the shingle. The sound seemed to be coming from there. He saw KK's eyes widen in astonishment.

After that, it all happened in a rush, so that it wasn't until much later that he could piece together how they had been rescued. The noise grew much louder and they saw that a crack was opening in the hill and widening, as if the whole hillside was splitting in two. There was a roaring sound from inside and then, pouring out of the opening, came bats large and small and birds of different sorts – crows and ravens, gulls, owls and jays. They swooped and dived around in great dark flocks, and some made towards the centre of the mere and began to dive-bomb the stone king, flapping their wings and plunging menacingly down, beaks forward. Others flew at the shingle and stabbed at it before soaring up again and diving once more. In the middle of the racket of beating wings and cawing and calling, Olly and KK felt themselves enveloped in a warm current of air and then being lifted up and carried swiftly forwards on the wings of dozens of birds, towards the opening in the hill. At this point, the stones seemed to wake all at once and the battle lines began to rumble and to move powerfully forwards and the ground began to shift and move with a great force. As it moved, every stone made a hard, hissing sound and the noise of hundreds of them together was menacing and eerie.

In the midst of the noise and the swirling water and diving birds, the beating wings and hissing stones and the churning shingle, Olly and KK were carried into what seemed like pitch-blackness inside the hill and then Jinx was behind them, running round and round and barking, but it was joyous barking now. The din from outside receded and grew fainter as the crack in the hillside through which they had been brought closed slowly like a pair of doors. From beyond it, they could hear muffled, furious screaming and hissing and the sound of stones rattling and hammering.

Olly felt himself set gently down on the ground, which was cool and soft. Jinx was licking his legs, which seemed to be fizzing inside as they came to life, as if he had been sitting on them for a long time.

All around, in nooks and crannies in the earthy walls, the birds had settled and were preening their feathers or fussing about getting ready to roost. Their bright eyes gleamed through the dark as they looked at Olly and KK.

'Well then, you two. I said to be careful but even I never expected things to take quite that much of a turn,' Nonny Dreever said.

CHAPTER FOURTEEN

Dark Tunnels and Gleaming Eyes

The back of the cave led to a winding passage which went for almost three miles through the middle of the hill. Nonny Dreever led the way. It was not dark because on ledges and in crevices all along eyes with golden chips at the centre gleamed with enough light for them to see by. Olly looked up every so often, trying to make out what was giving the light but he could never see far enough behind them to make out anything but vague and sometimes feathery shapes.

The passage smelled of earth, but although it was chilly and quite damp too, it did not have the dreadful sour mouldy mushroomy smell of the room in Gullywith which had the cold patches and wet bits of plaster on the walls. It smelled fresh and pleasant, as if someone had been digging and turning over the soil in spring. They stopped once for a break and Olly looked behind them, dreading that he would see the army of stones or even the stone figure from the mere marching to catch up with them, and for a split second he did indeed think that the stones had followed them and pulled at KK to look as well.

'Oh, yes, they're fetching up the rear. They'll always

look out for us in here and anywhere else for that matter,' Nonny Dreever said, seeing them.

The line of stones making slow and steady progress down the passage between the earth walls turned out to be a line of tortoises, golden eyes glinting.

Jinx was sitting at KK's feet, mouth open a bit to let his pink tongue pant out cheerfully.

It was quite a long time before they reached the end of the passage and saw a flight of steps cut roughly into the bank. Jinx scrambled up with some difficulty but the tortoises gathered together at the bottom, forming one very large bumpy boulder, and closed their eyes. At the top of the steps was a small wooden door without any handle or latch, but Jinx, who was first, simply pushed at it with his nose and it swung open easily, letting him in to what looked to Olly strangely familiar.

It was. The door turned out to be a panel in the back wall of Nonny Dreever's house on stilts and when Olly emerged into the room, blinking, he saw that he was standing beside the Christmas tree, whose lights were shining quietly away to themselves and whose baubles and ornaments swung slightly in the draught that came through the door from the passage below.

He looked round, taking in everything again, but as he did so, he saw that there were far more things not only that he had not spotted on his first visit but which he was sure had not been there at all. On a shelf near to his left elbow was a complete miniature circus with tiny lions and tigers, elephants and dancing bears, a ringmaster, clowns, trapeze artists and acrobats, and next to it was a troupe of Russian dancing dolls dressed in fur hats and high boots and which were twirling round silently, as if someone had wound them up seconds before. There was a church, lit from inside, and a parrot with vivid opalescent feathers, which clicked its beak and was definitely a real bird, as were the fluttering canaries which played about near the roof. The snake Olly was unsure about. It lay coiled lazily along the edge of the shelf with its head hanging down and its eyelids folded down over its eyes and nothing about it moved at all. It certainly did not appear to be breathing and not the slightest ripple passed over the length of its scaly brown and black and greenish mottled skin as long as he looked at it.

Below the shelf, also asleep on an old bit of blanket lay a fox with its ginger brush curled neatly round so that the tip just touched its black nose, but the fox was definitely breathing softly.

Twenty minutes later they were all sitting round the table eating scrambled eggs on toast with fried tomatoes and the most delicious mushrooms Olly had ever tasted, huge and flat with dark brown gills oozing juice. There was an old enamel pot of tea and a pile of toast and a slab of butter and a comb of golden honey and no sound at all except the steady one of munching and crunching and slicing and buttering and scraping and swallowing. Olly had never been so ravenously hungry. It was as if he had not eaten for weeks and it was only after two platefuls of eggs and mushrooms, four slices of toast, two of them with honey, a mug of tea and an apple that he felt even slightly full and wide awake.

As he drained the last drops of his second mug of tea, a cuckoo clock that hung high up on a hook above the sink whirred and whizzed and leaped into life as the little bird sprang in and out five times.

'I should think,' Nonny Dreever said, 'that by the time you've let your breakfast go down and made your way back, you'll get another hour's sleep before they wake up at your house.'

'But . . . but we left there hours ago. We went for miles and . . . it can't be only five o'clock!'

'Why not?'

'Because . . . it just can't.'

Nonny Dreever laughed. 'That's the poorest argument I've heard for a day or two, Oliver Mackenzie Brown. Try harder.'

'Because it was half past three when KK came and threw the pebbles at my window, and it must have taken us at least an hour to get to Withern Mere and . . . the time doesn't add up properly.'

'Time hardly ever does.' Nonny Dreever stood up and began to clear the table. 'Or so I find.'

Olly felt confused. He also felt, quite suddenly, extremely sleepy. Nonny Dreever looked at him sharply.

'Right,' he said, 'come and sit out there on the step. The dawn air is always chill and it will perk you up for the walk home. There are a few things we need to discuss.'

It was beautiful on the little landing above the steps. The dawn was breaking through a pearly mist, which was, as Nonny had said, chilly but not unpleasantly so, like the mist over the mere. Birds were singing and the sheep were grazing and it was hard to believe that any of what had happened earlier had actually happened. Indeed, it was hard to believe that Withern Mere so much as existed.

'But it did,' Nonny said, sitting on the old triangular canvas chair and lighting a small, curly clay pipe, as if he had read Olly's thoughts. It was something he had an uncanny way of seeming to do.

'This is no game, you two. They don't play games. I feel responsible, telling you to go to the Withern at all. I should have come with you. I should have seen something like this might happen. I had a bad feeling in my leg all night.'

'In your leg?'

'In my leg.' Nonny did not explain further.

'Well, thank goodness it's all right now,' KK said. 'You came in the nick of time and rescued us and I should think they were pretty scared.'

Nonny said nothing for a moment as he puffed carefully on the pipe to get it nicely alight. The thin wisp of blue smoke curled its way to Olly's nose. It smelled sweet, like apple peelings and chestnuts that had been singed together in a fire.

'Scared? I wonder. I'm not sure what scares them. They're pretty determined when they want something back.'

'But what do they want?'

'What do you think? Gullywith of course. Gullywith is

theirs. It began with them all those hundreds of years ago and lately they have got to feel it's come back to them, since no one has been there. They don't like your arrival one little bit and I don't think one visit from us is going to stop anything. They'll have retreated now. They've probably slipped down into the water and are lying at the bottom together. But they won't be lying quietly. They'll be plotting. Plotting their next move.'

'What was the thing that came out of the water – the stony-looking man?'

'The Stone King? Yes, I must say I was surprised he put in an appearance. No one has seen him for so long they put him out of mind. He's there in the books and stories of course, and you might find a few very old folk round here who still believe he exists but, on the whole, he's regarded as a sort of Loch Ness monster.'

'Have some of those very old people seen him?'

'Save us, Oliver Mackenzie Brown, it will be more than ten thousand years since anyone saw the Stone King. Maybe even longer.'

They were silent, thinking, remembering. Olly could still feel the stiffness that had crept up his legs and the way he had not been able to move his eyebrows or twitch his nose.

'Now. A word of advice. I don't suppose you'll either of you go back there in a hurry, but keep a weather eye out for any of them and especially if anything new happens, let me know. It's best I hear about everything from now on. I don't want another narrow shave.'

He stood up.

'It'll be sunrise before long. Time you were getting back.'

'I hope Lula hasn't woken up early. If she does, sometimes Mum takes her into my room to play a bit.' Olly scrambled up.

'She won't be awake for a while yet. But off you go, now. Skedaddle.'

He clapped his hands.

'Dad says scoot,' Olly said, making for the steps.

'Then do that as well. And watch out.'

'Thank you, Nonny, thanks for the great breakfast.'

Jinx was ahead, running fast, and they followed him, so full of energy they felt they could skim the ground.

Nonny Dreever watched them out of sight, puffing on his pipe. In front of his triangular chair was a large footstool and he nudged it towards him a little way. The footstool settled itself comfortably, opened its eyes once and closed them again.

'I don't know about you,' Nonny Dreever said to the tortoise, 'but I'm worried.'

CHAPTER FIFTEEN

The Arrival of a Letter

The sun was breaking through the early mist when Olly got back to Gullywith and everyone was still asleep. KK had left him at the crossing in the tracks to go in her own direction home. The house was still. Olly looked into the kitchen. The sun was shining on the marmalade jar and when Olly put his finger on the glass it felt warm. He remembered the scrambled eggs and the mushrooms that had tasted smoky and earthy and the pools of soft honey spiralling from the spoon down on to his toast and it seemed as if he had eaten breakfast at Nonny's in a dream. But there were toast crumbs round his mouth and when he licked his finger it tasted faintly of tomato.

He crept upstairs, afraid that the stairs would creak, which they generally did, because it was just that time of the morning when Lula might be woken by the slightest, tiniest sound and start singing out for someone to get her out of her cot and start the day. Olly slid into his own room. Nothing had stirred.

He felt a strange mixture of being tired and being wide awake, being excited and puzzled and troubled and disbelieving. He got into bed and curled tight under the duvet so that he could not hear the birds or see the light, and so that he could think. He needed to think. So many things had happened, he needed to go over them one by one, turning them and examining them, working out what they might mean. KK throwing the pebbles at his window, the walk in the moonlight over the hill, the climb down the steep slope to the fog-shrouded shore of Withern Mere, the . . . Olly felt himself fall down into a deep, soft cloud of sleep which wrapped itself around him and rocked him very gently.

The next few days were remarkable in being absolutely and completely normal. Nothing happened. KK did not appear. The sun shone. They unpacked the rest of the boxes and put things away. Olly went to the supermarket with Mum and twice into Fiddleup with Dad to buy paint and a new drill. They had an ice cream at the Bluebird Café the first time but the second they were in too much of a hurry to get back and they didn't go into the book-shop at all, partly because Helen Brown had said 'No More Books' but mainly because on each trip the door had been shut and a sign up saying, *CLOSED*. Dad had made a start on turning one of the barns into his office, as he was going to do all his software design work from home now, and there was the sound of drilling and hammering and banging from early each morning.

Above all, Gullywith felt normal, calm and cheerful and peaceful and there were no stones anywhere. When Olly went into the little damp room in the attic, the hole in the skirting board had been neatly plastered over and even the cold patches seemed to have disappeared.

Things only changed with the arrival of the letter. Olly had met the post van by the gate and noticed the type-written envelope with a blue emblem on the back, but as it was addressed to Mr and Mrs Peter Brown it had not, of course, crossed his mind that it was anything to do with him.

'Oh, listen, Olly, this is about your new school. It's from the head teacher.'

School. Something seemed to drop down inside Olly's stomach like a heavy coin dropping into a slot. He had deliberately kept his mind away even from the word 'school', not because he didn't like it – school was school, sometimes good, sometimes not, but you had to go there so that was that. But 'school' now did not mean what 'school' had meant before. Then, it had meant Peter's Road First School. Now . . .

'Fiddleup Middle and Upper,' read Helen Brown. 'Mole Hill, Fiddleup. Dear Mr and Mrs Brown . . .'

Olly turned away and started to tease Lula into eating up the last of her banana, mainly so that he would not have to listen, but he caught odd words like 'welcome' and 'Mrs Waller's' and 'uniform'.

None of it would have anything to do with him until the beginning of the new term and as that was not until September and it was now only July he preferred to take no notice.

Then his mother said, 'Listen to this, Olly – this is a good idea. "In order to help newcomers settle in well, we try to make arrangements for them to meet someone who is already at the school and will be in their form before the start of the new year. Accordingly, I have asked the Crust family to make contact with you. The Crusts have two children with us. They live in Pithersett, a village just a few miles from you. Mervyn Crust is the same age as Oliver and they will be in Mrs Waller's class together. They will also catch the same school bus."

'What a brilliant idea, Olly. It won't be half so weird going to a new school if you have a friend there beforehand.'

'How do I know he'll be a friend?'

'Of course he will be.'

'KK's a friend.'

'And does she go to Fiddleup Middle and Upper?'

Olly realised that he had not the slightest idea. The subject of school had never come up. He and KK had other, far more interesting things to talk about.

'When they get in touch, I'll invite him over. You'll be bored kicking about here on your own before long and you know coming to Gullywith means we're not getting away on holiday this summer.'

'I like kicking about on my own.'

'All the same.'

Oliver sighed, lifted Lula down from her chair and wiped her face with a damp cloth. He might have known it was pointless to say anything.

But nothing else was heard for the time being about the boy called Mervyn Crust, which was probably a good thing as from that day crisis after crisis hit Gullywith. The old barn which Dad was converting had damp rot and dry rot and sinking foundations. The old stable, which was going to be Mum's studio, had a roof which collapsed in on itself in the middle of one night, the same night that it started to rain as heavily as Olly had ever seen it rain, and it rained for days on end, by which time everywhere was a sea of mud, Pete Brown was in a permanently bad temper and Helen Brown was either in tears or in a rage.

It was on one of the blackest mornings of all, when Olly felt as if he wanted to go round kicking the walls and Lula had a nasty, runny cold and cough, that things came to a head.

'Unless you get a team of builders, a proper firm who can start now and finish yesterday, I'm going to Aberdeen and taking the children with me until this place is sorted out,' Helen Brown said. Olly could tell by the quiet, sweet tone of her voice that she was deadly serious. His grandparents lived in Aberdeen in a small flat at the top of a forbidding-looking grey house in the middle of the city. It was the last place in the world Olly wanted to be.

Pete Brown knew that she meant it too and in ten minutes he was in the car and out of the gate. He returned a couple of hours later and said that he had found a firm of Polish builders who were starting the next day. He also brought three pairs of pale green wellington boots with pink flowers on them, a small pair with ducks on for Lula, and a bunch of flowers, which Olly could tell had come from the petrol station.

The Polish builders, five of them, arrived the

following morning at seven o'clock. From then on, and apart from the wellington boots with pink flowers on in his size, Olly felt that things had begun to look up.

He also wished that KK would turn up again.

That night, the electricity went off, not because anyone had fused it but because there was a tremendous thunderstorm. Olly lay in bed, watching the lightning flash vivid blue, and even blue with red edges a couple of times, over the hill and hearing the thunder go crump. He loved storms. He thought it would be especially good to be in Nonny Dreever's house on stilts. He also wondered what Withern Mere looked like whipped up by the wind and rain of a storm. Withern Mere. It was strange to remember it. It was almost as though it had never existed. But it did. He was quite certain of that.

The lightning streaked down and went flash-flash-flash, turning his whole room electric-blue. But, in the opposite of the sort of thing that usually happened, the lights came back on. Olly's giraffe lamp started to glow in its peaceful, golden way, somewhat subdued in competition with the vivid blue and white lightning outside, and in its soothing light, Olly noticed that there was something on his bedside table, something that definitely, definitely had not been there earlier in the day or before the electricity had gone off.

It was a book, bound in dark blue, and with the title stamped in dull gold on the cover.

The Battle for Gullywith.

CHAPTER SIXTEEN

The Vanishing Book

Olly reached out his hand but he did not quite touch the book. Something that appeared and disappeared might do other things and he did not altogether trust it, however serious and solid it might look now. In view of everything that had happened, he lay and simply looked at the book for a long time. It was not a book he would have taken any notice of if it had not had such an interesting title. It looked pretty dull. It had dull gold writing on the spine and a dull dark cover and that was that.

The other thing about it was that, so far as Olly knew, all books had the name of an author printed on them but this had none. How could a book exist if no one had written it?

The thunder rumbled on.

Olly let his hand hover over the book but still did not actually touch it. He was longing to see inside, to read the story, to find out everything about the house and why there was a battle about it, but he felt that he might prefer actually to open it in the safety of daylight.

He fell asleep with his hand stretched out towards, but still not touching, the book.

The next morning, Dad had to go into Fiddleup and Mum made him take Olly and Lula, so that she could start sorting out her quilting things and trying to make a temporary workroom from one of the spare attic rooms until her studio was ready. The Polish builders had arrived again at seven and were cracking on so fast Dad was cheerful at the thought of everything being finished, including the roof and both workrooms, by the time Olly was back at school.

When they reached Fiddleup, it had stopped raining and Dad took Lula with him to the shoe repairer's, the post office and the chemist, leaving Olly to get the newspapers, a cartridge for the printer and a head for the mop. The plan was to meet in the Bluebird Café.

The jobs took half the time Olly expected and as he went back up the hill he saw that the sign on the bookshop said, *OPEN*.

He went inside, making the doorbell jangle, and as he went he glanced down, but there was no doorstop there, shaped like a tortoise or anything else.

There was no one else in the shop either. Olly went quickly to the shelves where he had seen *The Battle for Gullywith* the first time. There was the book about skylarks but now it was next to *Puffins and Other Coastal Birds* and *Hedgerows and Their History* had gone. *The Battle for Gullywith* was not there either.

But just as he turned away, Olly caught sight of something else. Slipped in between skylarks and puffins was a fat book in dark red binding. He turned his head sideways to read the title.

Legends of Withern Mere.

Like *The Battle for Gullywith*, this, too, seemed to have been written by no one.

Olly reached out his hand.

'Can I help you, young man?'

Olly jumped a foot into the air. The voice had come out of the ceiling. 'Is there something in particular you're wanting? We don't get many children in here.'

Olly felt insulted. 'My hands are clean and actually there is something I'm interested in. I would like to know the price of this book, please?'

He turned back to the shelf and took out the fat red book. The man, who had been perching perilously on the top of a stepladder changing a lightbulb, climbed down.

He was a small round man with glasses on top of his head and a yellow duster tucked into the front of his shirt and as he took the book from Olly, he gave him a long hard look.

'Twelve shillings,' he said. 'Or at least, that was the price when I last sold it. Apparently.'

Olly wondered if he was deliberately being confusing.

'Why do you want it?'

Olly almost said 'To read' but stopped himself and just said, 'It looks very interesting.'

'Is that all?' the man asked. Olly didn't know. 'I'm very careful who I sell some books to and this is one of those books. It doesn't do to let some books fall into the wrong hands.'

He pulled his glasses down from the top of his head into their proper place and peered at Olly again. Olly felt uncomfortable. He also thought that he was late to meet Dad and likely to be in trouble.

'If you could just tell me the price, please . . . I have to go. I have to meet my dad.'

'How much money have you got?'

Olly rummaged in both his pockets. In one he found thirty-five pence and in the other fifty. He also found the small heavy brass tortoise which had been his present from under Nonny Dreever's Christmas tree, which was surprising, as he did not remember putting it there.

'I'm afraid I've only got eighty-five pence but I can ask Dad if he would buy it for me so long as it wasn't too much. He always gives me money for books.'

The man was putting the book into a brown paper bag.

'Fine. That will be eighty-five pence, please. And it's a pleasure to do business with you.'

'Are you sure? I mean . . . that isn't much.'

'Quite sure.'

'Thank you. Thanks very much.'

Olly handed over his money. As he did so, he dropped the brass tortoise on to the floor and before he could stop it, it had rolled away and disappeared among the piles of books on the dark floorboards of the shop.

There was a very sharp pain in Olly's leg.

'I . . . ouch. I just dropped something. I think it rolled under there.'

'Yes,' the man said, 'it did. It'll have gone to seek its

fortune among the others.'

'Other what?'

'Other tortoises of course.'

Olly's leg hurt so much and he felt so muddled and upset that it was only when he had got out of the shop, banging the door so that the bell jingled violently, and into the Bluebird Café, that he realised he had done three things all at once: handed over all his money, lost the brass tortoise, and forgotten to take the book.

His chance to go back was thwarted by an urgent phone call from his mother as Pete Brown was wiping ice cream from Lula's front and trying to steer her away from the remains of his cup of coffee. Olly answered.

'Where's Dad?'

'Er . . . gone to the loo.'

'Where's Lula?'

'Here. She's fine, Mum.'

'OK, do you want the bad news first or the good?'

'Er . . .'

Dad handed him the wiping cloth and took the phone. Several customers were staring at them. Olly couldn't make out whether their expressions were sympathetic or annoyed.

'Right, on the way. Just got to, er, get stuff into the car.'

Which was how they came to be packed up and bowling out of Fiddleup before Olly remembered that he had not gone back to the bookshop.

'The bad news,' said Dad, 'is that the barn roof has collapsed and one of the walls, from what I could tell, and it's more or less a pile of stones and rubble.'

'And the good?'

'Can there be any?'

'She said.'

'Oh yes – a boy has arrived. Apparently he's your new friend.'

As they turned into the gateway at the top of the drive, they could see the barn, which was barely a barn any longer. The dust was still rising from it, though the rain was damping everything down.

Dad groaned. 'Sometimes,' he said to Olly, 'Fifty-eight Wigwell Avenue seems golden in the memory.'

The Polish builders had gone off to finish a job elsewhere. Olly looked at the heaps of stones, huge ones from the walls, great grey uneven blocks, along with tiles and some of the wood from the rafters. Dad took Lula inside and he was behind, carrying the shopping.

He knew what had happened, of course, and it had nothing to do with the weather. The lull in the Battle for Gullywith had been just that – now things had started up in earnest again and the stones were rising against them.

He needed to talk to Nonny Dreever urgently.

'Olly, what are you doing out there? Come and meet your new friend.'

Olly's heart sank. He told himself that a new friend would be great, someone to do things with, like Jamie had been in Wigwell Avenue, but he had a feeling it wouldn't be the same. He turned away from the ruined barn and, as he did so, kicked a small stone with his toe.

It went rolling ahead across the yard looking spiteful and he saw that it had the markings scratched on its surface. He wasn't surprised.

'Oh, there you are at last. Olly, this is the friend the headmaster told us about. His mother brought him over earlier so I said it would be really nice if he stayed for lunch.'

Olly looked at the boy standing beside the range.

'Well, say hello for goodness sake. This is Mervyn. Mervyn Crust.'

'Hi.'

'Lo.'

Helen Brown sighed. 'Honestly. Well, don't just stare at each other. Now –' She turned to Pete Brown, who was filling the kettle, always his first action when trouble swirled around his head. 'About this barn . . .'

The boy was a bit taller than Olly. His hair was black and stuck up here and there, and he had extremely pale green eyes and almost no eyelashes.

He wore shorts and a check shirt so terrible that Olly could only feel sorry for someone who was called Mervyn Crust and whose mother put him in a shirt like that.

Mum and Dad had gone outside and Lula was asleep in her buggy. It was quiet in the kitchen, apart from the rain spattering against the windows.

'Weird place,' the boy said. 'What'd you come here for?'

'It's not weird. It's a great place.'

'It's weird. Everything's got holes in, it's falling down

and the toilet smells of mushrooms.'

'Only the downstairs one. There's a lot to do, that's all. Nobody's lived here for a long time. Do you want to see my room?'

Mervyn Crust shrugged.

It was a long morning. Mervyn Crust told Olly a few things about school that he could have guessed because they were the same as things had been in his previous one. He picked fault with everything inside and outside Gullywith, and he was fussy about everything he was offered to eat and drink and complained that he was cold. After lunch, as it was still pouring with rain, they went back up to Olly's room.

'What's this for?' Mervyn Crust had picked something up from the bedside table. Olly looked. It was the brass tortoise, sitting neatly and quietly on top of the red book he had left behind in the shop.

'What's wrong? What are you scared of?' Mervyn Crust said.

It was one of those moments when things changed. In a split second, Olly went from thinking he would keep his mouth shut and tell Mervyn Crust nothing about any of it to saying, 'It's the tortoise I lost on the floor in the bookshop and that's a book I left behind there and I don't know how they got here but things like this keep happening, they've happened ever since we came to Gullywith, no, even before we came and since I met KK and Nonny Dreever and went to Withern Mere and . . .'

If he could have sucked all the words back into his

mouth and swallowed them the second after he had spoken, he would. What had possessed him to come out with everything to Mervyn Crust?

The other boy sat on the end of Olly's bed. He had a small, pleased smile on his little cushiony pink mouth. 'Another one,' he said.

'Another what?'

'KK. She's another weirdo. That's the sort of thing she'd make up. You wait till I tell them this one. Flying tortoises, moving books, underground passages in hills, evil stones. You want to be careful though. There's always been stories about this place and if you go making ones up something might happen. You never know. Truth is stranger than fiction, my mum says, and once you start you might find you can't stop. Then what?'

Olly took a deep breath. 'I don't know what you're talking about.'

'Don't pretend you didn't say any of it. I heard.'

'Oh, that.' Olly got up and went to the window. 'It was a joke. Don't you know when someone's doing that?'

He looked out towards the hill. The rain was slanting across the horizon, and the sheep were all in a huddle at the bottom. He held his breath and crossed his fingers. He'd been pretty stupid to start telling Mervyn Crust what had been happening and he only hoped he'd managed to convince him it had been made up for a joke. Mervyn was fiddling with an old model of a crane on the shelf, winding the handle to make it go up and down.

Olly wondered how long he would have to be here.

And then he saw something. Through the rain, right

at the top of the hill, something flashed, but it was not lightning, which had a blue-white flash, it was a golden light, fiery and brilliant. It flashed twice, then there was nothing.

Flashed again. Flash-flash. Flash-flash. Nothing.

'What are you staring at?'

'Nothing. Rain.'

'This is quite cool.'

Mervyn was still playing with the crane. 'Can I have it?'

He glanced quite casually across as he went on winding the crane up and down.

'Be careful, you'll break it if you do that too much. It's quite old. It was my dad's.'

'Can I have it?' It was as if Olly could read everything in Mervyn Crust's head, the words and the sentences and what they all meant, as if he could see them like writing on a page. 'A lot of people would be quite interested in all that stuff. Tortoises and stone men and books that aren't there and then they are. I can guess what they'd say when I told them. Did you know the police are interested in that Nonny Dreever?'

'What for? He hasn't done anything.'

'You don't know much.'

'You leave Nonny Dreever alone. And that crane. Stop doing that, you'll break it.'

Mervyn Crust wound the handle of the crane very quickly tighter and tighter one way then the other. Olly dived across to grab his arm and stop him.

The crane wire snapped and hung in two lifeless bits

and the crane slumped down on to its base with a bang.

Olly let out a howl of rage but Mervyn Crust simply got up and walked out of the room, leaving him feeling furious and helpless. And the person he was most furious with was himself.

'Mervyn . . . your mum's here,' Helen Brown shouted from downstairs.

'Good. Good good good. Good riddance and don't come back,' Olly muttered.

He went into the bathroom and locked the door. He didn't want to have to go downstairs and meet Mervyn Crust's no doubt awful mother, or to see them go.

'Oliver, come down here, please.'

'I can't. I need to stay in the toilet.'

'Oh, heavens. All right, all right.'

Eventually, he heard the distant sound of a car driving away and, after waiting a few more minutes to make sure the Crusts had gone, Olly came out and slipped across the landing.

The first thing he noticed was that the rain had stopped and the sky was brightening slightly over the hill.

The second thing he noticed was that the golden light was flashing again. Flash-flash. Stop. Flash. Stop. Flash-flash. Stop. Nothing.

The third thing was that the small brass tortoise had gone from where it had been sitting on top of the red book.

CHAPTER SEVENTEEN

Withernosaurus

'Why on earth did we come here in the first place, that's what I want to know. I mean, what was wrong with Wigwell Avenue?'

Pete Brown had his head bent over the paper, which was his way of letting the tide of Helen Brown's complaints wash over it. Olly was always impressed by the way Dad never, or almost never, answered back or pointed out the obvious fact that it was she who had pushed and pushed to leave Wigwell Avenue and come to Gullywith, she who had worn rose-tinted spectacles throughout the viewings, the auction and the move, she who had imagined the children tumbling in sunlit hay meadows while she made her quilts and wall hangings in a white-washed studio and Pete designed his software and the organic kitchen garden provided them with a never-ending supply of wholesome vegetables and an orchard with fruit. Possibly there was even a goat. There was certainly a bounding puppy and a fat cushion cat which slept beside the range when it was not ridding the house of the occasional mouse that dared to venture over the threshold.

Pete Brown had known the spectacles were rose-tinted but he had not had the heart to remove them because he knew she would have struggled to keep them firmly clamped in front of her eyes and also because he knew time and reality would restore normal vision.

'The place is damp and it smells, there's mould and mildew all over the place – no wonder Lula has that cold and cough – the electricity goes off and the range goes out, the roof has holes and the barn's collapsed in a heap. And there are stones everywhere.'

Pete Brown got up silently, crossed the kitchen to the range and set the kettle on to boil.

'There are no neighbours, it's a half-hour drive to get a pint of milk or a newspaper and I didn't care for Mrs Crust. She made remarks about the state of the house, which was rather rude. She knows that we've only just moved in.'

She sat down at the kitchen table and burst into tears. Pete poured out a mug of tea, spooned two sugars into it and set it down in front of her. He also handed her a clean tea towel to wipe her eyes.

Olly went round and gave his mother a small tight hug. 'Great,' he said. 'Great, Mum. Crust the Creep,' and went out of the kitchen.

'And that isn't called for, thank you, Oliver.'

Huh, Olly thought. A minute ago she was saying she didn't care for them.

It was still raining. Olly switched on his giraffe lamp and picked up the red book.

Legends of Withern Mere.
Chapter One. The Withernosaurus.

Two hours later, Olly was lying on his bed but now he was asleep, with the book beside him and he was having a muddled dream about the Withernosaurus, which was sitting at the table in Gullywith's kitchen being fed by Helen Brown with honey sandwiches.

Olly woke and lay still for a moment, smiling at the dream. It was pretty unlikely that anyone would have fed the Withernosaurus with anything at the kitchen table. The book chronicled the story of this monstrous beast which was said to have been dropped accidentally into the bottom of Withern Mere as an egg, from the claws of its parent flying overhead, and to have hatched out there in the murky waters under some boulders and spent the next seven thousand years growing until it first surfaced and was spotted by some men out hunting with stone axes for weapons and deerskins for clothes. The Withernosaurus had been several hundred feet long, with sharp pointed fins which pierced the surface of the water in a long line. Its scaly body was slime green and its eyes had been yellow and gleamed, and when its head had emerged from the water it had opened its mouth to roar and reveal thousands of scissor-like teeth. All of this was known because the men had raced away, fearing for their lives, to caves under the hill, and there one of them had scratched pictures of the great beast of the mere on the walls with sharp, pointed stones.

The Withernosaurus had not been seen again for

several thousand years, although stories had been told about it to frighten naughty children around the open fires at night. Many disbelieved in its existence and stories were made up about it simply for fun.

Olly did not like all books but when he found one that he did like he read it in the way a starving person will eat food, hugely, greedily, without any manners, to the exclusion of everything else, which was how he had devoured the opening chapter of *Legends of Withern Mere* and why, having finished it, he was so exhausted he had fallen asleep. It was as though he had read the chapter about the Withernosaurus with his ears and nose and mouth and stomach, as well as his eyes and mind, gobbling it up and reaching out for more, living with the men who had been hunting when the beast had first risen from the mere, feeling their horror and their fear, running home with them and telling the tale, then drawing the pictures on the cave walls, yet at the same time, he had been the monster, huge and powerful, lying low, deep in the cold green-black waters, plotting when to surface, and feeling the first of the air and light striking his leathery, scaly skin. He had breathed faster, his hands had gripped the book, and somehow the lashing rain on the windows had added to his excitement.

It was still raining but otherwise the house was very quiet. He smiled and rolled over, to reach for the book again. Chapter Two might be even better.

But there was no Chapter Two. He turned the pages over, then the book itself over, but although the title page – without any author's name – was there as before, and although the list of contents began with *The Withernosaurus*, there were no other chapters at all, just a couple of blank pages and that was that.

But when he had first seen it in the bookshop, he could have sworn there had been chapters called *The Stone King*, *The Rising of the Waters*, *The Drowned Castle*, *The Ghostly Bells* and more. The book had been quite fat and heavy, but now it was thin.

Maybe this was a different book, maybe he had left the thick one with all the other chapters in behind and come home with this?

No he hadn't. He hadn't come home with any book. He had dropped the brass tortoise on the floor and . . .

Olly lay on his back. Things were churning round in his mind again, with odd bits rising to the surface and other bits sinking down, and he needed to get some of it straight if he possibly could.

Now, the tortoise had been the present, wrapped in Christmas paper and with the label that had his name on in funny violet-coloured spidery writing when . . .

The writing! That was it. The thin, spidery, violet-ink writing was the same as the writing on the bookshop door notice, just smaller. *OPEN. CLOSED.*

He knew he'd seen it somewhere.

So, the next thing that happened had been . . .

There was the most tremendous rumbling noise. It seemed to be coming from deep inside the walls and to have started at a distance and to be growing as it came nearer and nearer. Olly leaped off his bed and went to the window. Nothing. Rain. Grey.

The rumbling grew louder and sounded oddly familiar. Then the walls began to shake and shudder and the floor rocked slightly under Olly's feet.

It must be an earthquake. They happened, he knew, even in this country.

But he had never heard an earthquake and, oddly enough, he knew that he had certainly heard this sort of rumbling sound before.

He was just wondering whether he should stay where he was or run downstairs, when the noise began to recede and in an odd way. It was as if it had started on one side of the house, in one wall, and was leaving by the other.

And then he realised that it had been a train. It was like the house of a friend in North London, where the tube trains ran deep below the ground and could be heard rumbling through from one side of the kitchen floor to the other. This rumble had been the sound of a train of some kind. Olly ran downstairs.

It was peaceful in the kitchen. Lula was in her playpen dropping felt bricks into a bucket, Dad was ironing a pair of jeans and Mum was cutting something out of a magazine.

'Did you hear it?'

'My goodness, you've been quiet.'

'The train.'

'What train?'

'Just now . . . a few minutes ago. I haven't heard the trains here before, maybe it was the way the wind blew, making it seem so near.'

'Some wind,' Dad said. 'The nearest train to here is

about twenty miles away.'

'No it isn't. I mean, it can't be, I heard it.'

'Were you asleep up there?' Mum said, putting down the scissors.

'Well, I was reading and then I think I might have been. Only for a bit though.'

'It only takes two minutes to have a dream. It was raining and blowing and in your dream it was a train. Would you like sausages and mash for supper?'

Olly sat down at the table. He knew he hadn't dreamed it. Dreams were quite different. The Withernosaurus eating toast and honey had been a dream but the train had not. He knew the difference.

He also knew that there was no point at all in arguing.

'Did you decide about Wigwell Avenue?' he asked instead.

'Wigwell Avenue? What about Wigwell Avenue?'

'If you wanted to go back.'

'What on earth are you talking about, Oliver? Of course we don't want to go back. Whatever gave you that idea?'

'Just what you were saying. Before. About wishing we hadn't come here.'

'I did not say I wished we hadn't come here. Why would I say that? Honestly, boy, the things you dream up. Why would we have gone to all the trouble to buy the place at all? I don't know what you're thinking.'

'But . . .'

Olly glanced up and caught Dad's eye.

'OK,' he said.

'Good. Now, Pete, if you give Lula her bath, I'll get the sausages on.'

'Right. Go and make a start for me, Olly – run the water and find a couple of dry towels.'

Olly got up. As he went out of the kitchen, he caught Dad's eye again.

Pete Brown winked.

It reminded Olly of the tortoise.

When Dad came upstairs a few minutes later, he was carrying Lula and a large white envelope.

'Forgot to give you this, Olls. Great, thanks for putting the towels out.'

Olly looked at the envelope. It was addressed to *OLIVER MACKENZIE BROWN* in spidery violet ink.

'Where did this come from?' he asked, putting his head round the bathroom door.

Lula was already sitting in the bath grabbing handfuls of bubbles and rubbing them into her hair. She waved a handful of them at Olly.

'Dunno. It was on the flags in front of the letter box when I went into the hall at some point. Someone must have dropped it off.' He rubbed soap on to Lula's sponge. 'Your new best friend, Mervyn Crust, probably.'

Olly made a disgusted face.

He took the letter into his bedroom. It felt interesting. Stiff, like a birthday card. There was no stamp.

He turned it over. At first he thought there was nothing at all on the back but when he looked closely he saw a faint watermark in the paper. He held it under his giraffe lamp but it was impossible to make out any words or even what the pattern might be.

He weighed the envelope in his hand. He smelled it. He shook it. He knew he was putting off actually opening it and he was unsure quite why, but after looking at his name on the front again very carefully, he slipped the envelope, still unopened, under his pillow and then followed the smell of sausages and mash down to the kitchen.

CHAPTER EIGHTEEN

The Invitation

It was not until quite a bit later that Olly opened the envelope. The Polish builders had wanted everyone to see how far they had got with clearing the heap of rubble and stones that had been the barn and starting to rebuild it, and they had got so far and everyone was so delighted that the whole thing turned into an impromptu party, with cider and a lot more sausages and mash and for some reason the Polish builders teaching everyone Polish wedding dances. The rain had cleared and the evening was fine with stars and a huge moon, and they sat about outside eating and drinking and laughing and dancing and listening to the builders tell Polish stories until after ten o'clock. Then all the Polish builders kissed all the Browns and then they kissed each other and went off in their trucks, waving, down the stony drive and away. 'Bed,' Helen Brown said, chasing Olly into the house. 'You haven't been up so late since I don't know when.'

She was in a good mood again, which was all thanks to the Polish builders. If they went on like this, the barn would be ready for Dad to work in and Mum's new studio would be finished too, before the summer was anything like over. It was good. Olly scrambled up the last stairs and into his room.

The envelope was propped up against his giraffe lamp, which was surprising, as he had left it under his pillow, but he was used to things moving about of their own accord in Gullywith – not to mention other things appearing and disappearing again.

He put on his pyjamas and got into bed but he still held the envelope in his hand for some minutes before he opened it. He was excited by it and he sensed that it was important and that once he had opened it things would have changed, though this was not a feeling he understood.

Very slowly and carefully Olly slit open the envelope and slid out the stiff card from inside.

He laid the envelope down on his bedcover, turned the card over and read.

The Pleasure of the Company of
OLIVER MACKENZIE BROWN
is requested at
A MIDWINTER REVEL
In the Ice Caves of Withern Hill
On Friday 5th August
From Midnight
Wear non-slip boots and warm clothing.

The lettering was embossed on the card in silver but his own name was written in the familiar spidery violet ink.

Olly lay back on his pillows. The moon was huge and washed over him with its cool, eerie light.

Where had the invitation come from? Who was giving the party? How could there be a Midwinter Revel in August? Where and what were the Ice Caves of Withern Hill?

His head buzzed and whirred with questions and after a while he slid the card back into the envelope and got up and put it at the back of his wardrobe behind a suitcase. He had a feeling no one else had better find it. Not yet.

There were two people he badly needed to talk to about it. One was Nonny Dreever. The other was KK.

He had no idea where KK lived and he doubted if he could have found his way to Nonny Dreever's house on his own. He would just have to wait until KK appeared at Gullywith again. But the Midwinter Revel was on Friday night and it was now Wednesday. If he didn't get news from one or other of them, it looked as if he would miss it. He knew Withern Hill was the steep one that led down to the mere but he would never find that on his own in the dark either. It was very disappointing.

CHAPTER NINETEEN

The Cellar

'Olly! Olly!' His mum was shouting and there was the smell of frying bacon. The sun was shining.

As he went into the kitchen, Dad came through the front door in a hurry.

'Have we got any sticking plasters? One of the builders has gashed his hand.'

Helen Brown produced the plasters and Dad shot out again. Olly went after him in case Mum had it in mind to get him to feed Lula her egg, which would mean more egg over him than in her mouth.

As they crossed the yard, there was a shout from the barn and three of the builders shot out of it. There was a rumbling noise, a crash and a cloud of dust rose into the air.

The stone wall which the Polish builders had just finished was now on the ground again in a broken heap.

As they reached it, the last builder emerged, hopping and holding his toe, his face red and screwed up with pain.

It took a while to plaster up the cut finger and for the builder with the toe to get his boot and sock off and take a look at it.

Pete Brown stood looking at the collapsed wall in despair.

'Unlucky,' Maciek, the team leader, was saying, waving his arms at the barn, 'everything is unlucky. We build, it collapse, we build again, it collapse again, we repair, it break. Stones not fixing together, nothing works. Unlucky.'

Unlucky. Olly went nearer to the barn. The dust was settling a bit. The stones were tumbled together but as he looked more closely he could see that, as he had expected, some of the smaller ones at the bottom of the wall had the faint, weird scratches on their surface.

'Olly, come away from there. We've had two accidents already, we don't want another.'

Olly glared down at the stones. 'Just go away,' he whispered. 'Just stop trying to do this. You can't win. You won't win. We're here and we're staying here and there's nothing you can do, so go away.'

'Oliver!'

Half an hour later, the entire team of builders had gone. There was nothing else they could do until a surveyor came and checked the building. They did not look happy.

Helen Brown was not happy either. The morning which had begun well was in ruins and the plans to have a studio, a workroom and a warm, bright, tidy house by the end of the summer seemed to be in ruins too.

Olly went upstairs, not wanting to hear the whole

argument about 'Why did we ever come here?' all over again.

On his bedside table, on top of the red book, was an envelope. The last envelope had been large and stiff but this one was small and floppy. The writing with his name on was the same as usual though, spidery and in violet ink.

Olly closed his bedroom door.

Inside the envelope was a ticket dated 5th August.

RETURN. GULLYWITH TO WITHERN HILL.
ONE PERSON. 11 P.M. RIDE OUT. 7 A.M. RIDE
BACK.

Olly put it back into the envelope and tucked it away at the back of his wardrobe with the invitation. The ticket seemed to solve the problem of transport to the Midwinter Revel but what kind of transport it would be and how he would find it was not clear. One thing was though, and that was his own mind. He had made it up. He was going. Things at Gullywith were not much fun, what with buildings falling down, walls collapsing, arguments, dashed hopes and rain. He had not seen KK again and he certainly did not want another visit from Mervyn Crust. There had been alarming talk of Olly going to spend a day at the Crusts' house and the thought was not a happy one.

Somehow, he had to leave the house at eleven, taking the ticket and the invitation, find the ride and go to the revel.

His eye fell on the red book again and he picked it up.

Legends of Withern Mere.

It would pass a boring morning to read about the Withernosaurus again.

But when he opened the book that chapter was no longer inside. Instead, the first page was headed:

CHAPTER TWO
THE DROWNED CASTLE

Thousands of years ago, there had been a castle on top of Withern Hill. It had had ramparts and turrets and fortifications and battlements, a drawbridge and a large internal court, round which the stone walls had been constructed. It was huge and it was impregnable. Army after army had attacked it and tried to storm it but been repelled. No one had ever found a chink in the castle's defences. The entire district had been both ruled over and protected by the castle and its armies.

The situation had remained like that for hundreds of years until in the middle of one winter, there had been a storm, one of the worst storms ever, with winds of such force that they had done what no army had ever succeeded in doing and not so much damaged or even demolished the castle as blown it away. The entire castle and all its inhabitants had been lifted up and hurled down Withern Hill into the mere. It had sunk many fathoms down. No one had ever seen so much as a stone of it again but from time to time people had heard sounds coming from the mere – sounds of battle, sounds of an army being routed, sounds of the drawbridge creaking open and closed again.

Olly read on, imagining the terrible scene of the storm and the castle flying through the air and being pitched into the mere, hearing the strange noises coming from deep under the water. He wondered how recently anyone had heard them, who they were, what it was like. The whole place was becoming more and more extraordinary, more and more exciting.

He was desperate to find out what happened next but just as before, when he reached the end of the chapter about the drowned castle, there wasn't anything else in the book. The one about the Withernosaurus had disappeared, and been replaced by this one. What would come next? All he could do was wait until Chapter Three chose to appear in the red book.

'Olly! I need you to come and give me a hand, please.'

Pete Brown was in the hall. 'There's a crack in one of the flags in the kitchen and it's sunk down a bit. I don't want it to sink any more, someone might break a leg. I need to investigate in the cellars.'

'What can I do?'

'Hold the torch. Hand me things. Whistle. Tell me jokes. Fetch and carry. You'll be my gofer.'

'What's that?'

'Don't you know what a gofer is? A gofer is pretty important. I say, "Go fer this . . . Go fer that." And you go fer it.'

The steps to the cellar were reached through a door in the back of the hall, a very low, rickety wooden door. Pete Brown had to bend almost in half to get through.

The stairs were narrow and steep and had a bend halfway, with a weird niche with a ledge in front.

'Like in a church,' Dad said.

'Why's it there?'

'Dunno. Be careful here, Olls, it's slippery.'

The steps were damp and uneven and there was nothing to hold on to and as they neared the bottom, the cellar smell seemed to rise up to meet them.

'Shine the torch down here.'

Olly did so. They were near the bottom. The floor was made of ancient flagstones and what looked like cobbles here and there. They were worn and damp and the smell was dreadful, of damp and mould and mustiness.

'You OK?'

'Course.'

'Well, I can't see how I can do anything from down here. Shine the torch on that side of the ceiling, Olly.'

The ceiling was made of ancient beams with slates between and the whole thing was almost black.

'Looks almost as if it's been smoked. I wonder if there was ever a fireplace down here . . . people maybe even lived here. Rum, isn't it?'

Olly swung the torch about. There was a tiny, filthy pane of glass high up in the wall but it let in no light. There was nothing in the cellar at all.

'You'd have to put in a damp course or even tank it down here to use it as storage. Good job we've plenty of other space. Right, well, this was a wasted journey.'

They started to climb back up the steps carefully. But as they did so, Olly's torch beam picked out a patch on the wall beside the first step.

'Look.'

There were faint scratched markings all over several of the stones.

'Like writing.' Dad took the torch and peered more closely. 'Almost like runes. Weird. I suppose they used some old stones for building. They wrote on stones long before they had anything else of course – long before clay or wax tablets or parchment.'

'Would someone know what it says?'

'Oh, some professor of ancient runes somewhere maybe. Probably not very interesting though. It might say "Smith and Smith, Stone Merchants. Carving and memorial work. Tombstones a speciality." Early advertising. Come on.'

Olly wished he could copy what was on the stones. It had to mean something. Maybe there was something in a book which would help.

Dad had reached the top of the steps now and gone across the hall. Olly shone the torch back into the cellar for a moment and as he did so something caught his eye, a movement in one corner. He moved the torch beam.

Yes. There against the far wall. Some stones, which were in a small pile, were separating themselves into a line and the line was making its way across the cellar floor.

Olly snapped off the torch, ran up the last few steps, and when he reached the top, slammed the cellar door shut.

CHAPTER TWENTY

Journey on the Sleigh Train

Several times during Friday, Olly went up to his room and checked that the invitation and the ticket were still in the back of his wardrobe. They always were but he didn't trust anything not to disappear now. Not that he had any hope of being able to go to the Midwinter Revel. Maybe there was no such thing anyway, maybe it was all someone's joke. But whose? Who would have a beautiful invitation printed in silver on card? Who would have a ticket made?

Pete Brown had spent the last couple of days trying to get a surveyor to come and give a proper assessment of the barn, in order to get the Polish builders back. Helen had whitewashed the temporary workroom in the attic. Because of the decorating, Olly had had to spend quite a lot of his time looking after Lula. KK had not appeared but there had been three phone calls from Mrs Crust, trying to fix a day for Olly and Mervyn to 'play together', as she put it. The thought of playing with Mervyn Crust was not appealing.

Late in the afternoon, he put Lula in her buggy and went for a walk down the track leading to the field. It was warm and the sky was blue and Lula was singing herself to sleep quietly. Everything seemed peaceful, summery and normal. Behind them the sun touched the stone walls and roofs of Gullywith and made it look homely and snug. Even the great heap of stones from the collapsed barn seemed honey-coloured instead of their real slate grey. Olly stood pushing the buggy gently to and fro. It wasn't possible that some of the things that had happened had . . . well, happened. It certainly was not possible that some small evil stones were trying their best to ruin a beautiful summer and a happy family home. Because just then, Olly felt sure that was what it was going to be.

He laughed. Maybe it was clever Nonny Dreever who had made up the Midwinter Revel and somehow managed to print the invitation and the ticket – in among everything he had in his house there was sure to be a printing press as well.

The swallows were swooping into the old stable and out again, to feed the young in their nests, and swifts were soaring high in the sky above the chimneys of Gullywith. The sky was a pearly blue and it was warm. There were white daisies in the long grass.

Lula was asleep by the time he was pushing her back towards where his mother was looking out from the doorway.

'Isn't it lovely?' she said to Olly. 'Everything is so peaceful and still. Imagine hot, sticky noisy London on a night like this. The weather forecast says it's going to be even warmer tomorrow. Maybe we can find your tent and you could sleep out – I think I know which of the packing cases it's in. Maybe you'd like Mervyn Crust to come over and camp out with you.'

'Mum!'

The evening seemed to dwindle slowly down towards dark and Mum and Dad sat outside on the wall for ages talking. Olly knew nothing was going to happen. He just knew. But he still wanted it to be dark and night. Midnight. Just in case. He wondered whether to get undressed or not. If something happened, he didn't want to have to start pulling his clothes on in a rush. In the end, he waited until his mother had been up to say good-night, and then he put on a T-shirt and pants and left his jeans on the chair. Then he remembered.

'Wear non-slip boots and warm clothing.'

He got a jumper out of the drawer. His winter clothes were still packed away but after a lot of rummaging in one of the packed boxes he found his old parka and put that out too, and a pair of woolly socks which didn't match, and his boots.

All the time he was creeping about his room trying not to let the floorboards creak, he told himself how ridiculous he was being. Nothing was going to happen and in the morning, he would just have to pack them all away again.

All the same, he got the two envelopes out from the back of the wardrobe and put them on top of the red book.

Then he lay down on the top of his bedclothes and

tried to go to sleep. The moon was coming in through the window again and two owls hooted in the trees outside. Olly felt excitement in his stomach, as if it were Christmas Eve.

'Stupid,' he told himself, 'you're being stupid.'

He turned and turned, lay on his back, lay on his front, lay on his left side, lay on his right side, the owls hooted, the moon shone in, and he couldn't sleep, he couldn't sleep, he couldn't sleep.

He fell asleep.

It might have been any one of several things that woke him. The light from the flares. The rumble of the train. Or the sound of the pebbles spattering against his bedroom window. He sat bolt upright in bed.

The train was rumbling somewhere and seemed to be getting nearer. Whatever anyone said about the old line having been closed and there being no station within twenty miles, trains definitely ran nearer to Gullywith. This was the second time he had heard them. But as he listened to the noise, it changed. It came nearer and nearer but then it slowed down and became a quieter sound, more of a bumping than a roaring and rumbling. He waited. It slowed and slowed and then stopped. Outside. Then, through the darkness, came the gentle sound of horses whinnying.

When Olly had gone to sleep, his room had been washed with still, silvery moonlight but now it was illuminated by something quite different. A burning, deep golden light flickered round the walls. And then the spatter of pebbles against the window came again.

Olly leaped off his bed and went to look. Far below, he could see KK standing in the yard and holding another handful of pebbles. She saw him at the window and waved her arm to beckon him down.

But it was not only KK outside. Olly stared and stared but then he remembered. It *was* happening after all!

He pulled on his clothes quickly, grabbed his parka and boots and the two envelopes, containing the invitation and the ticket, and went as softly as he could down the stairs, across the hall and out of the house, closing the front door behind him without a sound.

Then he stood and gazed.

Beyond the yard, near the gate and the entrance to the field, was something he had never seen before and could barely have imagined.

A number of huge sleighs made of carved wood and joined together by silver chains were waiting. Each sleigh had a high curved back to it and a seat within. At the front were six horses and at the side of every sleigh, slotted into tall silver holders, were huge flares. It was the light of the burning flares which had made the red-gold flickering shadows on his bedroom walls.

'Come on,' KK was whispering loudly. 'Come on, Olly, we don't want to be late.'

Olly followed her. KK clambered up into the first sleigh. It had a small wooden door, like the door of a carriage. She opened it, stepped up and waited for Olly. Then they both sat on the slatted wooden seat beneath the high curving canopy. He had glanced behind and seen shadowy figures in the other sleighs, huddled in rugs and furs, and now Olly noticed that there was a fur rug on the seat, and fur foot muffs and gloves. But the night was warm and the sky above the flares starry. He didn't even need his parka, let alone a fur rug.

'But what . . .'

He had hardly begun what he wanted to say when the horses whinnied again, and the sleigh train began to move forward, slowly at first and bumpily over the uneven cobbles of Gullywith yard, but then they were through the gate and across the field and picking up speed. The air rushed past them, cool on Olly's cheeks, ruffling through his hair. The burning flares streamed backwards and now and then a trail of tiny golden sparks glittered away into the night.

Olly couldn't speak partly because of excitement but also because the speed at which the sleigh train was now going took his breath away. He glanced at KK, who had a huge grin on her face. She yelled something at him but the words flew backwards on the air.

The field, which did not seem particularly large the last time they had crossed it, now became miles long and as their sleigh whooshed across it the night grew colder and colder so that they were glad of the fur rug and then of the muffs and hats. The sky above them crackled with frost and the stars glittered. After a while, they left the flat fields and started to climb and as they climbed up the hill, Olly saw that they were driving not across grass and earth but over hard packed snow which gleamed by the light of the flares. They climbed higher and he could see other hills around them which were snow covered too. They sped downhill and then began to climb again and this time there were steep banks on either side of them and the banks were dense with trees. Snow lay along the branches and thick opalescent icicles hung from them. The tree bark glistened with frost. And then they were down again and running, running, and ahead of them something shone. They were taking the track down to what he was sure was Withern Mere but it was a Withern Mere of ice. For a moment it seemed as if the sleigh train would plunge across it but at the last minute it veered and followed the path that ran round it. Olly looked down. He could hear the sleigh runners whistling beneath them and feel the bitter cold that came off the frozen mere – a dark, iron cold, quite unlike the shining frostiness of the surrounding night air. He shivered.

Then he saw the hill, Withern Hill, the one they had escaped into from the Stone King, and the sleigh train was heading towards it – indeed, for one moment, it seemed as if they were going to charge straight into the side of Withern Hill and come to a terrible end, but as the horses raced ahead, Olly saw the two great doors swing slowly open. The sleighs shot through and the flares lit up the tunnel of darkness ahead of them.

CHAPTER TWENTY-ONE

The Midwinter Revel

For a few minutes the sleigh train ran on through the dark tunnel but then Olly saw light ahead, bright clear sparkling light, and then they were whooshing into the most astounding place he could have imagined and running smoothly to a stop beside a small landing stage. KK was laughing at him as he stared and stared in astonishment, completely unable to speak.

They were in a vast cavern whose walls were sheer ice. It was lit by dozens of flares let into the walls and posted all round the edge of a massive glittering ice rink, which formed the centre of the cavern and had tiers of benches round the edge like in a football ground. As well as the flares, there were hundreds of eyes gleaming like jewels out of ledges in the ice walls and shining down from the domed ice roof high above them. But braziers with red-hot blazing coals set all round the edges meant that the cavern was not cold.

'Come on,' KK said. 'We're here and the other sleigh trains are coming in. Everyone will be coming. It's all going to start.'

'Oliver Mackenzie Brown,' boomed a voice. Olly

looked at the figure, which had the voice of Nonny Dreever, but it was a very different Nonny Dreever who stood before them. He seemed several feet taller and he wore white fur boots over white chaps, a silver jerkin with white fur edgings and an amazing high white fur hat. But the face was Nonny Dreever's, the face and the topaz-centred eyes.

'Welcome to the Midwinter Revel, Oliver Mackenzie Brown.'

There was more noise as sleigh train after sleigh train shot into sight and stopped, to unload crowds of creatures and strange people in fancy dress, with masks and jewelled hats, high boots and sparkling costumes. Olly glanced down at his own jeans and shirt but then KK was pulling him along towards the stalls which were dotted around the cave, stalls with food and drink, hot roasted chestnuts and strange cups into which drinks were poured.

'What is it?'

'Revel Cup. Taste it. It's the best drink you've ever had.'

The cup was made of thinly beaten silver and pointed so that you couldn't have set it down and the liquid smoked with a curious blue-white smoking flame that danced over the surface. Olly held it away from his mouth.

'No, it isn't too hot . . . look.' KK tipped the silver beaker to her lips and drank and grinned. 'Yum.'

Olly hesitated, then quickly did the same and the smoking flame seemed to burst into a sweetness around his mouth. The drink was warm and fizzy and tasted of – he looked at KK, who said, 'Honey, lavender and sarsaparilla.'

The other stalls had hot bubbling cauldrons of what looked like fudge, little cubes of melting cheese, tiny portions of crisp batter, hot soup, small crunchy chips, bubbling chocolate. They took a bite of this and a paper cone of that and a sip of the other, licked their fingers and wandered on to the next stall, and by now the cavern was filling up and people were stepping on to the ice floor to slide and skate. But then a loud echoing drum roll and a fanfare which seemed to come from inside the ice walls sent everyone to the tiers of wooden benches and the flares changed colour, from white to purple, then red, then gold, then blue, then silver, then purple again. KK pulled him towards the benches. The flares changed colour again and seemed to double in size, lighting the whole cavern so that the walls shimmered.

'What's going to happen?' he whispered.

'The acrobats. Look!'

There was a strange high singing and the air was filled with figures swinging and swooping over their heads, over the great circle of ice on thin shining wires. Seconds later, they were joined by butterflies and birds, which fluttered and soared and wove in and out with the acrobats. The ice below was full of changing lights and among the light beams were skaters dancing and skimming.

Olly had been to a circus once in London, where there had been acrobats and high-wire artists, and once to an ice show, but none of it had been like this. The ice sparkled and crackled and the blades zipped and fizzed over the ice, trailing showers of silver sparks and stars.

The show finished in a blaze of fireworks and brilliant changing light and then there was a scramble for the ice and in a minute Olly, who had never skated, found himself spinning round and round with KK, and balancing easily on the ice as if by magic, laughing among the others. He held his breath and closed his eyes, then opened them quickly, expecting to find himself waking up in his bedroom, fresh from a dream. But he was here still, in the ice caves, among the revellers and dancers, skating so fast that the flares and gleaming eyes whirled round like a kaleidoscope before him.

'Come on, let's find the roundabout.'

They left the ice by a short ramp and slid into a second cave, smaller than the main one. In the centre was a huge carousel, with swingboats, dodgems on ice, and a helter skelter round it.

'Ice cream!' Olly said, 'Who wants ice cream at a winter revel?'

'Get some, you'll see.' The ice-cream stalls had queues and while they were waiting in one, Olly looked at the people in front of them. It was difficult to tell if they were human or animal – some of them might have been people dressed in animal costumes but others looked suspiciously real. And then he saw someone looking back at him, someone he was sure he recognised. The only trouble was, the person looked more like a fox than anything else and Olly was pretty sure he didn't know any foxes.

He looked at the hundreds of small lights in the niches of the ice walls and saw that every pair of eyes belonged to a tortoise which was nestling there quite snugly, blinking from time to time, which was what made the whole cave glimmer.

There were huge ice sculptures too, figures and animals carved out of great blocks of ice and lit up with neon colours of purple, green and blue. Lanterns made of ice with flares inside sent up spirals of vivid rainbow smoke every now and again. One of the ice walls had a freezing waterfall cascading down into an ice pool, showering tiny silver and white sparks as it fell. Everywhere Olly looked he saw something new and wonderful made of snow and ice and frost, something beautiful, something exciting.

They reached the front of the queue and got their ices. They were scooped out of a bucket made of ice into silver cones and, again, blue lights danced over them like the flames on a Christmas pudding. The cone was cold in Olly's hand but when the ice cream touched his lips it was hot. KK watched him, laughing again.

'Told you! Look, there's Zed and Xylo.'

'What are Zed and Xylo?'

'My brothers of course. Come on.'

Zed and Xylo were dressed as a chipmunk and a bear, but eyes exactly the same as KK's peered at Olly out of their furry headdresses.

'I didn't know you had two brothers.'

'I don't.'

'You just said –'

'I said they were my brothers. I've got four more.'

They all laughed but no one could talk because the band was playing again very loudly in the main ice cavern and when they went through they saw that everyone was dancing, and that a troupe of Cossacks in scarlet tunics and bearskins were weaving in and out in a long line on the ice, roaring out a Russian song and dancing with knees bent, each leg shooting out and back in turn as they went. The music got louder and faster until everyone was spinning round and then the room was full of Gypsies in long, full, coloured skirts which they held up as they twirled about. Olly found himself caught up by one of them and danced away with across the ice, laughing and breathless. But as they danced and as he was enjoying himself so much and whirling so fast he couldn't think, he caught a flashing glimpse of the fox, and knew that somehow, somewhere, he had seen the face before. But not on a fox.

Before he could work out who it was though, they had gone and now he was dancing with one of KK's brothers and then with KK, faster and faster. He ought to have slipped and skidded and crashed on to the ice but his feet were firm and sure and he didn't slither once, only danced and leaped and jumped in his excitement. The brothers were clapping him and now he was one of the line of Cossacks, holding on to the waist of the Russian in front and being pulled along to the music.

'Go, Olly, go go go!' KK shouted, clapping them on

from the sidelines, and now everyone else was clapping in time to the rhythm of the music. He caught a glimpse of Nonny Dreever, taller than everyone there in his white fur hat, clapping, and of Gypsy dancers and ice-cream sellers and acrobats and white rats and otters and beavers and stoats, standing on their hind legs and clapping, and he was whizzing round the ice rink laughing and singing to the clapping and the band until his ears rang.

'Hurrah!' he shouted out to them all. 'The Midwinter Revel. Hurrah!'

There was a great roar back. 'Hurrah! The Revel! The Revel!'

And, at that moment, the whole cavern went black.

CHAPTER TWENTY-TWO

Everything Goes Black

Not only was everything black, there was also sudden and total silence. Olly did not know how long he stood there trying to work out what had happened or was happening and trying to get his bearings. The dark was like no dark he had ever known, thick and heavy and without the slightest chink of light. He began to feel round. He put out his hands slowly to see if he could find something or someone, and gradually extended them, so that he was circling round himself with his arms. But there was nothing. He moved a tiny step forward, then another, and then turned slightly, and began to feel again. Where had everything gone? Where were KK and Zed and Xylo and all the hundreds of others? The flares and the lamps?

He inched forward holding out his right arm and after he had been doing so for what felt like miles, his fingers touched something hard and slippery, cold and wet, like a rock wall with water running down it. He felt a little higher, a little further along, and it was the same. He was frightened now because he had no idea which way to turn to find anything else. And then he felt something take hold of his other hand.

'Who's that?'

'Oliver Brown,' he said firmly.

'It's Zed. KK and Xylo are behind me. Are you OK?'

'Yes. What . . . where is everything?'

'We –'

'Look!'

Olly gripped Zed's hand as he saw a pair of gleaming yellow eyes above him.

'What is it?'

'I can't tell.'

The eyes stared.

'There's more.'

There were several pairs of eyes here and there in the blackness, and all the same, all small and oval and yellow and gleaming.

'Olly . . . Move forward a bit. Keep your hand on the wall, don't move away. If we all edge along like that, we might find the opening. If we keep together like this.'

Olly waited, then slid his hand forwards. The cold wet rock went on and on. He felt the others move close behind him. Once or twice he glanced up. The eyes were still there.

'Oh . . . it's here. I think . . . the wall stops. There's an opening.'

'Go forward very very slowly. When you put one foot forward, touch the heel with the toe of the other. Keep your hand stretched out in case you feel a door or the wall again.'

'Where's Nonny Dreever?'

'I don't know where anybody is, Olly. Just keep going, go on. We're all right.'

Keeping his feet close behind each other and only moving forward a cautious few centimetres at a time, and with his hand still out, Olly went on. The blackness was beginning to make him feel odd now, as if it was swirling and spinning him round. There was only space ahead of him, space and darkness. No wall. And now the gleaming eyes had faded too. There were no more ahead. He stopped.

'What's the matter?'

'It makes me giddy. I don't know where I'm going.'

'Wait a minute, then. Stand still and close your eyes.'

He did so. At first the blackness still swirled in front of him but gradually it calmed and he felt steadier. He opened his eyes again and took a small step forward.

The next moment there was a loud rumbling round immediately behind them.

'What's happening?'

'It sounds like a lot of stones coming down. Like a sort of avalanche.'

'Move on, move on, we don't . . .'

But as they pressed forwards, the rumble became a strange roar that seemed to go from one side to the other and then there was a great clanging sound as a great heavy door closed right behind them, shutting them in.

They froze, huddling together. There were no gleaming eyes. There was only the blackness again.

'I don't like this,' Olly said very quietly.

It was cold but not the wonderful cold of the ice cavern, which somehow had not been cold at all and in any case had been cheerful. Here the cold was damp and dismal and dark. They were in a small space, they could feel it. The walls seemed to close them in.

And then Olly heard something. He didn't say anything in case his ears were playing tricks. But after a few seconds, KK said, 'Listen!'

It was an odd sound and it came from low down, close to the wall and the floor just ahead of them, a faint scratching, scraping sound. It started and stopped, started and went on for quite a few minutes, then stopped again.

'I wish we could see.'

'I can . . . I can see something,' one of the boys said. 'Look . . . look, it's getting brighter.'

They watched. Just ahead of them, from where they had heard the sound, they now saw first one and then another tiny light. The lights were in pairs and they glinted a faint gold. They couldn't see anything else at first but one by one more tiny lights came on, until there was a whole ring of them, then a ring within the ring and then yet another ring, and they were all gleaming and glimmering and lighting up the space on the ground around. Behind the circles came other pairs of tiny lights, moving towards them very slowly, and joining to make another circle.

Then the noise started up again, the scratching and scraping.

Olly hesitated, then let go of Zed and crouched down. He moved slightly forward and reached out his hand very carefully. One of the pairs of lights winked off and on again slowly as Olly's hand touched the cool, hard, patterned shell of a tortoise.

'What are they doing? Olly, can you see?'

'I'll try but I don't want to hurt them or break up their circles. Hang on.'

He got down on his hands and knees and moved forward carefully. The floor was stone and not only cold but uneven and with sharp edges here and there. He felt like a giant down among the small, busy tortoises but after a moment the light they were giving became slightly brighter, as if half a dozen candles had been lit. The noise, which had stopped, started up again and he leaned towards it.

The lights of the tortoise eyes were enough for him to see that at the base of the rocky wall was a small hole and in front of the hole was a hollow in the ground. Six or seven tortoises were digging steadily with their front feet and the hole was growing bigger. They did not have the digging power of terriers or moles but they were solid and organised and persevering. Olly watched them in amazement for some minutes. The front row began to tire and dig more slowly, at which point they retreated and another group took their places and began to dig. It was an extraordinary sight.

'But what are they digging for?' Zed asked.

'A tunnel of course,' KK said. 'They're going to dig us out.'

'But that could take days – weeks probably.'

'Not at the rate they're going,' Olly said. 'Ouch!'

He yelped with pain because something hard and

sharp had hit him like a sting on his nose. A second later, he felt it again, this time on the top of his hand, and then on his arms, more and more little hard sharp things pinged on to him.

'Ow!' Zed yelped. 'One hit me then. They really hurt.'

'Stones,' Olly said. 'We might have known.'

'Where are they coming from?'

'What does it matter? The roof somewhere. They can obviously fire down with a good chance of hitting us even in the dark.'

'I'm pretty hungry. And thirsty. And tired. I could lie on the floor and go to sleep.'

'I wouldn't, Zed,' KK said. 'Go to sleep and anything could happen.'

'It already has,' Olly said.

The stones were hitting them hard now, each one bouncing off them on to the rock floor with a hard little ping and then there was a sudden blue-white flash and a long, low rumbling noise.

'Thunderstorm,' Xylo said.

'We wouldn't hear it inside the hill.'

There was another zigzag flash. Olly looked up. The thunder came again. He waited. Another flash and this time in the split second of light, he could see a jagged hole in the roof.

'That's the sky,' he said. 'I saw it. So if the sky is there – we could climb up.'

'How?'

'I don't know. One of us could climb on another's shoulders?'

'No. We stick together. We stay here,' KK said.

'I think that's stupid. If we stay here, we might –'

'Look!' In the dim light given off by the tortoises, they could see that the hole they had been digging was much bigger. 'I reckon we could get through that now.'

'But it's just a hole. What would be the point of that?'

'Let me have a look.'

KK knelt down and edged between the tortoises, who parted their tight circles to let her in. The boys stood looking down. The lightning flashed up near the roof once or twice but the thunder was rumbling further away. The little stones had made a shingle on the stone floor so that once or twice KK let out a sharp cry of pain as she knelt on a sharp edge.

'What is it?' Zed whispered.

'Just a minute . . .'

Olly wondered what time it was. It seemed hours since he had got on to the sleigh train outside Gullywith and he wondered why daylight was not already showing through the hole in the rock roof above them.

'It's really clever,' KK said, standing up beside them. 'They've dug a hole large enough for us to get through one at a time and it leads to some steps going down. I can't see any further than the top two – they seemed to be cut into the earth and it's quite narrow, like a tunnel. But we could get down.'

'We wouldn't be able to see where we were going.'

'We'd have to feel our way along the walls.'

'No,' Olly said, 'we'd take one of the tortoises. Quite a few tortoises. They'd give us enough light.'

'We're not taking the tortoises,' KK said. 'They're taking us. Look.'

The tortoises were moving. One by one they trundled towards the hole they had dug and clambered through. The circles unwound and formed an orderly queue and the gleaming eyes went down into the dark.

'What shall we do?'

'Wait.'

When about three quarters of the tortoises had gone through the hole, there was a pause.

'They're waiting for us to go,' KK said. 'The others will come behind us. You go first, Zed.'

'Why?'

'Because you're the biggest. If you can get through the hole, the rest of us can. Go on.' As she spoke, there was a low roaring rumbling noise in the darkness behind them and this time it was not thunder coming from outside, it was something behind the doors that had clanged shut on them earlier. 'Hurry up!'

Zed was on his hands and knees and crawling towards the hole. The others watched him in silence. The remaining tortoises had dropped back and gathered into a group.

Zed put his head through the hole, then wriggled his shoulders.

'It's fine,' he said. 'I've got room. I can stand up enough to get down the first step. I can't see much. OK, I'm going.'

And the next moment, Zed was completely swallowed up by the darkness inside the hole.

CHAPTER TWENTY-THREE

Bright Blue Bats

At the moment that Zed vanished and just as the others were moving forward to follow him, Xylo, who had said almost nothing for the entire evening, said softly, 'It's them.'

He did not need to say any more because a split second later, Olly and KK saw what he meant. From high above them came the sound of what Olly thought at first were mice squeaking. But it was not mice. The bright blue bats, which had been hanging upside down from the roof, had started to fly round and round, faster and faster, above them and as they flew faster they also flew lower. Then, in ones and twos, they started to swoop and dive.

Olly remembered what his grandmother had once told him about bats liking to get tangled in your hair, though he didn't know if blue bats did it as well as the usual black ones, but he still ducked suddenly as one came particularly close. He heard its squeak against his ear and felt the zip of its leathery wings against his skin.

'Get down the hole, quickly, after Zed. You first,' Olly said, pushing KK forwards. He had a feeling she might scream, because girls did scream at things like bats, and that any screaming might madden them.

'Why?' KK hissed. 'You think I'm scared of a few bats or something?'

No. Of course he didn't. He knew enough of KK, even after a short time, to realise that of course she was not.

He got down and, with the bats diving for him, crawled to the hole the tortoises had dug and peered down. Below the first step he could see glimmers from the line of tortoise eyes which gave him just enough light to see by and he climbed carefully in and began to feel for the second stone stair. It was covered in loose soil and quite slippery but, one step at a time, Olly crept down between the earth walls which pressed in on either side. Behind him he could hear the others, and the angry squeaking of the bats.

A few minutes later they were all in the tunnel, which was quite narrow so that they had to go single file, but the roof was high enough for them to be able to stand up and they could see quite well by the glow of the tortoise eyes.

'Where does this lead to?'

'Under the hill,' KK said behind him. 'But I'm not sure which way we're going. Tell Zed just to go on. Trust the tortoises.'

They went on for a long time, hearing nothing but the sound of each other's footsteps and breathing. It was damp and cool in the tunnel and smelled earthy.

Then Zed said, 'Oh.' The next minute, he was no longer immediately in front of Olly.

They had come into a place where the tunnel widened

right out into something like a room. The tortoises had placed themselves round the edge and a few had clambered up into niches on the walls and once they had all arrived, they could see that they were indeed in a sort of underground room. There was an old rickety table with a couple of chairs, a couch covered in a faded rug, and another rug on the floor. On one wall hung a set of shelves, with a few tin beakers, old biscuit tins, and then a couple of rows of books. On the opposite side was what looked like a large picture in a frame.

Olly went over to it and, close up, he could just make out a very old map. The writing was not in English, or even in the alphabet. All the place names of open fields, steep hills and thin lines of rivers or streams were in thin spidery writing but they were not a language he could understand. In the middle of the map was a large blue area that looked like an inland sea.

'Withern Mere,' KK said.

They all peered at the map.

'Might be.'

'And that's where we are – under here. That's Withern Hill.'

Olly tried to make sense of the marks but gave up quickly and turned back into the strange little underground room.

Xylo was opening the canisters and peering into the mugs. Zed was sitting at the table with his head on his hands and his eyes closed. Olly felt suddenly exhausted, with a heaviness in his legs and soreness round his eyes as if he had not slept for days. The couch and the rug looked extremely inviting and the tortoises, which had positioned themselves obligingly round the room and up on one of the low ledges, now began to half close their eyes one after another. The effect was that of lamps being dimmed. Olly sat down on the couch. It was surprisingly soft. The cushions and rug were old and slightly scratchy but they were dry and felt quite warm. He burrowed down into them a little and yawned.

In his dream he was cuddled up with a dozen bats which were forming a warm blanket over him and also protecting him from some giant tortoises, as high as houses, which were trying to peel the bats away and clamp an empty shell around him which would be attached to him forever. One of them carried a lot of iron rivets which would attach him to the shell, another carried a headpiece with tiny slits in, the only spaces out of which he would be able to look.

The bats clung to him, squeaking in fright and . . .

'Get off, get off, don't do that!'

Olly woke with a yelp. KK and Zed were sitting at the rickety table with a small enamel pot and two mugs in front of them and Xylo was on the floor, apparently teaching a couple of the tortoises to dance on their hind legs.

'How long have I been asleep?'

'Hours and you must have been having quite a dream, you were waving your arms about and squeaking and mumbling. Do you want some of this drink?'

Olly got up and almost fell over.

'My leg's gone fizzy. What's in that?'

'Tastes like Revel Cup . . . only it's gone a bit flat.'

'Do you think you ought to drink it? You don't know how long's it's been sitting there. You might get an upset stomach.'

KK snorted with laughter.

'You sound like Mervyn Crust,' Zed said.

Olly stared at him.

'He goes to our school.'

'I know. He's supposed to be my friend, he had to come to Gullywith to sort of introduce me to everything.'

Xylo, who had now succeeded in getting the two tortoises to dance together very gingerly on their hind legs, said, 'Yuk.' Which, Olly had begun to realise, was a long sentence for him.

He took the Revel Cup KK had poured out for him, tipped back his head and drank it in two or three long gulps. 'Ha,' he said, wiping his mouth, 'I'd like to see Mervyn Crust do that.'

'The only thing is,' Zed said, 'you do have to be careful what you say. Mervyn Crust has very sharp ears and a pretty long nose. He got wind of something once, something private to do with Nonny Dreever and the Midwinter Revel and the mere and he told his mother and she came up to the school and there were some pretty worrying moments before it all blew over. Mervyn's into everything. Mervyn and his friends.'

'Yuk,' Xylo said again. He had now got three tortoises and was trying to make them dance in a ring but every time they started to shuffle round, one of them collapsed back on to four legs and he had to start the whole thing over again.

'Who are his friends?'

'Errol Bingly and Georgina Yurt,' KK and Zed said together. They all looked at Xylo, but he was too involved in a tricky manoeuvre with two separate trios of tortoises to say 'Yuk'.

Olly looked round. It was cosy in the room and the drink, although rather flat, had brightened him up. KK and Zed seemed to have invented some sort of game with paperclips they had found on the floor and Xylo was humming a strange little melody to himself.

'Hellooo?' Olly said. 'What's going on? Only I thought we were heading down the tunnel trying to find a way home or out or – anywhere.'

'I like it here,' KK said, pushing one of Zed's paperclips on to the floor with a deft flick. 'What's the hurry?'

It was Xylo who sorted them out. He stood up, swept the paperclips into his hand and replaced them on the shelf with the mugs, straightened the rug and cushions on the couch, all without a word. Then he clicked his fingers. The tortoises which had been learning to dance scurried back among the others and the whole lot of them opened their eyes very wide, giving out quite strong beams of golden light.

'Right,' Xylo said.

KK and Zed looked slightly embarrassed.

The tunnel which had led them into the room did not lead them out again but there was a low archway on the other side and now the tortoises had lined up and were moving steadily towards it.

'Your turn,' KK said, digging Olly in the back.

Olly bent his head and pushed himself through the low archway. Immediately facing him was a wall of rock and let into the wall was a narrow iron ladder. The tortoises were now milling about at the bottom of the ladder and Olly realised at once that although they had managed to clamber down the stone steps into the tunnel there was no way at all that they could climb an absolutely vertical iron ladder.

'What shall we do?' he whispered as the others came up behind him.

There was a dreadful silence. The tortoises all seemed to be looking up at them.

And then Olly realised something.

'It's getting cold,' he said. 'Colder and colder.'

He realised that his hands were beginning to feel stiff with the cold and that his face was stiff too, as if it were freezing over. His legs felt oddly heavy.

He looked at KK. Her face had turned very pale and she seemed to be trying to smile but unable to move her mouth.

'The tortoises!' Zed said.

They looked down. The eyes of the tortoises, which had been gleaming and blinking slowly from time to time, were now fixed and the light from them had become dull and glazed.

'Quick,' KK managed to say, though her voice sounded as if she had been to the dentist and had a dozen fillings. 'Climb, Olly, climb!'

Olly heaved first one heavy leg and then the other forward, wondering how he could possibly lift them up enough to reach the first rung of the steep iron ladder let alone get up to the top. His leg weighed a ton and now his head would not turn from side to side and the air was freezing so hard it was hurting.

He heaved his right leg with a tremendous effort, and then his left. As he did so, there was a creaking noise from somewhere above, at the top of the ladder, and then a patch of light which grew wider as a trapdoor was opened. Light and warmth flooded down on them and at once Olly felt his face begin to thaw and the stiffness to ease in his legs.

'Climb,' KK said, in her proper voice. 'Hurry up, Olly. Climb up there as quickly as you can.'

Olly climbed up the iron ladder and stepped through the open trapdoor, the other three on his heels.

It was not until they were all at the top and the trapdoor was safely shut again on the cold and darkness below that they looked at one another in horror.

They stood, saying nothing but each one of them picturing the scene they had left only a few minutes before, with Xylo humming his strange little tune and some of the tortoises dancing solemnly on their hind legs while the rest of them looked on through gleaming, golden eyes.

CHAPTER TWENTY-FOUR

Mushrooms

Olly picked his way carefully through the heaps of huge stones and old tiles which had been most of the walls and roof of the old barn. The trapdoor they had come through was in the middle of it and from where they were standing now they could see the house and the front yard in the pearly dawn light.

'Right, you'd better go in, Olly, and we shouldn't be here.'

'Where are you off to?'

'Home of course. Won't take long.'

'But . . . we can't just leave them. The tortoises. They were turning to stone. We can't –'

'We can't go back down there either or the same thing will happen to all of us. Can't you see, this is what they want – they only have power over us when they make us like themselves.'

'But –'

'Listen, you're new, but the tortoises are ancient and they've been in this battle before. They have centuries of experience in defending themselves against the stones. They have to do this on their own. We can't help them now.'

Olly felt doubtful.

'Why don't you go and see Nonny Dreever later on,' Zed said, putting a comforting hand on Olly's shoulder. 'He'll say the same and he'll know what you need to learn to defend this place too.'

'Will you come as well?'

'If we can. Can you find your way?'

'I think so.'

'Take your brass tortoise with you in your pocket. That's like a magnet straight to Nonny's house.'

Olly felt cold in his stomach.

'What? Olly, you haven't lost it?'

'No. At least . . .' He thought back and suddenly it was all quite clear. 'I didn't lose it,' he said. 'It was stolen. And I'm pretty sure I know who did the stealing.'

It was the most beautiful morning, with a sparkling dew on the grass. Olly stood watching KK and Zed go off down the track, his head swimming with everything that had happened. But he was more confused and unable to sort out everything that had happened than tired.

Once again, no one was stirring in Gullywith and he slipped in through the back door and upstairs to his room.

On his bedside table was *Legends of Withern Mere* and this time there were two chapters, not the usual one. The first was 'The Ice Age' and the second was 'The Withern Bats'. The only problem was that, apart from the titles, the chapters were in a strange old-fashioned English.

'Olly? Are you awake?' Pete Brown called softly as he came up the stairs. 'I'm going to look for mushrooms. Do you want to come?'

'Where?'

'I don't know. In the fields, I suppose. Isn't that where you find mushrooms? Only if you want to come, hurry up and be quiet or we'll have to take Lula and I think that would hamper our search.'

They crept out and down the stairs, trying not to make a sound and trying not to giggle. Then they were outside and clambering over the low wall into the paddock at the back of the house and Gullywith and its remaining inhabitants slept peacefully on.

They plunged about the long grass in the back field for ages without coming upon so much as a toadstool but Pete Brown was quite cheerful about it and Olly enjoyed spending time with his dad, who was daft about every-thing – the fields, the sky, the birds, the wet grass, even the absence of mushrooms – telling Olly how good it was for them to be living in such a beautiful place, how much better for them all than London, how much he was enjoying the relaxed life, how . . . Olly wondered what Mum had been saying to make him go on about it so much.

'You like it here, don't you, Olls?'

'Yes.'

'Don't want to be back in good old Wigwell Avenue?'

'No.'

'Sure?'

'Yes.'

'Quite sure?'

'Dad!'

'Look, here's . . . oh. No. It isn't a mushroom. Oh well.'

'What is it?'

'Mushroom-shaped stone.'

Olly bent down. The stone was nestling innocently in the long grass. Olly touched it. The runic markings were quite clear. 'Got you,' he whispered, and picked it up quickly and slipped it into his pocket. Stones with markings were safer in his keeping than wandering freely about the world ready to cause trouble.

As they crossed the paddock, mushroomless but quite cheerful, they heard Helen Brown calling from the house.

'What have you two been up to?'

'Nice early morning stroll. Why not?'

'I thought we could have breakfast out here. It's going to be hot later. Can you change Lula please and, Olly, you can help me bring the crockery. It'll be wonderful to eat in the fresh air. Do us a power of good.'

Olly groaned.

He groaned even more when he was halfway through his egg.

'Oh heavens, I nearly forgot. Olly, Beryl Crust rang. She's picking you up at half nine.'

'What? What do you mean, she's picking me up? I don't want her to pick me up.'

'You're going to spend the day with Mervyn. She thought it would be nice for you both.'

'Do I have to?'

'Yes. If you can't find friends for yourself, other people will find them for you.'

'I can find friends, I've got a friend.'

'KK? I thought she was great. I like independent girls like that. I wonder why she hasn't been back?'

Olly opened his mouth to say 'She was at the Midwinter Revel, she . . .' and shut it again fast.

'Egg,' Lula said, holding out her spoonful of it to him. 'Egg egg egg. Olly. Olly egg.'

'Thanks,' Olly said gloomily.

CHAPTER TWENTY-FIVE

A Day with Mervyn Crust

'Please put your feet on the paper, Oliver,' Mrs Crust said. Olly looked down. There was a sheet of newspaper on the floor of the car. 'It's to make sure any mud on your shoes comes off there, not on the mats.'

Olly stopped himself from saying there was no mud on his shoes and stepped on the paper.

'I hope you don't mind being in the back, dear, only Mervyn has to sit in the front or he's sick.'

Yes, thought Olly. Of course he is.

'No, that's OK, I'm fine.'

'Just put your seat belt on before I move off.'

Olly put his seat belt on. It smelled of polish. The entire car smelled of polish. There was not a single thing in it apart from a map tucked into the pocket on the back of the driver's seat. He thought of their car. What on earth would Mervyn say if he ever had to travel in that?

The Crusts lived in a bungalow halfway up a short hill on the outskirts of Fiddleup. It was a dull-looking street and a dull-looking bungalow and inside it was so exactly like the Crusts' house of his expectations that Olly started to grin the moment they stepped inside the front door.

'Take your shoes off, Oliver. Put them there, on that mat.'

'Do you mean wipe them?'

'No, dear, I mean take them off. We don't allow outdoor shoes in the house. Would you like to borrow a pair of Mervyn's slippers?'

'No!'

Mrs Crust glanced round sharply.

'No, thank you. I don't mind having bare feet.'

'Oh dear, Oliver, it is bare feet, isn't it. Did your mummy forget to put any socks out for you this morning? Poor boy.'

Put out any socks? There'd probably be clean socks in his drawer and if not in the basket on top of the dryer, and if not there, in the dryer. He wondered exactly what putting them out meant.

'I'm fine, thanks.'

'Now, come and get your drink and biscuit in the kitchen, then you can play where you like. Mervyn has to have a drink and a biscuit by eleven or he feels sick.'

The kitchen was like a kitchen in a showroom. Everything gleamed. The work surfaces, which were pale beige, the floor which was pale beige tiles, the cooker, the windows, the polished wood of the table and chairs. Mrs Crust went to fill the electric kettle but before she filled it she wiped it vigorously and after she had filled it she wiped it again. The pale beige biscuit tin was full of pale beige biscuits. Plain ones. Olly dug about hopefully in case the chocolate and cream ones were at the bottom but they were all the same. Pale beige. Plain.

'Oliver! Other people have to eat those, dear, and you didn't wash your hands.'

Sitting on the other side of the table, Mervyn smirked.

Eating and drinking in the Crust house was very stressful and Olly wondered what a whole lunch was going to be like. Mrs Crust had wiped the table, the worktops, their chairs when they got down, the kettle twice more and cleaned their mugs and plates thoroughly before putting them in the dishwasher.

They wandered outside in the back garden. There was a long stretch of shaved stripy lawn with neat orderly rows of shrubs on either side.

'We could play footie?' Olly suggested after they had stared at it for a minute.

'I'm not allowed to play ball games in the garden.'

Duh, Olly said to himself. Stupid me. Of course you're not.

'Where do you play them, then?'

'I don't really.'

'OK, what are we going to do?'

'I've got things to tell you anyway. Come on, we'll go into my room.'

It was bright and warm, even if the garden was neat and boring and entirely without leaf or blemish, and Olly thought it might be better than being stuck in Mervyn's room but he realised when Mervyn went back in through the kitchen door that he wasn't being given any choice.

Mervyn Crust collected things. He collected rubber

dinosaurs, model tractors, shells, pencils, space invader characters, I-spy books and cricket balls. His collections were arranged in immaculate order on shelves and the model tractors were labelled. Everything else, like shoes and clothes, was out of sight in drawers and cupboards.

'Tell me, then,' Olly said.

'OK, but you have to promise you keep it dead, dead secret.'

Which was exactly the kind of thing Mervyn Crust would say.

'Dead secret,' Olly said.

'Cross your heart and –'

'Look, just get on with it.'

'Right.' Mervyn curled himself up in his chair and hugged his knees.

'It's about your house.'

'Gullywith?'

'Gullywith,' Mervyn said in a deep spooky voice.

'Are you boys quite happy in there?' Mrs Crust poked her head round the door, her nose coming quite a long way in front because it was that kind of long and pointy nose. 'Don't mug inside too long on such a lovely day. I'm going to the supermarket after lunch, you can come with me. Enjoy yourselves now.'

Olly would have shrieked in protest if Helen Brown had just come into his room like that, but then, she never would. She just didn't. But Mervyn said nothing at all.

'The thing is, if I were you I'd be very very careful at Gullywith. I mean, no one round here would even have gone there. No one round here would have bought it, I can tell you.'

'Obviously not, since it was empty for so long. What's this about?'

'It is about . . .' Mervyn lowered his voice to a hoarse whisper and rolled his eyes dramatically. 'Ghosts.'

'Oh.'

'I said G.H.O.S.T.S.'

'I know, I heard you.'

'Gullywith is haunted.'

'Right.'

'Gullywith is a Haunted House. That's why no one from round . . .'

'. . . here would buy it. Right.'

'It's the truth. Cross my heart and –'

'Yeah, yeah.'

'Everybody knows about Gullywith's ghosts.'

'OK.'

'Have you seen one yet?'

'Nope.'

'Heard one?'

'Nope. Can we go outside?'

'It's only a matter of time. They're there and you'll know about it one of these days and then you'll wish you'd never set foot in the place. Your mother and father will wish they'd never bought it. You'll leave. You'll leave very fast. Everyone leaves Gullywith fast. You'll see.'

Olly went to the window and looked out on to the street. There were a few dull cars. A lot more bungalows. A woman with a pushchair. A man with a dog. He thought hard for quite a long time and while he thought he said nothing. Mervyn fidgeted about then said, 'Aren't you bothered? You know what it means, don't you, living in a haunted house? It's pretty horrible, it's very scary. You –'

Olly turned round. 'Why are you saying all this stuff?'

'It's true, everybody round here knows it. Gullywith's got ghosts.'

'Even if it was true, which it probably isn't, but even if it was, I don't get it. I don't know what you're going on about it for.'

Mervyn shrugged. He seemed a bit surprised that his story about spooks hadn't made Olly scream with fright. 'I'd be really scared,' he said now.

'Well, I'm not. Anyway, what sort of ghosts are they meant to be? Do they come walking through the walls? Do they have their heads under their arms? Do they drip with blood? Do they –'

'Shut up!' Mervyn slid off the bed in a hurry. 'I don't know, do I? It's only what everybody says, I've never been there.'

'Yes you have. You have been to Gullywith, Mervyn Crust. Only you didn't see a ghost.'

'No. OK OK, it was a game, OK? Come on, we can ask if we can go to the corner shop and get something.'

And he whizzed out of the room.

Olly smiled to himself. That was probably the end of that.

But as he went towards the door after Mervyn, something caught his eye, something gleaming very faintly. He looked round, then went over to the shelves on which the collections were arranged. In among the shells and the pencils and half hidden behind one of the tractors was a small brass tortoise. His small brass tortoise, he was absolutely certain of it, the small brass tortoise which had been his present from under the Christmas tree at Nonny Dreever's.

He picked it up and put it into the pocket of his jeans.

'I expect you're really looking forward to going to your new school,' Mrs Crust said, whipping out a cloth to wipe up a spot of sauce Olly had dripped on to the table.

Fortunately Olly did not have to answer because his mouth was full of fish pie.

'It's a very good school and you'll make a lot of friends and Mervyn will make sure you don't get in with the wrong set, won't you, Mervyn?'

Mervyn smirked.

'What's the wrong set?' Olly asked, having swallowed.

'Just the sort of children you'd be better off not making close friends with.'

'Errol Bingly,' Mervyn said.

'Well, Errol can't help what happened in his family, Mervyn. You do have to make allowances.'

'What happened in his family?'

'Oh, just a bit of upset, dear, we don't need to go into it.'

Olly saw where Mervyn got his way of hinting at dark secrets. It was extremely irritating.

'KK and Zed,' Mervyn continued.

Mrs Crust gave a snort as she rubbed away at an invisible speck of dirt from the door handle of the fridge.

'Yes, you'd certainly be better off without knowing those two, but then, I imagine you have more sense to start with.'

Mervyn was looking at him through slightly narrowed eyes.

'Why shouldn't I be friends with them?' Olly asked.

'Gypsy types. Not that there's anything wrong with Gypsies, but that family . . .'

She sniffed and took a wet cloth to the fridge door handle.

Olly felt anger bubble up inside him. He wanted to shout out that KK and Zed were his friends already, his best friends, and that there was nothing wrong with them, that . . . but he swallowed the bubbles down and finished his slice of lemon meringue pie. Mervyn was still watching him.

'Now, you can watch television quietly for twenty minutes while you digest your lunch and before we go to the supermarket. Mervyn can't go in the car straight after a meal, Oliver, or . . .'

'. . . he's sick.'

'How clever of you to know that, dear! You're quite a sensitive little boy, aren't you?'

Television was a choice between an ancient black-and-white film with women wearing crinolines, a bowls match, or a programme about chickens.

Olly took the tortoise out of his pocket and held it up to show Mervyn.

'This is mine,' he said. 'You took it from my room.'

'No, I didn't. I've never seen it before. I expect my

mum bought it for me . . . yes, it was a present, my mum put it on the shelf for a surprise present.'

'How do you know it was on the shelf if you've never seen it before?'

Mervyn went red.

'And you'd better stop saying things about KK and Zed. They're my friends. Very very good friends.'

'Well, you need to be jolly careful knowing them. Weird things happen when they're around.'

'What sort of weird things?'

'Just weird. You'll find out.'

'Like I'll find out about all the ghosts at Gullywith? Right.'

After that they sat and watched the programme about chickens and didn't speak.

'Boys, please go to the toilet and then wash your hands properly before we leave!'

The rest of the day was distinctly boring until Helen Brown came for Olly at five o'clock. It was only as they were going that Mervyn slunk up behind him and whispered, 'They won't wake up for ten thousand years.'

'What?'

'They're frozen. In a stone sleep. You'll read about it in the book. A stone sleep lasts ten thousand years.'

Instinctively, Olly put his hand in his pocket. The small brass tortoise was still there.

Mervyn Crust smirked. 'Not that one,' he said, shaking his head. 'Just the others.' He turned away. 'And there's nothing you or any of your friends can do about it.'

CHAPTER TWENTY-SIX

Back to the Strange Bookshop

It was all very well to think Mervyn Crust was a stupid mummy's boy and a thief and a liar, which he was, but Olly spent the rest of the weekend thinking about the ghosts of Gullywith, his stolen present, KK and Zed being weird and, worst of all, the stone sleep into which the tortoises had fallen for ten thousand years.

Mervyn's face, with its narrowed eyes and sly smile, and Mervyn's whispering voice kept getting in between him and sleep.

'There's nothing you or your friends can do about it.'

But Olly was sure that the tortoises would be relying on them to help. He remembered their little faces looking up towards the trapdoor, their heads already stiffening, their gleaming, topaz eyes slowly closing . . .

He had to see Nonny Dreever. KK and Zed would help as well, he knew, and although some surprising things happened when they were around, he didn't believe for a minute that they were weird or not to be trusted or befriended, as Mrs Crust had warned. But somehow he was certain that the best person to ask for advice was Nonny Dreever.

Although he thought he could find his way to the house on stilts, Olly was not totally confident about it. He needed a map – a really good, detailed large-scale map of the few miles round Gullywith. Olly had a passion for maps, any maps. He had got it from his grandfather, who collected them and had sets of special map-drawers and walls covered in old maps and umbrella stands stuffed with rolled-up maps. Helen Brown said she had been put off maps for life after living with them and, seeing Olly looking at an atlas one day when he was three, had telephoned her father to tell him that the map passion was back, having skipped a generation.

On Monday morning Olly went to find Pete Brown in his makeshift office in one of the spare rooms. He was fiddling with the wires and plugs around his computer systems, as usual. It was a mouldy little back room with peeling flowery wallpaper and brown damp patches and a view of the pile of stones that had been the barn, but Olly knew his dad wouldn't even notice, probably wouldn't even look out of the window. It was strange really. Dad had probably been one of the first boys in the whole of the country to have his own computer, when most people didn't even know what they were, and he had been designing software and programming since he was about twelve. Computers and what they could do were his passion. And Olly had no more interest in them than he had in table tennis. He almost never went on one, he didn't know how to play games, he didn't have an e-mail address like most of his friends – he just found them boring.

Now he waited until Pete Brown had noticed him, which was quite a while, as usual.

'Oh, hi, Olls. Come to have a lesson in computer programming? OK, joke.'

'Can you take me into Fiddleup?'

'Er – Thursday? I ought to get a dentist appointment before this loose filling starts hurting. We should get you registered with a dentist too.'

'I meant now.'

'Now? What's so urgent? I was planning to spend this morning getting the back-up systems running properly.'

'I need to go this morning.'

'Right, tell me why and I might negotiate.'

'I want to buy a map.'

'You've got plenty of maps.'

'You've got plenty of computers.'

Pete Brown sighed. 'I tell you what – let me get this sorted this morning without interrupting me again and we'll go this afternoon. I can do the dentist thing and you can look for your maps.'

'And we can have tea in the Bluebird Café.'

'If I don't sort this first, we no go, so scoot.'

Olly scooted.

They had to take Lula with them, which Pete Brown said was fair because Mum had had her all morning and now it was her turn to get on with some work. But Lula was no trouble when she was out because she was always interested in everything and liked to see a lot of new people and smile at them charmingly. They always smiled back charmingly and a lot of them wanted to stop and talk to her, so their progress through town was slow but cheerful.

At the top of the hill, Dad and Lula went to find the dentist's surgery.

'Meet up in the Bluebird at three o'clock,' he said, giving Olly a five-pound note for his map.

'See if this month's issues of my magazines are out yet, Olls. I haven't got round to ordering them yet.'

'Er . . . if I can,' Olly said vaguely.

'You know which . . .'

But he shot down the street out of earshot. He wasn't going to the newsagent and stationer's, he was going to the second-hand bookshop and he was pretty certain they would not have Dad's computer magazines in stock.

The bookshop looked exactly the same as it had the first day they had found it, with the door closed but the sign saying *OPEN* and the notice on the counter saying *Please Ring for Attention*. Olly glanced round as he opened the door and the bell jingled. The tortoise doorstop was no longer there.

He thought he remembered where the map section had been and was just going round to the other side of one of the book bays when a frail quavery voice said, 'Good afternoon. You'll find the maps over there now, not behind that stack.'

'How . . . how did you know I was looking for a map?'

But he wasn't sure at first who had spoken to him because he couldn't see anyone behind the counter, though that was certainly where the voice had come from.

'Did you want a map of Gullywith, of Withern or of the entire district? No, probably you wouldn't need the latter. In that case try the third shelf down, on the left-hand side.'

Olly hesitated then went to the counter, climbed on to a convenient pile of heavy books rather gingerly and peered over the edge. The counter was quite high but on the other side of it, seated on a stool and mending the broken back of a very big old book, was the small round man. Everything about him was round. He had a round head which was entirely bald apart from a few wisps of grey hair sprouting like fluff from the sides, a rounded back, bent over the book which was on a ledge in front of him, and, when he looked up at Olly, a very round face with very round spectacles.

'Ah,' he said, 'there you are,' and pushed the spectacles on to his forehead to peer at Olly. He had very blue, very round eyes and a small pursed mouth that somehow seemed round too.

'I was wondering when you'd turn up again, Oliver Mackenzie Brown.'

Olly was no longer in the slightest bit surprised when this sort of thing happened. He had stopped bothering about how people like Nonny Dreever and now this bookshop man knew his name, just as he had stopped trying to work out how there could have been caves full of ice in the middle of Withern Hill in August.

'Well, here I am,' he said, ' so . . . well, I'll just have a look at the maps, then. Thanks a lot.'

'Aren't you going to ask where it is?'

'Where what is?'

'You mean to say you didn't notice? I find that hard to believe, sharp lad like you. Of course you noticed.'

'Oh. The tortoise.'

'What else?'

'No. I mean yes. Where is it?'

'Vanished. Taken I imagine.'

'You mean stolen.'

'Do I? Yes, I probably do. I must learn to speak precisely.'

'The thing is, what use are the tortoises to anyone? To people who keep stealing them, I mean.'

The round man laid down the book he was mending and looked at Olly hard for quite a long time before he said, 'I am astonished – *astonished* – that you should need to ask me that. *What use are the tortoises to anyone?* The tortoises are the most useful, most valuable, most wanted, most sought-after . . .' He shook his head, and then picked up the book again, muttering to himself. 'What use are the tortoises to anyone? What use . . .'

'Yes. Right. I'm very sorry. I shouldn't have . . . I mean, that was a really stupid question. I'll just look for the map, then. Thank you. Thank you very much.' Gabbling in embarrassment, Olly slid off the pile of books and went to where the maps were.

As he squatted down and started to look past 'Ordnance Survey to Monmouthshire 1973' and 'A Map of Barcelona' and 'Road Map of the Scottish Highlands and Islands 1947', which he really wanted to pull out and look at, the quavery voice behind the counter said, 'A bit further to your left, I think you will find.'

Olly looked along the row.

'A Map of Withern' had a faded red paper cover. Next to it was a map made not of paper but of cotton cloth, yellowing slightly with age.

'Gullywith'.

He took them out with slightly shaky hands. He was excited. And scared.

'You won't have room to spread them out in that corner. But you'll find they are what you need.'

Olly took the maps back to the counter. The small round man had laid the half-mended book on the bench and was standing up waiting.

'Would you like those in a bag?'

'I don't know if I've got enough money to buy them and how did you know –'

'Sadly, most shops have these devices now, you know. Thieves and so forth. Not that it stopped the tortoise from being taken.'

Olly followed the man's glance up to a carefully placed convex mirror which reflected what was going on behind the book bays back to the area behind the counter.

'I have some rather valuable volumes. It does act as something of a deterrent. Though not, sadly –'

'The tortoise. No. How much are the maps, please?'

'How much money do you have?'

Oliver rummaged in his pocket. 'Four pounds nineteen pence.'

'Then that is how much they are. But let us say that the nineteen pence is discount.'

'What's discount?'

The round man sighed. 'Money off,' he said, and tutted again between his teeth.

He put the maps into a paper bag and handed it across the counter but as Olly reached out to take it, he held on to it for a second.

'Use them wisely and when you have found out everything you need to know keep them out of harm's way. The bats will show you.' He let go of the bag.

'The bats?'

But the small round man had gone through the door at the back of the shop. The door had a glass panel but the glass panel was covered in a lace curtain so that Olly could not see anything of the room behind.

He waited but the man did not come back. The shop was entirely silent, except for the slight creaking of the books in the shelves and the settling of the wooden floorboards.

Olly went quietly out, holding his paper bag with the maps inside it, and the bell on the door jingled gently behind him.

CHAPTER TWENTY-SEVEN

Ancient Maps

An hour or so later, having eaten a toasted teacake and a toffee-fudge ice cream at the Bluebird Café, Olly lay on his bedroom floor with the maps spread out in front of him, blissfully happy. The map of Withern was creased and faded. The writing, which was in curly lettering and violet ink, was faded slightly too but Olly could still make out almost all of it. But what was more exciting were the drawings. They decorated the entire map, all round the edges like a border, and were dotted among the place names and lines for roads and tracks and streams and hills. There were drawings round the edge of and in Withern Mere, pictures of tiny figures and animals. There were pictures over the shape of Withern Hill. Pictures of stones with runic writing, of bats and strange long-haired figures, pictures of what looked like wolves. Tortoises were here and there with runic markings on their shells, and there were wasted bare-branched tree trunks, caves, underground tunnels with bends and twists, each one named, streams with writing running down the middle. There were names with which he was already familiar – Withern and Peagarth, which he knew was where KK and her brothers lived. Fiddleup, though, did not seem to exist – there was merely a strange pile of stones and the word 'Iron' and then again 'Quarry'. Beyond what was now Fiddleup was a range of high hills, dotted with stretches of water, leading away into the far distance and off the edge of the map.

Olly thought he could make out the track leading to Nonny Dreever's house on stilts.

He refolded the map carefully, opened the one with the red cover and labelled Gullywith and gave a small gasp. If the Withern map had been pleasingly decorated, the one of Gullywith and its surroundings was bare, pale and strangely sinister. There was a small, dark brick shape more or less in the middle with the name, Gullywith, in dark, spiky lettering. There were two other smaller brick shapes near to it which looked as if they were the barns and the stable. And there was the hill at the back of the house. Otherwise, the whole area was criss-crossed with very faint brown-coloured dotted lines. Some of them led off towards what must have been the field and the track, where they were criss-crossed by other faint dotted lines in grey and some, not dotted, in very pale blue.

A shadowy outline looked as if it might stand for the hill where the sheep grazed now, the hill down which KK and Jinx had first come, but that was all. Beyond that was nothing except a few more lines, spidery and wandering off in several directions but ending nowhere.

But there was something else, something that seemed a bit like a watermark printed into the thick paper. Olly picked the map up, went to the window and held it up to the light.

The whole map was traced over with the outlines of what looked like stones and among the stones the faintest outlines of what he thought were plants – at least the shapes were vaguely leaf-like or tree-like – it was hard to tell.

But when he put the map back down on the floor the shadowy outlines disappeared.

He stared at the map for a long time. There was nothing at all beyond Gullywith. It wouldn't help him in the least to find his way to Nonny Dreever's house – the one of Withern would be better for that, though still not of very much use. He would take them both with him but he could see that in the end, he was on his own and would have to work out the way without help.

He knew that he could do it and he knew that he would do it tomorrow. Meanwhile, he went on looking at every detail of the Withern map for a long time.

It was only when he was putting them both carefully away among his books – tucked in between two very tall ones, one about endangered species and the other about Iceland – that he happened to glance up and almost shrieked.

In the corner, between the wall and the ceiling, hung a bat.

CHAPTER TWENTY-EIGHT

A Serious Breakfast with Nonny Dreever

The bat was still hanging there quietly when Olly got up the next morning just after six o'clock. He wanted to get on his way before anyone else woke and he had written a note to say that he had gone to see KK about something urgent. He left the note on the kitchen table and crept out of the house. He had brought the map of Withern. He was pretty sure it wouldn't help him much but it seemed better than nothing.

But as he went through the gate on to the track that led across the first field, something brushed past his head. He swotted at it with his hand but as he did so, it brushed past him again on the other side. Then it went round and round just above him.

He could hear the bat squeaking very close to his ear.

'I thought bats didn't come in daylight,' he said. The bat dived in front of him, squeaking more loudly and began to circle and swoop a few metres ahead. From that point on, it led the way.

They went to the end of the track and started up the

hill and the bat was always slightly in front, occasionally circling, occasionally diving, occasionally zooming past Olly's ear until it dawned on him that the bat was playing. He ducked down and then started to run and the bat, squeaking joyfully, ducked as well and sped off, did a sharp brake, spun round and came whizzing back. They went on like this to the top of the hill.

'OK, you'd better settle down and show me the way to Nonny Dreever's . . . I'm not sure I know the right path after we leave here.'

Obligingly, the bat stopped squeaking, slowed, and flew to the east and kept going, turning once or twice, as if it was looking over its shoulder to check that Olly was following, but mostly just flying on.

The places started to look familiar. He recognised the second track when it turned towards the trees.

It was a cloudy morning, without any sun, and cold up here on the hills. Olly was glad he'd remembered to put on his sweatshirt. He had also remembered, at the last minute, to bring an apple, a mini chocolate bar and the small brass tortoise. What with those and the map, his pockets were quite full.

There were no sounds except the bleating of the sheep and the faint moan of the wind now and again but Olly felt perfectly happy and unworried because of the tortoise in his pocket and because of the bat. He was not far from Withern Mere but nothing could frighten him.

When they reached the path that led to Nonny Dreever's house on stilts, the bat suddenly charged ahead towards it, squeaking loudly in excitement so that by the time Olly reached the steps up into the house Nonny was waiting for him, leaning over the half-door. The bat was resting on the ledge above his head, hanging upside down.

'Hi, Mr Dreever!' Olly called out cheerfully.

But Nonny Dreever did not look cheerful. His expression was what Helen Brown would call grim. Olly stopped at the bottom of the steps.

'Good morning, Oliver.'

'Is . . . is it not convenient – it's fine, I mean, I can go back home straight away. I suppose I shouldn't have just called on you without warning. I'm sorry if I'm causing you trouble.'

'It is not,' Nonny Dreever said, 'a question of causing me trouble. It is not inconvenient. Besides, I had warning. I always have warning. You'd better come in.'

Olly went in feeling extremely small.

The house on stilts was in many ways exactly the same as when Olly had last been inside it and in other ways different, though he didn't notice the differences for a few minutes.

'Sit down,' Nonny Dreever said, and pointed to the chair in front of the wooden table. Olly pulled it out and sat down. Then Nonny Dreever went to the stove and turned his back to him. Olly sat in silence. The bat was still hanging upside down in the porch. He could just see the tip of its wing and one tiny ear through the open door.

He looked round the room. There was the circus.

There was the cuckoo clock and the Ferris wheel and the . . . he stared. The acrobats. But they had changed. They were now wearing glittering white and silver costumes, the same ones the high-wire acrobats had worn at the Midwinter Revel. Then he looked along the row and saw the sleigh train. It was exactly the same as the one he and KK had ridden in but very much smaller. A model sleigh train. There was a tiny ice-cream seller. There were the flares, with bits of coloured fluff for smoke coming out of the top. Everything was there, even a tiny ice rink with skaters – except that it was a piece of mirror-glass and the skaters were made of wire and thread.

And then he realised. Everything was the same except . . .

'That's right,' Nonny Dreever said, as Olly drew in his breath. 'No tortoises.'

Not a single tortoise. Olly put his hand into his pocket but his own, small brass tortoise was still safely there.

'Where have they all gone? Did someone steal them? What happened to them, Mr Dreever?'

Nonny Dreever said nothing. He was busy doing something at the stove and the work surface. Olly saw him take down a pan from the shelf above his head and a jar out of a cupboard. He smelled something frying.

Nonny Dreever started to whistle and at once the bat righted itself, flew into the room and hung itself on to a low beam immediately above Olly's chair.

'You see? He knows.'

Nonny Dreever brought two plates of toast with fried eggs and mushrooms to the table, went back for a pot of tea and two mugs, then sat down.

Olly waited. He knew that Nonny was either upset or angry or both and that it had something to do with him but he had no idea what he might have done.

'Eat while it's hot.'

Olly picked up his knife and fork and for a while, the two of them ate in silence. Once, the cuckoo popped out of its clock, cuckooed seven times, then popped back, and once, a small model of the Tower of London suddenly struck up a marching tune. Otherwise, and apart from the clink of knife and fork on china or the sound of tea being stirred, it was quiet. The sun moved round and shone in through one of the windows on to the table.

The bat hung quietly, its eyes closed.

The mushrooms tasted as fresh and delicious as before and the eggs had orange yolks and were cooked exactly how Olly like them best, a little bit runny in the middle for him to dip his toast into them, but not too much. He enjoyed them but all the time he was eating he kept glancing at Nonny Dreever, who ate steadily, poured the tea out for them both, and said nothing at all.

But when they had both finished he picked up his mug and nodded his head for Olly to join him on the little verandah at the top of the steps. It was still cloudy but it was warm enough to sit outside all the same. The bat seemed to be sound asleep.

'Oliver Mackenzie Brown,' Nonny Dreever said. 'I have a lot of very serious things to say to you and many things to tell you. I think it is time you were told.'

'Are you cross with me, Mr Dreever?' Olly asked in a

small voice. 'I can't think what I've done wrong but if I have done anything I'm very very sorry.'

Nonny Dreever sighed a long, deep, slow sigh. Then he stretched out his legs in front of him.

'No, no, Olly. I'm not cross. I'm sorry if I appeared so and I'm sorry not to have been very chatty this morning but the truth is that I was relieved to see you, very relieved. When I heard that you had set off, I was worried. Very worried. You were not to know what day it is, and what seems to be in the air. You were not to know. The fact is that these are dangerous times, and you should never venture far from Gullywith, let alone anywhere near Withern, by yourself. What was it your mother said to you the first day you arrived?'

'Always make sure you can see the house and don't go anywhere near water.'

'Always make sure you can see the house and don't go anywhere near water.'

'I thought – well, I've been here before.'

'Of course you have but you were not on your own. KK was with you. With her you were much safer – not entirely safe but safer. Today you had the bat. The bats can lead you here and they can warn me that you're on your way but they only have limited powers to protect you from . . .'

'I had my tortoise. The one you gave me for a Christmas present.'

'The one who managed to escape, with great difficulty, and who is the last one left who is not, at present, in a ten-thousand-year stone sleep. It would be as much as he could do to save himself, Oliver.'

Olly sighed. His mind was confused, and although Nonny Dreever had said that he was not cross, he still felt the shadow of his disapproval just as he knew that he hadn't done as his mother asked him.

'I didn't disobey her on purpose,' he said now.

'I know that. You just didn't think. You left your wits behind. And you need your wits about you all the time now more than ever. Never forget that.'

'Why now more than ever?'

Nonny Dreever got up and went into the house. He returned with a fresh pot of tea and a large book bound in cracked leather, which he set down on the table beside him.

'Drink your tea,' he said, when he was back in his chair, 'drink your tea and listen.'

As he started talking, the sun glowed faintly from behind a bank of cloud, struggling to shine, but after a moment or two gave up and faded back again. A faint chilly little breeze sneaked round them, making the bat stir in its sleep.

Olly drank his tea.

'Many many moons ago, Gullywith was a very different place. Everything here was different. Gullywith was not the farmhouse you live in. It was a small stone castle, a satellite to the great castle on the hill. Both belonged to the stone people. The whole area was ruled by them. They were hard masters and they liked battles. Their aim was to extend their rule further and further on all sides – not an unusual ambition. I won't go into what happened in detail – besides, I don't know everything. Nobody knows. But the castle toppled into Withern Mere and was swallowed up. There it lies, many fathoms down, far beyond the reach of man. And there, so the legend goes, it is still governed by the Stone King whose ambition is either to rise and take over his old kingdom, or to bring everything else down into the bottom of the mere and be under his power there. He would prefer the first of course but, as a last resort, he would accept the second.

'We fight a never-ending battle here, Olly, and the battle has become fiercer. Now you have joined in.'

'Because we came to Gullywith?'

'Partly. Partly because of the time.'

'Time?'

'The time. The time according to calculations and legends in the books and maps and written on the stones. Some of it may be fancy. Some of it may be rumour. Who knows? Few people know about any of it and if they were told they would laugh their heads off. But you have seen enough to know better. Now things have become serious. Silly, petty little skirmishes have turned into real fights. They love nothing more than fights and battles, Olly. They live for them. They love forming into battle lines and marching about, they love threatening and playing sinister little games.'

'Like putting the stinging stone in my pocket and getting in through the hole in the wall.'

'Exactly. But the stones' powers are fairly limited, even when they mass together. It is the Stone King who has the real power. But by drawing strength from him, they have managed to freeze the tortoises into the ten-thousand-year stone sleep and that is the most dangerous and worrying thing they have done so far. I had no idea the threat had grown to be so big.'

'We must rescue the tortoises. Surely we can? KK said they could look after themselves.'

'KK knows a certain amount, though not as much as Zed, but she was being too optimistic.'

'We have to save them, we have to. If they fall too deeply into the sleep, it'll be too late. We have to do something now!'

'Sit down, Oliver Mackenzie Brown.'

Olly sat. But inside him, determination was bubbling and boiling.

'You mean well, I know. You understand the importance of the tortoises to us – they are on our side, of course. So are the bats, which I know came as a bit of a surprise to you. But the tortoises are far more important, they have greater strength, they have determination and cunning and of course there are far far more of them. Without them . . . but the stones hate them because the tortoises are far more ancient than they are. The runes they have on their backs come from a time aeons before those scratched on some of the stones. Many of those are fake by the way but the runes on every tortoise prove its ancient lineage without any doubt. Remember that.'

Olly shivered.

'Ultimately, Oliver, it is between the two of us. Him

and me. But my powers are waning. I can feel it. They are not the powers I had before the castle sank into the mere. He drained some of it out of me and sucked it down with him many fathoms deep. I have no way of getting it back. But I do have some left. I have the power to help people have fun. I have all sorts of tricks up my sleeve. But they may not be enough.'

'They have to be, they have to be, Mr Dreever. We can win. I'll help, you know I will.'

Nonny Dreever chuckled. 'You're a good boy, Oliver. Maybe you're my successor. Who knows? That's another legend . . . that someone will come to take over from me and restore Gullywith, banish the Stone King for ever. It is in there somewhere.' And he pointed to the leather-bound book on the table.

'My book . . .' Olly said. 'Maybe it's all in *The Battle for Gullywith*.'

'No, I'm afraid not. That's an interesting story and there are some recent legends in it. But that book is far more recent – only a few thousand years old. This one is known as the Great Book and above everything else they want to get their hands on it again. They believe it is theirs and theirs only. This book,' he stroked it gently with the palm of his hand, 'who knows when this one was written and bound? In fact, it was starting to fall apart. It was in a very bad way. But it's been well repaired.'

Olly remembered the little round man in the bookshop, sitting behind his high counter with a book on the bench.

'Yes,' Nonny Dreever said, 'that's the one.'

Olly gave a low whistle.

'You have work to do, Olly. I want you to keep an eye out for things . . . I know some of what goes on but I am powerless once I leave here and in any case I can only go as far as the top of that hill.'

'Why?'

'It was one of the things that happened in the battle. I am tied here, and I can never go on to the other side of the hill, let alone as far as Gullywith.'

'I wish you could. You could take some mushrooms and show my mum how to cook them. Anyway, we'll win and you'll be free and then you can come.'

'I'd like that.'

'What else do I have to look out for?'

Nonny Dreever was silent, his head bent, thinking hard.

'You can tell me, Mr Dreever. I won't say anything. Unless . . .'

'KK and Zed know, you don't have to worry about that. I don't want to alarm you unnecessarily.'

'I'm not frightened of anything.'

'Oh, easily said! Don't ever underestimate them, and don't ever become too confident. What does pride come before?'

'A fall.'

'Precisely. Just be aware and report anything unusual, anything that doesn't seem right to you, anything that hasn't happened before. They're always up to new tricks but there are other things . . . we have other enemies. So do the stones. This isn't entirely straightforward. It would be easier if it were.'

'You have to give me a clue or how will I know?'

'You'll know. You've got your wits about you. One other thing . . . Mervyn Crust.'

Olly groaned.

'Mervyn Crust is a low-grade spy. He works for them but they don't treat him well. They laugh at him behind his back and use him to do menial jobs – but Mervyn Crust is not a bad boy. You must bear that in mind. He is weak and silly and not very bright and his head is easily turned. But he is not a bad boy. Do you understand me?'

'I understand.'

Nonny Dreever stood up, turned to the east, and put his fingers in the corners of his mouth. Olly heard nothing. He had never been able to whistle that way, only by pursing his lips in front. He waited. The bat stirred slightly and moved its wings, before settling back.

'How about some Revel Cup?' Nonny Dreever said. 'I think there's still a bit left over. We can drink it while we're waiting for Zed and KK. They'll be going back with you. And don't look like that – I know an arguing face when I see one, Oliver Brown.'

CHAPTER TWENTY-NINE

Plots and Plans

'Don't forget to look in the book,' KK said. She and Olly were putting the plates into the dishwasher and Zed was wiping down the table. Lula was in her high chair, throwing bits of eggy bread at him.

They had all come back from Nonny Dreever's house an hour ago – Olly being forbidden to walk the track alone again – and at Gullywith the house was not stirring so KK and Zed had got breakfast for everyone. Olly was surprised that he managed to eat a second lot of eggs and toast but the walk back had made him hungry again.

'It tells you all about the fair. You need to get a costume – everyone goes in fancy dress.'

She clicked the dishwasher door shut.

'Come on, Zed, we've got to go. Bye-bye, Lula.'

'Are you going, KK? You've only just arrived,' said Helen Brown, coming in to collect Lula. 'Stay for the day. Olly gets fed up by himself.'

'No I do not!'

'We can't today. Stuff to do. See you.'

'See see you you see see see see,' said Lula.

When they had gone off down the track in what was now a drizzly morning, Olly went up to his room and pulled out the *Legends of Withern Mere*. There were chapters about the places all around – what had happened in the past, what stories had been told, what customs and sayings people had made up. He turned over pages about the drowned castle and about the mere sprites, which many people claimed to have seen not only around the mere itself but in their own gardens. One story told of a mere sprite which had taken up residence in a cottage in Pennymore, another of an old woman who had kept a sprite in her pond. Some of the tales had almost certainly been either completely made up or at least embroidered and exaggerated.

He had not noticed the chapter KK had told him about any previous time he had looked in the book – but that didn't surprise him. He was used to the way things came and went.

CHAPTER ELEVEN
FIDDLEUP FULL MOON FAIR

The chapter told him that the fair's origins were lost in the mists of time but certainly went back as far as the age of the Stone King and that it was celebrated every five years on the top of Fiddleup Mount, the great hill behind the town.

There were lots of stories connected with Full Moon Fair – stories about runaway pigs rolling down the hill and through the streets of Fiddleup, stories about cats and dogs changing shape and children being changed into sprites and grown men being spirited away at midnight.

There was also the legend about the return of the Stone King, when he would rise from Withern Mere and march on the fair to regain his kingdom, in the year the moon turned blue and Gullywith was 'liyted as a beacone to be sene fur monny moon miles rund'.

Olly read on and on, struggling here and there with the weird spellings but able to follow most of the story.

When he went downstairs again, Pete Brown was in the kitchen reading the paper.

'Here, Olls, this ought to be good. We should go.'

Olly went and looked over his dad's shoulder.

'Town Gearing up for Full Moon Fair.'

Olly felt a little shiver run down his spine.

'Spooky,' he said.

'Why?'

'Oh, just KK and Zed were talking about it, that's all.'

'I should think everyone's talking about it. The Fiddleup Full Moon Fair only happens every five years . . . A lot of the children who'll be there weren't even born when they had the last one.'

'Will we dress up?'

'Don't see why you shouldn't . . . not sure about your mum and me of course.'

'Oh go on, Dad . . . you'd love it!'

'We'll see. It isn't for a week or so and there's something else you might like to know about before that. It's been quite a business getting us all up here and, as you know, a few things have gone wrong and Mum has had to work pretty hard. It doesn't look as if the house is going to be the way she pictured it for a while . . . so I think she deserves a break. We're having a week in the sun. Spain. There's no knowing when we'll manage to get away again and by the time we're back, it'll be school uniform and new shoes and off you'll be.'

Olly wandered outside and sat on the wall to think. A week by the sea might be OK but as soon as Dad had mentioned it he realised how attached he had become to Gullywith and how he didn't really want to leave it even for a short time. He also realised that anything might happen while they were gone.

He had taken Nonny Dreever's warnings seriously. Gullywith was under threat. The book made that clear as well.

He thought perhaps KK and Zed would keep an eye on the place but they couldn't live in it for a week.

Besides, there was something more important still. The rescue of the tortoises. The time for that was running out and he knew KK, Zed and Nonny Dreever were working out some sort of plan, though when he had asked KK about it, she had only said that nothing was decided, everything was being worked out.

'We only have one try,' she had said, 'so we have to get it right.'

Whatever the plan was, Olly didn't want to miss anything. He worried about the tortoises and he knew that the longer they stayed as they were, the deeper their stone sleep was becoming and the more likely that they couldn't be woken.

The more he thought about it, the more he was sure he did not want to go away, even for a week on a beach in the sun.

CHAPTER THIRTY

An Amazing Scooter Ride

This time what woke him was a strange whirring noise, like the blades of a propeller whizzing in his ears. A bat was flying round and round his head and occasionally dipping down to touch the tip of its wing against his cheek, but the sound was coming from outside. Olly went to the window.

KK and Zed were below, mounted on what looked like scooters and it was from these that the noise was coming. Another couple of bats were hovering round them too.

It was raining when he joined them. The scooters were not very large and had high, curved windscreens and runners rather like those on a sledge, instead of wheels.

'What's happening?'

'Get on the back, quick. We don't have a lot of time. Nonny Dreever sent a message. He's heard that the tortoises are going to be gathered up and driven down into the bottom of the mere tonight or perhaps tomorrow night – he wasn't sure. Once they get there they'll be shut into the drowned castle and we can never reach them. We have to rescue them tonight.'

'But how can we do it? Their sleep is getting

deeper and deeper.'

'I know but Nonny has found the Undoing Sleep Rune in the Great Book and told it to me. He thinks it will still work, though it's ages since it was last used. The point is we have to try, we don't have a choice, we can't leave them like this. Get *on*, Olly. Unless you want to ride behind Zed and be boys only.'

'Don't be stupid.'

Olly climbed on the back of the scooter. There was a small bar for him to hold on to and a rest for his back. It was rather comfortable.

In a split second, the scooter rose in the air a few centimetres. The whirring of the engine increased and then they surged forwards and began to move very fast just above the ground. It took a minute to cross the field and power up the hill. Zed was alongside and the air and the soft, light rain were cool on Olly's face.

'This is terrific!'

'I know. Hold on!'

The blades made a whooshing sound and they rose a little higher and picked up even more speed. When they came down the hill very fast with Withern Mere gleaming below, Olly's stomach turned over and over.

They went on to the path that wound round the mere and towards a dense belt of dark trees.

'Where are we going?'

KK turned her head and said something but her words blew away on the night air and Olly just held on tight and waited to find out.

Now they had turned off the track and entered the

trees, and he saw that they stretched on all sides and far ahead, huge thick trunks with great spreading branches, mainly like pine and spruce trees. The path was sandy now. He looked to the right and the left, peering to see if there was any life here, but all he could see were endless trunks, endless heavy branches, endless sandy track leading off into blackness on either side. But the number of bats increased all the time. Now there were dozens of them, swirling round their heads making their high-pitched squeaking and chattering. Once a bat came and perched on Olly's shoulder, and later another on his head. He supposed they were taking a rest. It was strange that he had once been frightened of them, hating their blackness and their leathery wings and the way they flapped. Now, he didn't mind them in the slightest. They were friendly and he was quite used to their squeaking and their weird little pointed, mousy faces.

He wondered how KK could find her way so easily among so many identical trees and how she knew which path to take when they went off to right and left, weaving in and out and criss-crossing one another every so often. She never hesitated but shot first one way, then the next. Zed was either beside them or just behind.

They were making one of the sharp turns on to another section of the sandy track when Olly happened to look at one particular tree as they passed it and saw what he was certain were eyes gleaming out of one of the holes in the trunk. A minute later, he saw them again, from the high branches of another tree – hard, staring, electric-blue eyes with dazzling points that hurt his own eyes as he stared into them.

Then there was a long stretch of track between the great trees and the whirring of the scooters as they skimmed the ground until KK turned sharp left and slowed down in front of a steep bank of earth with tree roots set in it like bony fingers.

The scooter sank to the ground. Zed pulled up beside them, and everything went quiet. The bats, which had been keeping pace with them the whole time, now gathered, fluttering round their heads.

'Where are we?'

'Withern Forest of course. This is the only way we can get into the tunnels without being too close to the mere and the hill at first. This is an entrance we don't think they know about – and even if they do, there's no sign of them here and their strength will be pretty weak, so far away from the water.'

'What are we going to do now?'

'Make our way in – some of the bats will guide us, the rest will stay here and send a warning if anyone comes. We have to find them and lead them into the Echo Chamber. When we're in there, we can repeat the rune and the echo should do the trick.'

'Hope you haven't forgotten it then,' Zed said with a grin.

KK made a face at him.

Olly liked Zed. He had a cheerful face and strange ears that were folded forward a bit and crinkled at the edge. He was older than both of them, and he had a great way of making them laugh even when he hadn't said a word. It was something about the expressions he did.

He did one now, making his nose turn up and his ears wave slightly.

Olly's laughter sounded strange in the huge, empty forest, as if it were running away and away for miles, getting fainter and fainter between the trees.

'Do stop showing off,' KK said, 'and concentrate. This is deadly serious.'

She didn't usually speak snappily to anyone and Olly realised that she was nervous.

He looked round. They were in a very small clearing among trees but he knew he could never find his way there again, or back to the place if he got lost – every tree looked the same and every one of the paths. He looked up. The trees reached high above them into the dark night sky and Olly could barely see a single star.

KK was standing still with her eyes closed and her lips moving slightly.

'It's got to be absolutely right,' KK whispered. 'Every single syllable has to be the same as in the Great Book or it probably won't work.' She opened her eyes. 'Fine,' she said. 'Now, Olly here, Zed behind Olly.'

Several of the bats were hovering about them. The rest were in the branches but wide awake and quivering slightly.

'Keep quiet from here. Quiet as you can. Creep. Are you ready?'

They nodded.

'Good. Now, follow me.'

To Olly every tree looked exactly the same as every other

tree but KK went over to one which had a large oval hole low down on the trunk. The hole looked dark in the centre. KK put her hand in, then her arm, felt around carefully and then nodded. 'This is it.'

She put one foot on the thick root at the base of the tree and slowly began to clamber up and then to climb into the hole, disappearing slowly until only the sole of her shoe could be seen sticking out.

'Now you.' Zed gave Olly a little poke in his back. He knew them both well enough now to trust whatever they did and he climbed up quickly and put his head and shoulders into the hole.

They were in a passageway which widened so that they could crawl along comfortably and it quickly became high enough for them to stand up. Zed was behind. A few of the bats had come in with him and were flitting about just ahead of KK, who had a small torch with a powerful beam which shone a long way ahead. The passage seemed to be empty for as far as they could see and was rather like those they had gone through to escape on the night of the Midwinter Revel. For a long time they trudged along without saying anything. Various low narrow tunnels led off on either side. KK went past several of them but then she stopped, hesitated, and then turned right.

Now it was much harder going. The floor was slippery and stony and the ceiling was so low that once or twice it touched their heads.

'Shhh.' KK stopped. 'Listen.' At first there seemed to be no sound at all but after a moment, they heard the faintest sound, a bit like a stream trickling, a bit like a breeze rustling gently through leaves.

'That's them.'

'What?'

'The tortoises. It's the sound of them dreaming. They must be very near.'

'Which ones?'

'All of them. Come on, but don't say anything else. We don't want to frighten them – they might just be able to hear us. And we don't want anyone else knowing we're here.'

'How far away are they?'

But KK shook her head without answering and began to move forward again.

The next moment she had stumbled and they had come out into a small high chamber-like space. It glowed dimly, though they couldn't see where the light was coming from. And all around them, still and silent and with closed eyes, were the tortoises. How had they got here, Olly wondered, how had they managed to escape? But he was learning fast that the tortoises had the most extraordinary powers. When he saw them, Olly had let out a little gasp and the gasp went round the walls and bounced back over and over again.

'This is it,' Zed said. 'This is the Echo Chamber. Now all you have to do is say the rune. You haven't forgotten it, have you?'

KK shot him a black look.

The bats had taken up their positions above the entrance, hanging upside down on a tree root that ran across the opening. Then others joined them and hung from the first row so that very soon the bats had formed a curtain. No one would be able to come through without them knowing.

Olly touched one of the tortoises nearest to him. Its carved back was very cold.

He touched another and it was even colder and it occurred to him that they were already too late and that they had gone several hundred years down into their sleep already.

He wondered about the Great Book from which KK said the Undoing Sleep Rune was taken. How did Nonny Dreever understand the runic language?

KK was in the middle of the Echo Chamber now. She had closed her eyes to concentrate. Olly reached out and gripped Zed's arm.

Her voice was a whisper but the whisper went round and round the chamber, as if it were a spinning ball going round a basin, and echoes of the whisper bounced off the walls and the ceiling and echoes of the echoes, getting fainter and fainter and being overtaken by other echoes.

The rune was like a rhyme and it seemed to send tiny electric sparks through Olly's hair and down his back. It made no sense and he couldn't have remembered any of it afterwards. KK was frowning with concentration.

Then her last words went round the chamber and the echoes of the words faded and faded as she fell silent.

They waited. The faint sound of the tortoises' dreams was like the sea curling over on shingle far away but gradually it too died away until there was only an immense silence, as deep and heavy as the sea itself.

CHAPTER THIRTY-ONE

The Waking of the Tortoises

For a long time nothing happened. They stood in silence waiting. Olly looked at KK. Her fingers were twisted together and her face was puckered in concentration, willing the rune to work.

Then he heard a very faint creaking sound. Then another. Then a noise like an eggshell breaking open.

Slowly, slowly, one by one, the tortoises were beginning to wake. First one, then another twitched and stirred very slightly. Their shells creaked a little. Their eyes began to open, though at first they seemed glazed and lifeless. Gradually a little, dim gleam came from them and then one tortoise put out a leg and then another, and tried to move forward. It was obviously difficult at first, as if they had been frozen and were thawing out.

They watched, scarcely daring to breathe, as the whole Echo Chamber filled with gentle movements.

'It worked!' Zed whispered and his whisper ran round the Echo Chamber.

'Fantastic!'

'We haven't a lot of time,' KK said. 'We can give them

193

a few minutes to come more awake but then we have to move. It isn't safe here. The stones may find out what's happened at any moment.'

She went round touching the tortoises gently as they poked their heads out of their shells, stroking them and talking to them in a low voice.

All of them were moving a bit now, as if they were limbering up to dance, stretching their legs out and shaking their heads. The brightness was growing stronger from their eyes, though they still seemed to have trouble seeing and bumped into one another now and again as they started to move about.

'I'll go first, Zed, you come behind me, Olly, you go last and make sure we've got every single one. Check before you leave – we don't want to leave a single one sleeping somewhere. Then come after us. Some of the bats will go on ahead, the rest will keep along with us as we go.'

'Go where? Where are we heading now?' Olly asked.

'We've got to reach the iron ladder. We came a very long way round but it was the only chance we had to try and avoid the stones. It's going to take some time but the walking will wake them up more and by the time we reach the ladder they'll be alert enough to climb on one another's backs and get out through the trapdoor. Once we're there they're pretty safe – for the time being anyway. They'll regroup and make a plan. You've got to remember that their greatest strength is that they are so much older than the stones. They know the runes by heart. They know the Great Book because their ancestors wrote it and they are very wise. But what the stones lack in wisdom and age they make up for in trickery and cunning. Now, let's go.'

Their progress through the passages was slow and steady. Olly followed at the back after making sure not a single tortoise had been accidentally left behind and he soon caught up with the others. Now the glow from the eyes of the tortoises was quite bright as they plodded along. The bats were mostly at the front, though the odd one flitted back as far as Olly occasionally and brushed his head and face briefly before fluttering back to the others. The tunnel was dry and warm and after a time walking along it was rather soothing. Once they reached the iron ladder and got the tortoises up through the trap-door their mission would be accomplished, he could get some breakfast and even enjoy thinking about a week in the sunshine of Spain.

He was in such a daydream that when Zed stopped suddenly he banged his nose crashing into him.

'Ouch!'

'Shhh,' Zed hissed over his shoulder. 'Didn't you hear what she said?'

Olly hadn't. He had been lying on a lilo on a warm blue sea.

But if he hadn't heard KK, he did hear the sound coming from far behind them in the warren of passage-ways. It was a faint, steady, rhythmical drumming and as he listened it grew louder. Louder and nearer.

'What is it?'

KK had turned and come close to them, so that they

stood in a little huddle together while the tortoises went on ahead.

'It sounds like an army marching.'

'That,' KK said, her face creased with anxiety, 'is exactly what it is.'

At that moment, a bat came swooping along the tunnel from behind them and flew madly round their heads, before dipping down to the ground and up again, then disappearing back into the darkness, returning, flying, dipping to the ground again.

'What is it trying to tell us?'

'That's often the problem with the bats. They mean well and they're anxious to please but they get confused and they don't always find it easy to communicate. Hold on . . . I'll follow it a little way back. Don't worry, I won't go far but I might hear something or it might show me what it's found. You stay there.'

They did not have to wait long. Within a minute, KK was back, scurrying down the passage.

'Go on,' she said, 'quickly.'

'What is it?'

'The stones are on the move but there's worse . . . it's the water. I think that's what the bat wanted to tell us. Just a little further back the ground is wet and after another few metres it's ankle deep and it's not far from us. The mere is rising.'

CHAPTER THIRTY-TWO

The Iron Ladder

The bats flew up and down squeaking in agitation but it was hard to get the tortoises, which were still quite sleepy, to move any faster and now they could all hear the water lapping in the distance.

Once or twice they stumbled as the floor of the passage became stonier and more uneven and Olly, remembering it from before, realised that they were not very far away from Gullywith. The walls narrowed here and the ceiling was close to their heads so that the bats had difficulty flying and kept catching on everyone's clothes and hair. The drumming sound was still behind them too, a regular, even beat.

Olly had never longed for anything so much as he longed for the sight of the iron ladder – let alone for home and his own bed. He was glad that one of the bats had stayed with him, fluttering at his shoulder and squeaking into his ear in a cheerful way to keep up his spirits.

And then, there was the iron ladder, gleaming faintly just ahead of them. The tortoises crowded together at the bottom.

'I'll go up first and open the trapdoor,' KK said. 'Zed, you put the first tortoise on the ladder and leave the others to come after. Olly wait until the last one has climbed on, then make sure no one has been left behind before you get up yourself.'

KK went like a monkey up the rungs set in the wall and after a moment there was a downward rush of air as the trapdoor opened slowly.

Zed lifted the first tortoise and then stood back and the two of them watched as one by one the creatures used one another as mounting blocks, lumbering on to each other's shells and so rising up steadily in a column towards the open air. The only noise they made was a slight scratching sound of claw on shell and occasionally a tiny grunt.

'Go, tortoises!' Olly whispered. 'Go go go.'

It was a slow, steady business and as they stood watching, Olly felt something cold at his feet. He stepped backwards and into water.

'Zed. It's round my ankles. Can you feel it?'

But Zed was chivvying the last few tortoises forwards and now he had both of his own feet on the bottom rung of the ladder.

'Make sure there's no one left then come up after me.'

Far above their heads Olly could see KK peering down at them. But now the cold, lapping water was rising round his knees and then he realised that the drumming had come much closer so that it sounded through the passageways right behind him, like the steady onward marching of an army.

He was about to grab the iron ladder after Zed when a slight movement in the shadows caught his eye. Pressed against the side of the tunnel trying to keep out of the water was a small tortoise, its eyes half closed. Olly touched it and saw that it was barely awake and that its front leg was hanging awkwardly.

'Zed, here.'

'Hurry up.'

Olly picked up the tortoise and headed for the ladder but as he reached it he realised that the water had been growing colder and colder so that it now felt freezing. He saw that the tunnel behind him was filled with sharp beams of white light.

'Zed, take it, take it from me.'

Zed turned. He hung on to the ladder with one arm. 'I'll pull you up. You keep hold of the tortoise.'

'No, you can't, my legs are frozen solid in the water, you'll never get me up. Take the tortoise. Go ON.'

He held out the small, injured creature, which was by now cowering back into its shell. Zed grabbed it and for a second tried to grab Olly's wrist too but he almost came off the iron ladder.

At the same moment, the drumming sound became deafening and the passage was suddenly swarming with small stone soldiers, holding shining white lances and hissing angrily.

'Zed, move.'

Olly looked up and saw Zed clamber up the last few rungs, clutching the tortoise, and reach the open trap. He saw KK's arm reach out to him. A few of the stone men were trying to climb up the ladder but the bottom rung was too high and they could not reach it or grab hold of the sides.

Then the trapdoor at the top banged shut and Olly was alone in the tunnel with an army of small, malevolent stone figures pointing their lances at him, beaming the white lights into his eyes and chattering furiously.

A small part of him felt frightened but a much larger part felt angry – very angry. He looked down at the stone soldiers, many of which were now grouping together on an outcrop of rock set against the wall, and was about to try and push his way through the others to get to the iron ladder when he felt himself pinned by his legs and lifted up. The water was still lapping around them but seemed to be receding like a tide and becoming shallower at this end of the tunnel. It was too dark for him to see much but he realised that he was being placed in what seemed to be some sort of hammock, then hoisted up. There was a sound of movement as the body of soldiers regrouped, then swung together, turned and began to go back through the tunnel the way they had come. Olly shouted and tried to sit up but he was pinned down by a criss-crossing of fine and, as far as he could tell, invisible threads which were stronger than steel and held him fast. He lay huddled down, the roof of the tunnel sometimes almost touching him, and beneath him went the sound of marching feet in steady rhythm. He supposed that eventually they would emerge through the tree hole and out into the forest, where perhaps by now KK and Zed would be waiting, but now they were turning left and going down what felt like steep steps so that he was tipped forward and at one moment thought he would slide off feet first on to the ground. But then they were level again and twisting and turning sharply so that he lost all sense of where they were and closed his eyes because the movement was making him feel sick.

He opened them when he felt cool air on his face. Above him was the night sky, thickly clustered with bright stars. The marching sound gradually ceased and there was complete stillness except for some low murmuring from the stones gathered behind and the faint sound of lapping water.

Then he was being lowered slowly. The lowering was a bumpy business and what seemed to be various orders and warnings came in hard little scratchy voices. Olly expected to find himself upright on firm ground but then realised that he had been lowered into a long boat which rocked gently on water. After a moment in which he felt very sick again, but then not sick at all, he opened his eyes.

The boat was shaped like half a walnut shell and Olly was on a wooden seat that went across the middle. But it was not the boat or the flotilla of others like it bobbing round and packed with the stone men which made him catch his breath, but the whole scene before him.

They were on the edge of Withern Mere and the light from a huge full moon was silvering the water and the silver broke into tiny slices of light that broke up shimmering with the occasional movement of the surface of the water.

The mere stretched away into the darkness, gleaming and strange, and on the far side, Olly could see the great rows of tree trunks that marked the beginning of the forest.

The stone people were all standing up in the boats and holding their lances upright and the moonlight caught on them and they glinted like a thicket of tiny needles.

The night air was soft and cool and every so often a faint breeze sifted across the water towards them and the army of tiny boats rocked gently.

It was so beautiful and so tranquil that Olly forgot that he was captive, forgot that he had been taken from his friends and had no idea where he was going, forgot to feel afraid. He simply gazed at the moonlit mere in great wonder.

And as he gazed there was a movement at the centre, a deep stirring, and he remembered the time that he and KK had seen the whirlpool and the figure of the Stone King arising from it through the grey mist. Perhaps it was happening again.

As he stared, the movement strengthened and it suddenly reminded Olly of a film he had seen on television about humpback whales. There might be a vast humpback emerging from the mere. Or a Withern Monster.

As he watched, a strange low humming sound began to come from the army in the boats. It did not grow louder but continued steadily like the humming of bees in a hive.

Then, slowly, something began to rise from the water.

At first it was impossible to tell what it was, though it did not seem to be any kind of sea creature and it was far far larger than the Stone King, but then Olly made out the shape of a pale grey turret, then another and so, bit by bit, the walls and ramparts and battlements and towers of a castle emerged from the depths of the mere.

As it rose, the waters of the mere fell away from its sides in great cascades, sending waves which washed against the boats at the edge and made them rock violently. The boat in which Olly was held rose and fell but seemed in no danger of capsizing.

It took a long time for the entire castle to stand clear of the water and when it had done so it was so vast that Olly felt the boats were toys and he and the stone soldiers made in miniature. The moonlight fell on the great grey walls and bathed them in a soft silver. After a pause, there was a curious sound as if something metal were clattering on to paving. Olly could not think what was making it but as soon as it began there was an urgent stir and bustle among the boats and his own began to turn and pull away into the main waters of the mere. The entire flotilla was making its way round beneath the walls of the castle to the other side and soon Olly saw that the drawbridge was being slowly lowered on great chains, down, down until it came to rest not far from land on the forest side. The boats sailed steadily towards it, his own only two or three from the front, the others massed up close behind. None of the stone soldiers had taken any notice of him whatsoever. They had taken him captive and moved him about and now they were bringing him to the drawbridge of the castle, efficiently and as if they were of one mind, but there had been no speaking, not even a glance. They faced stonily in one direction and worked like some impersonal machine.

Now, they were at the drawbridge and one of the boat's wooden benches was lifted out and placed between the boat and the edge of the bridge. Several of the stone men formed up in front and cut the strings of the hammock with the sharpened edges of their stone lances. Then, Olly felt himself being pricked in the back by the lances of the others so that he got up quickly and jumped from the boat, barely touching the plank, and on to the wide drawbridge of the castle.

In seconds, the rest of the army had formed up behind and the drumming rose as they began to march on the spot.

Then they were making their steady, orderly way, with Olly surrounded and made to keep time with them, up the slope and through the high arch with its raised portcullis and so into the great round courtyard of Withern Castle.

CHAPTER THIRTY-THREE

Withern Castle

The inner walls of the castle rose steeply above Olly's head and the whole courtyard, which was cobbled, was lit by huge flares held by what seemed to be stone statues standing at intervals all the way round but which after a moment he realised were guards. Two of the largest flares were placed on either side of a high entrance door and it was through this that one column of the soldiers now marched, with Olly in the middle of them and a second column behind. The rest stayed outside, standing stiff and silent, watching the procession go in.

Olly had been inside castles before. They had visited a ruined castle with his class from school once and he and Dad had been to an unruined one in the country the previous summer so he thought he knew what to expect. But Withern Castle was far bigger than either of those and the great hall in which he now stood was the most awesome place he had ever been in. It had banners fluttering from the walls and torches flickering in sconces which made the shadows leap up high into the darkness overhead. There was a great dais at one end made of slabs of grey stone, with steps mounting up to a vast stone seat with a high back which had to be some sort of throne. The seat had markings and patterns cut into it like the marks scratched on to the backs of all the stones. Elaborately carved stone pillars stood behind. But unlike any other throne he had ever seen in pictures, this had no rich hangings or velvet seats, no painted panels or vividly jewelled insets. It was like everything, just stone, grey, cold-looking and without colour. Even the banners hanging from the walls were grey and pale and marked but not coloured in any way. The whole castle was cold and ghostly and eerie. The strange thing was that it was not streaming with water and covered in green slime and algae after being submerged deep in Withern Mere for thousands of years. Olly looked down. The flags of the floor, which looked exactly the same as the flags on the floors of the hall and kitchen and passageways at Gullywith, were not even damp.

He was startled by the sound of trumpets, a mighty fanfare which rang round the great hall and boomed in his ears, and then by the familiar sound of drumming as a procession emerged from an entrance on the far side, more stone men in formation, with their stiff grey faces and set heads and dead eyes focused in the same direction. They were leading in the Stone King, the same immensely tall, strange figure with robes carved in unmoving folds and long hair in sculpted strands which reached his shoulders but did not sway or shine. On his head he wore a stone crown carved like that of a chessman but without any gilding or jewels. He walked slowly and ponderously towards the dais, where the stone men had formed a guard on either side of the steps, and mounted them to sit down on the grey throne. Then the great hall fell silent and still. The only movement came from the light of the torches and the flickering shadows on the walls and over the standing stone figures.

Olly stood and waited. He was not afraid, neither of the Stone King nor of the stone army, but he was cold and tired and hungry, he was worried about the others and he wished he had somebody to talk to.

'Oliver Mackenzie Brown.'

Olly jumped. It was strange, hearing his full name spoken out loud in the great hall by the Stone King, who was staring directly at him.

'Yes, Your Majesty.'

'Come here, Oliver.'

There was a rustle of movement among the soldiers. Oliver walked straight up to the dais very boldly, and stood at the bottom of the steps, looking up at the high throne.

The face of the Stone King was without any expression, so that Olly could not tell if he was angry, friendly, threatening or even smiling. His eyes were stone eyes, though they had tiny pinpoints in the centres indicating sight. The rest of the figures stood to attention, looking straight ahead.

'Up here, please.'

Olly climbed the steep stone steps towards the King. When he reached the throne, he bowed instinctively and stood, waiting.

'Do you know where you are?'

'Yes. I am in the great hall of Withern Castle.'

'Good. But do you know why you are here?'

'No, Your Majesty. And I hope I'm not going to be kept here for too long. I do have to get back home and I want to make sure . . .'

He faltered. He had started to chatter as if the Stone King was some long-lost friend but how could he be? He might be about to do anything at all and, whatever it was, he had a vast army to help him.

'Of what?'

'Nothing. Just . . . to get safely home.'

'And perhaps you will. But let me tell you what I want, Oliver. What the stone people want and must have because it is our right. Have you any idea what it might be?'

Oliver was about to say Gullywith but bit the word back, shut his mouth and shook his head.

'Come and sit down here.'

The Stone King pointed with his long, stiff stone finger to a spot on the floor at the foot of the throne. Olly went there. It was very cold. All the stone was cold. But dry. He was still puzzling about it when the King began to speak again.

'Withern Castle has risen again, Oliver. Withern Castle has risen and stands great and proud over Withern Mere after century upon century. The new Stone Age is dawning. The stones are ancient. Others make claims to greater age, greater wisdom, claims to supremacy, and so we have enemies. We have enemies who wish to stand in our way. We have enemies who have taken possession of territories which belong to us, as it is written, and these territories must be restored. If they are not restored, we will repossess them. But we would rather there were no battles. We would far rather be given back what is ours and to have our rule peacefully restored. You cannot know what was done to us. It began with the theft of the Great Book and after that nothing was safe.'

He spoke in the same strange even tone, his voice never rising or falling, but when Olly glanced at the Stone King he saw that now and then the tiny pinpricks of light in the centre of his eyes seemed to spark.

'You could help us, Oliver.'

There was a long silence apart from a very faint expectant stirring among the stone soldiers, like the wind whispering through reedbeds.

Olly bent his head, thinking carefully. He knew what the Stone King wanted him for now. He wished the others were here and Nonny Dreever most of all. Nonny would know not so much what he ought to do – Olly was quite sure of that himself – but what he should say. He sat with his head down, saying nothing, for a long time until eventually the Stone King said, 'You are a very wise boy, Oliver. Wise to think carefully. I can see that you would do well amongst us. Stone Prince!'

Olly looked at him in horror in time to see the sparks fly from the King's eyes.

Then he said, 'That sounds very grand.'

The Stone King clapped his hands. It made a hard, cold sound.

'Then grand you may be.'

'What would I do?'

'To be Stone Prince? Help us. Help us to regain what is ours.'

'Why is it yours?'

'Because it was always ours.'

'By fighting?'

'No. We want back what was stolen from us but we want it to be given back freely. There should be no battles. Not unless they become necessary. If you help us, they will not.'

'And if I don't help you, then what?'

'There are others. We are not friendless, Oliver. But you are quick and clever. You would be of the greatest possible help to us.'

'How would I? I don't understand.'

But the Stone King moved his arm and then rose from his throne to tower above Oliver.

'That is for you to learn on another occasion. First, you must eat and you must rest. You will be taken to your chamber and given food and a bed, and while you eat and rest think carefully. Think how best you can help us. Think of who you know. Think of who you must speak to. Think of how you can persuade them to hand over to us what is ours. These are things only you can do, Oliver, and that is a great power. A great responsibility and deserving of great reward. Stone Prince!' He waved his arm slowly over Olly, turned and strode down the steps of the dais. As he passed, Olly felt a draught of bitter air waft over him, chilling his face and hands so that they went stiff and numb.

Then the Stone King was gone, followed by the procession of marching attendants, their footsteps echoing loudly down the stone passageways into the distance.

CHAPTER THIRTY-FOUR
Taken Prisoner

There was no time for Olly to wonder what might happen next because it was happening. He was surrounded by the stone guards and marched out of the great hall and up a steep stone staircase which wound round and round and went on for so long that he was both giddy and out of breath by the time they got to the top. The spiral staircase was narrow too and he realised that they were almost certainly climbing up inside one of the castle turrets.

At the top they went through a low door set in an archway into an extremely curious room. It was round with the usual stone walls and a pair of iron grilles set high up and it might have seemed like a prison cell except that it was the first part of the castle which was not made entirely of cold bare stone. There was a high couch with a couple of steps leading up to it, and the couch was draped with thick fur covers. At the foot was a fur rug. And here and there round the walls were huge maps, maps like the ones Olly had seen before, intricately drawn maps with spidery lines and small square markings, maps of Withern Mere and Withern Hill and

Gullywith, as well as of other places he did not recognise. The place names were all in the runic language and it was runic language in which the scrolls that also hung from the walls were written, long long lists of what might have been names or even verses, he had no idea.

On the stone table beside the couch was an oil lamp which gave out a soft tallow light that flickered comfortingly round the stone walls.

Beside the lamp was a stone bowl filled with nuts and fruits and a stone vessel full of something liquid.

The next minute, the door of the chamber had swung shut and was being bolted on the other side and Olly found himself entirely alone.

He stood looking round. He was tired and now he was by himself, he could acknowledge that he felt slightly – but not very – nervous. But he was also interested in the chamber, wanted to look at the maps and to lie on the couch among the great thick fur covers and, above all, wanted to eat and drink.

The fruit was fresh and delicious, dark sweet red berries and large plump yellow berries, small dark thick-skinned wrinkled fruits that looked weird and tasted delicious, knobbly little banana-like things and nuts which split open easily and were milky inside. He ate and ate and then he lifted up the stone cup in which the drink bubbled and fizzed very slightly as he put it to his mouth. It gave off a slight smoke. Olly drank it all. It was almost but not quite the same as the Revel Cup with one of the flavours missing and a different one he did not recognise in its place.

He had been very hungry and thirsty and at first he felt revived and quite excited, and roamed round the chamber looking at the maps and picking up some small ornamental stones carved with runes which were placed in niches here and there, and then he noticed that the stone floor was scratched with runes in a pattern that might have been some kind of game. He was studying it and thinking about it when the giddiness that he had felt on reaching the top of the spiral staircase came over him again. The soft light from the oil lamp seemed to swerve about and dance wildly on the walls and the maps began to undulate.

He climbed up the stone steps and lay down on the couch, pulling the great fur covers over himself and sinking down. The lamplight steadied itself again and just flickered gently, soothingly and once or twice gave out a little popping phuttering sound.

Olly closed his eyes.

He woke out of a strange dream which ended with something silky brushing against his face.

The light from the lamp had burned quite low and was a dull red like the embers of a dying fire. Olly watched it for some minutes. Then he looked round carefully. He was alone. The fur rugs were wonderfully comfortable and warm and he was about to sink down into a delicious sleep again when his face was touched briefly by something. He sat up. Nothing. The chamber was still. He looked everywhere. Then it came again, a flutter and a swoop downwards.

The shadow of the bat skimmed across the light for a

second. Olly looked up and saw that it now hung on the narrow ledge beside one of the iron grilles set high up in the wall. He was pretty sure it had not been there earlier.

He listened before sliding off the couch but there was no sound anywhere. Presumably the stone men were all asleep, though surely there must be a guard both inside and out. All castles had guards on watch.

He waited a moment longer, then gave a very short low whistle. At once, the bat flew down and round his head, making tiny squeaks, before flying back up to the grille, down and back, down and back.

But if it intended him to escape through the grille, it had miscalculated badly because there was no way that he could climb up the bare stone walls. He sat down again and, for the first time, a terrible despair came over him. He was in the turret of a vast castle belonging to an enemy, it was the middle of the night and he was a long way from home and without any means of escape, even if he did have the company of a well-meaning bat.

The next thing he heard was a faint scraping sound. It stopped and started, stopped and started and was coming from somewhere above his head.

The bat flew round and round the chamber madly before diving down and dipping its wings several times.

The scraping came again and was followed by a tapping, then a creak, tap, creak, tap, creak. Silence. Scrape scrape scrape.

Something was working away at trying to remove the iron grille.

Olly's heart was beating very fast, partly with excitement,

partly with anxiety that the sounds, however faint, must surely waken some of the stone soldiers and bring them up the spiral staircase into the chamber. He got up and crept to the door. But after he examined it carefully, feeling it all over with the palm of his hand because the light from the lamp had got very low, he found nothing which could be dropped down or turned to lock or bar it from his side.

The small sounds went on above him for a long time and the bat had stopped flitting about and vanished into one of the dark shadows in the roof.

Olly wondered who was out there in the night, trying to open the grille, and how they had climbed up in the first place. KK and Zed? Nonny Dreever?

It had to be one of them.

He badly wanted to lie down and go to sleep again and the red glow from the lamp was fading quickly now, leaving most of the chamber in total darkness.

He burrowed his legs into the pile of fur rugs and closed his eyes.

It was the bat's chirruping which stopped him from falling asleep again. It was hovering close to his ear and its tiny shining eyes had an imploring look in them. Then it left him and seemed to fly at the wall. Olly waited for the sound of it hitting the stone but it did not come. He got up and groped his way off the couch and the dais and across the chamber. Now the bat was at his shoulder, now ahead again, now touching his face, now his hands, guiding him forwards. He could see a little in the last glow from the lamp. He put out his hand and touched first the wing of the bat and then something else.

The next moment he was clasping a thick, strong, heavy rope which must have been let down from the grille above. There was a large knot in the end, enough for his feet to grip and to take his weight as he jumped up and grabbed the rope with both hands. The bat was chirruping madly now, flying joyously round and round Olly's head as he climbed steadily, knot by knot, up and up. The rope swung a little but felt quite safe. Once he glanced down. The lamplight had sputtered out and the red glow had gone. But when he looked up he saw a patch of silver moonlight behind the grille and made steadily towards that. It was a tiring climb and his legs and arms ached and his hands were burning on the rope but eventually he reached the grille. There was a wide stone ledge in front of it and he managed to get off the rope and on to it, though once there he had to crouch down and put out a hand to reach back for the rope to steady himself.

He was not sure what was going to happen next but as he waited there was a slight noise from outside and the grille was lifted away, revealing the sky, the moonlight and a large opening which he could easily get through.

The bat went first, diving out into the night and wheeling round and round.

Olly wondered if there was another rope on the outside. Or a ladder. Or a staircase. Or . . .

He peered out a little way but all he could see was the

sheer wall of the tower plunging downwards, which made him feel so giddy he closed his eyes and ducked hastily back in. But surely whoever had managed to get the rope down to him and take away the iron grille was not going to just leave him there.

He waited but nothing else happened and no one came and even the bat seemed to have flown off into the night.

Olly was holding on to the stones at the side of the opening for dear life and wondering what he should do next when, from far below, he heard the noise of angry voices and then of marching feet. A flare went up, whizzing past his nose and blazing out into the darkness. Olly ducked back. Another and then another and the third one came close enough to the opening to reveal him in its few seconds of vivid yellow light.

There was a roar of triumph from the courtyard and the next minute the sound of hundreds of small stone soldiers clattering up the spiral staircase towards the chamber.

CHAPTER THIRTY-FIVE

On a Bat's Back

It was the strange low whistle which made him turn. It came again, from immediately outside the window. Olly peered a little way out very cautiously and looked down and was startled that he could no longer see the courtyard lit by the flares and full of the angry stone battalions. Something dark was blotting out the view below and the whistling noise seemed to come from it but now it changed and became a sound he knew well, a bat-like squeak.

He stared down until in the moonlight he saw the mousy outline of a body and the wide wings like those worn by the paragliders he had once seen jumping off a cliff in Wales and flying, flying.

Squeeeeeeak. It came more loudly and urgently and now the noise of stone on stone came loudly up the last steps of the spiral staircase.

There was only one thing Olly could possibly do and he did it. He clambered out of the window and lowered himself down on to the back of the great bat, expecting it to tip over sideways with his weight and send him crashing down. But it was like climbing on to a leather sofa. It was firm and strong and it held him as safely as if he had been held by rope. He gripped the ribs of the bat's wings and gave a little jerk. Just in time, as he heard the door of the chamber burst open, he felt the bat rise up easily and soar, flapping its wings evenly and steadily, up high over the castle towers and turrets.

As they rose into the sky, Olly shouted out as loudly as he could 'Ha-Hah! You'll never win and you'll never get Gullywith. Never never!'

Flares were sent up one after another and there was the distant sound of roaring as the stone army watched their prisoner escape effortlessly into the night, crossing the path of the moon, swooping over Withern Mere, and vanishing from their sight.

The flight did not last long nor was it especially enjoyable. The bat's back only resembled a sofa for the first few moments. After that, it was like a sofa whose springs were sticking through, with upholstery coming away from the framework. Olly was terrified of falling off and he felt extremely sick. The bat swooped in a most alarming way and took corners at an angle, which made his head spin and his stomach part company from its moorings.

He dared not look down much but they had certainly soared a good distance from the castle before they started to drop down and down but he had no sense at all of where they were – perhaps over Withern Hill, perhaps close to the mere.

Landing was even more alarming. One minute they

were flying in the open air, the next they were bumping heavily down on to something hard. The bat showed every sign of being about to hang upside down and in the process of doing so, tipped Olly off its back through a narrow space that felt like a letterbox before swishing away into the darkness.

The letterbox turned out to have been his half-open bedroom window and the hard place his bedroom floor. He lay on his back, unhurt but puzzled until he recognised the odd sloping bit in one corner of the ceiling and then the pattern on the rug beside his left hand.

The moon was shining on to his bed and from downstairs he heard the little cough-cough Lula often made in her sleep. He undressed quickly. He was not tired at all but he needed to think over everything that had happened and bed was his thinking place. But it also seemed to be full of stones.

He shifted about and turned over and over but in the end sat up and put on his lamp. There were no stones – he investigated very carefully, or at least none that he could see but it felt as if the mattress and the pillow were stuffed with them, and when he looked at his leg he saw angry little red marks where they had quite clearly dug into him.

Legends of Withern Mere was where he had left it on the bedside table but he had certainly not left the long thin strip of paper which was now sticking out from the top.

The Mere is Rising it said in spidery, violet lettering. He looked down at the open book.

221

CHAPTER ELEVEN
FIDDLEUP FULL MOON FAIR

The origins of this ancient celebration are lost in the swirling mists of antiquity but anthropological scholars have calculated that

The book had not been so boring as this before. It went droning on for pages but Olly had long since fallen asleep.

CHAPTER THIRTY-SIX

A Pop-Up Book

The week in Spain did the whole family a power of good. It was hot and the sun only stopped shining at night, the villa was cool and shady and very comfortable and when Olly was not on the beach or in the swimming pool with Lula he was eating baby squid and fresh sardines and a spectacular chocolate ice cream called a Trufficono in waterfront cafés later at night than he had ever been allowed up before.

Gullywith, KK and Zed, Nonny Dreever's house on stilts and the bookshop, not to mention the Midwinter Revel and the night he was held captive in Withern Castle seemed to belong not so much to another life as to a story he had read recently but which was fading from his mind.

It came up bright and fresh as paint again the day they returned home and he found a card in an envelope addressed to him among the waiting post.

'Saturday night. Keep watching.'

He did not recognise the writing and there was no signature.

The next morning they were in Fiddleup by five past nine. Lula was being taken to the clinic by Mum for her next lot of jabs, Olly was being taken to the dentist by Dad for a check-up, after which they were both being taken to the shoe shop and the hairdresser's. Only after that was all over did they meet in the Bluebird Café. But at least Olly's favourite fish and chips and Dad's favourite roast pork chop were on the menu.

'This,' Olly said as they sat waiting, 'has been the most boring morning of my entire life.'

'Yes,' Helen Brown said vaguely, 'I'm sure it has. Now what about this costume?'

'What costume?'

'Or don't you want to be in fancy dress?'

'Mum . . .'

'She's talking about the Fiddleup Full Moon Fair,' Pete Brown hissed at him.

Helen Brown took out the local paper.

'Six o'clock on Fiddleup Mount, the lighting of the beacon. The Fiddleup Games. Seven thirty. Torchlight procession down into Fiddleup. The crowning of the Fiddleup Queen, who opens the fair.'

'It doesn't say anything about dressing up.'

'Theme. WEATHER. Prizes for the best costumes. Section One. Adult. Section Two. Twelve to sixteen years. Section Three. Under-twelves. Section Four. Babies and toddlers up to two years.'

'Weather?' Olly said, as his plate of golden crisply battered fish and chips was put down. 'What sort of fancy dress is that? *Weather?*'

'Oh come on, Olls, think about it. You can go as a little raindrop.'

Pete ducked as the chip flew past his ear.

'Oliver Brown!'

'Oliwer Wown,' Lula said rather sadly. She had put her spoon down without eating any of her cut-up omelette and her cheeks were very pink.

'Oh dear, the jabs are making her feel horrid already. Better get her home soon.'

'Can I go into the bookshop when I've finished this?' Olly said, stuffing five chips into his mouth.

'I'll come with you, I want to see if he's got any more of those car manuals.'

'No you do not, Peter. You've got far too many as it is. We need to get Lula home.'

'Why don't you take her home and Olly and I can get Tinker's taxi back later? They've got a sale in the outfitter's and I need some new T-shirts.'

'Fine, only I'm warning you, any more old car manuals . . .'

'Apple crumble or syrup pancakes, Olly?' Pete Brown asked, winking at him under cover of the menu.

Fifteen minutes later, Mum and Lula were heading for home, Dad was in the outfitter's trying on sports jackets and Olly was opening the door of the bookshop. The bell jingled as usual but the small round man was not behind the counter, nor did he come out of the room at the back when Olly started to wander round.

The first thing he noticed was that the tortoise was

back in its old place behind the door, but although he kept looking at it, and even went to stroke it on the back, it did not wink at him and there was not the faintest of gleams in its eyes.

Olly doubted if it was even the same tortoise.

At first there was nothing of interest at all on his usual bookshelves. No maps. No *Battle for Gullywith*. No *Legends of Withern Mere*. There was a dull-looking history of the county and a couple of 1970s AA guides but that was all. He went round to the next bay, then the next. At the very back was a section of children's books and he began to look along those rather half-heartedly to see if there was anything he might enjoy, as Dad had given him four pounds to spend.

There were adventures of boy scouts, polar explorers, Roundheads and Cavaliers and Vikings, boarding school stories, Red Indian stories and, in Olly's view, far too many fairy tales. He didn't want to spend good money on any of them, or even on the old copies of the *Beano*, *Eagle* and *Boy's Own Annual*, and he was about to give up and go to find Dad when he saw it. Like everything else he had found here, the book was tucked away almost out of sight, this time between one about dogs and *Bible Tales for the Very Young*. It was the faded gold lettering on the thin spine that gleamed slightly, as if to catch his eye.

'Be very careful!'

He almost jumped out of his skin and he did drop the book.

The small round old man tutted as he bent down, picked it up and dusted the faded cover very carefully.

'I'm really sorry but you made me jump like anything. You weren't there a minute ago.'

'I don't think any harm is done.' He handed the book back to Olly.

'It's four pounds by the way.'

His eyes gleamed like topaz behind his small round spectacles.

Olly looked down at the book in his hand. The cover was a dull brown and he couldn't make out the writing it was so rubbed away. He opened it carefully and jumped again. From between the pages emerged the paper model of a castle, the battlements, towers and turrets rising up slowly from their folds, the drawbridge, held by two fine pieces of thread, lowering itself in front of him. It was a pop-up book of Withern Castle. Through the arched entrance he could just make out the great hall.

He folded the book and the castle folded too, flattening itself back so that it was an ordinary page again.

If there were any other pop-up pages, he would wait until he got the book home to discover them.

'Ah, I thought that one might tempt you, Oliver Mackenzie Brown.' The small round man reached his hand over the counter to take the book and wrap it. Olly put down his four pound coins.

'You're lucky today. This is Special Offer Day. Buy one, get one free, as it were. I think that's what they say.'

He bent down and disappeared somewhere beneath the high counter and Olly heard him rummaging around.

As he did so, the shop door bell jingled and Pete

Brown came in, carrying a handful of shopping bags, which he dumped down in front of the counter before disappearing towards the shelf labelled 'Automobiles'.

When the small round old man emerged, he had not a book but a box in his hand. It was square, not large, and had a coloured label on the top which was very faded and which Olly could not see clearly before the box disappeared into a paper bag along with his book.

'Please hold the bag this way up, things may tip out.'

'How much is the box, please?' Olly asked, looking round for Dad.

'That is the trouble with boys, they don't listen. The only worse things for not listening than boys are girls. What did I say a moment ago?'

'That today was Special Offer Day.'

'Correct. And?'

'Buy one, get one free.'

'You see? Which means the book costs four pounds and the box is free. Goodness, sometimes boys make me quite worn out.'

He handed the carrier bag over the counter. Olly took it gingerly, holding it upright.

'Good. I think you will find,' the man now said, coming round from behind the counter and heading towards Pete Brown, 'a 1962 Mustang manual in excellent condition, there, third from the left. Ah yes.'

The boring car conversation droned on and on. Olly stood by the shop door looking out on to the street, watching people go into the Bluebird Café, a boy on rollerblades go whizzing down the hill, and a woman get the lead of her dog wound round a lamp post.

'Dad, can I go outside?'

Drone, drone, drone.

'Dad?'

'What is it, Olly? You know it's rude to interrupt.'

'Can I go outside?'

'What for?'

'Just outside.'

'All right, all right, but not far. Now, the 1960 model, that was . . .'

Olly escaped.

The sky was mud-coloured and it would probably rain. So long as it didn't rain for the Full Moon Fair . . .

Olly wandered up the hill, looking in shop windows at nothing in particular, holding his carrier bag carefully. At the top he crossed over and started to wander down the other side again and he had only passed the shoe shop and the florist's when he came to what Helen Brown called the 'funny shop'. It was small and the window was a mess of bits and pieces – sets of old fire irons, croquet mallets and golf clubs, piles of ancient Bibles, tin trunks, coal scuttles, an ancient garden bench with flaking green paint, two piles of old brocade curtains. Olly stopped to look.

He saw the statue at once, even though it was at the back of the window, between a copper warming pan and a pile of old carpentry tools. It was a statue of the Stone King, grey, stiff, about a metre high, and unmistakable. Its face was his face, its hair was carved like his long, wavy stone hair. And as Olly looked, its eyes glinted with a hard, frosty glint right at the centre.

CHAPTER THIRTY-SEVEN

The Stone Game

By the time they got home in Tinker's taxi, it was pouring with rain. Olly dashed through the mud and puddles to get his bag with the book and the box in it safely to his room but, as he was shooting through the hall, Helen Brown appeared with Lula under her arm.

'Olls, will you take her upstairs and put her in her cot, please. She's feeling horrible from the jabs and I've got to ring someone about a design by three o'clock. I've given her some Calpol, she'll just need you to sing to her till she drops off.'

Lula felt hot and sticky but she clung on to Olly with her arms wound round his neck and her legs tight round his middle, so that he was terrified of dropping the carrier bag on the stairs. He went into his own room first and let it slide from his hand on to the bed before lugging his sister into her room, but she started shouting and waving her hands to stay and sleep on his bed and it was quite a while before the battle was over. The rain was rolling down the roof and lashing against the windows and once they were in her room Lula wanted to watch it and then she wanted to play hiding under the covers and jumping on the mattress and altogether it was rather a long time before she felt in the slightest bit sleepy. Olly had to sing 'She'll Be Coming Round the Mountain' and 'Ten Green Bottles' and 'The Wheels on the Bus' three times each, getting slower and slower and singing more and more softly before her eyes closed, and then they sprang open again several times as he was trying to creep out of the room.

By the time he got away safely, the rain was even heavier and he could hear Dad thundering around downstairs shouting about leaks and buckets.

Olly closed his bedroom door.

He took the pop-up book out first and opened it flat on his small table to examine it. The castle was incredibly true to life. Everything he remembered about it seemed exact – the drawbridge, the turrets. There was a page with drawings of how the bridge worked, where the arrow slits were and so on, and on the next page, another pop-up, this time of the great hall. He looked at it closely. Yes, it was right. There was the dais. There were the archways leading off to the passages and the one to the spiral stone staircase. There were the banners.

Some of the stones on the floor of the great hall had runic markings, so did one or two on the walls.

Whoever had made this book must have been inside the castle.

And yet the castle had only re-emerged a day or two ago from Withern Mere after lying fathoms deep underwater for thousands of years.

He turned to the front of the book. There was a title and a publisher whose name was in a language Olly did not recognise, but there was no author or date of publication. He turned to the back.

At the bottom of the last page was a small box with four lines of runic writing.

That was all.

He turned back to another page. The spiral staircase unfolded and rose out of the book, and when he turned the next there was the chamber in which he had been imprisoned, with the high bed draped with fur covers, the furry-looking rugs on the floor, the lamp, the grille up in the wall. And hanging upside down by a cotton thread from the stone ceiling of the chamber was a very small black paper bat.

He put the book on the shelf next to *Legends of Withern Mere* and turned to the box which the bookshop owner had said was a special offer.

It was a wooden box with a faded peeling picture on top but Olly could not see what it was meant to be, though he thought he recognised the end of the word 'Game', or possibly 'Home' or even 'Dream'.

He slid the lid across to open the box. On top was a flat piece of wood and as Olly took it out he saw that it had a hinge for the wood to open flat, like a chessboard. But printed on the surface were not the black and white squares of a chess game but a series of lines criss-crossing this way and that. He was sure he had seen something like them before but couldn't remember where. There was a large ring of pale blue in one corner, a clump of dark green trees in the one opposite. Round the edges were what looked like the ladders of a snakes and ladders game, but lying flat, like a border. Inside each segment between the rungs were small symbols and pictures. The pictures were drawn like black silhouettes – silhouettes of a castle, a bat, a tortoise, a stone with runic markings and a flaring torch. There were five of each and in between the pictures were runic markings.

Olly went back to the box. The stone pieces, like chessmen, were in two layers. In the top layer were stone soldiers, wearing helmets and visors. Some had shields and lances and all of them were scratched with the faint runic markings on their tunics and shields. There were sixteen soldiers and in the layer below, sixteen identical tortoises. In a side section of the box were a lot of very small, irregularly shaped stone pieces, scratched with the runes.

And at the bottom was a single stone king, larger than the other pieces and identical to the real Stone King, and to the one Olly had seen that morning in the shop window.

He looked inside the box again and at first thought that it was empty but then he found another section with a lid and a tiny knob.

The pack of cards he took out was unlike any other he had ever seen. There were no diamonds, hearts, spades and clubs. There seemed to be different suits, and apart from four stone kings, there were weird symbols instead of numbers and little groups of runes in formation. One card was all white without anything on it at all and another was the same but all black.

There was also a dice. It was like any other dice except that instead of a six there was a tortoise.

Olly tipped the box upside down but nothing fell out, no other compartments sprang open, and there was no leaflet with instructions for playing the game or games.

After looking at everything again and turning all the pieces over and over, he packed it all back. Maybe KK would know about it. Or Nonny Dreever. He probably had half a dozen boxes like it in his house. It was the kind of thing that sat about casually there, as boxes of matches and packets of tea bags sat about in everybody else's.

He had not seen any of them since he had been dropped back by the bat into his bedroom the night of his escape from Withern Castle. He felt rather hurt. Even if he had gone to Spain for a week, they might have left a message. How did they know he wasn't still being marched along tunnels knee deep in water by the stone soldiers? He might even have been drowned.

He sat on the edge of his bed swinging his feet and feeling sorry for himself for some time while the rain battered against the windows.

CHAPTER THIRTY-EIGHT

A Great Flood

'Flood Warning . . . Four centimetres of rain in twenty minutes . . . Downpours continue . . . Rain and heavy storms forecast for the next ten days.'

'Looks like the fair will be washed out, then,' Pete Brown said, switching off the television.

'Well, don't sound so pleased. I'm halfway through making Lula a sunbeam costume. It could stop by tomorrow night.'

But it won't, Olly thought, staring out of the window. It hadn't stopped since they'd come back from Spain.

He felt as if he was in a cage. He had been out a few times when the rain had been normal rain but now it was washing down in such a way that nobody could enjoy anything. Water came down the lane towards the house in a flood, carrying stones and sand and branches; there was a lake in the middle of the yard where a small hollow had been and the field was so waterlogged he couldn't see the path going across it towards the hill.

The phone had been cut off twice and the lights kept flickering and going out, there were buckets under several leaks in the roof and a small bit of fungus had started to grow out of a damp patch in the attic.

It was only Helen Brown who ignored it all and carried on sewing Lula's sunbeam costume.

'And you'd better hurry up and decide what you want to go as, Olly, or I won't have time to make you anything.'

'A monsoon,' Pete Brown said, passing through.

Olly went back to his room to get out the game again and try to figure out how it was played and what he was going to go to the Fiddleup Full Moon Fair as while he was doing it.

He laid out all the game pieces on the board on his table and moved them to and fro a bit while pictures of weather went through his head. Thundercloud. Lightning. Sun.

Rainbow. Yuk. He thought of all the little rainbows there would be, holding hands with the sunbeams.

And then, as he threw the dice and moved a stone down the dotted line in the direction of the mere, it came to him. He put the game hurriedly back in its box and raced downstairs.

An hour later they were plunging through Fiddleup in macs and wellies looking for several things on Olly's dressing-up list and Dad was waving a wet shopping list and moaning. In the Bluebird Café, after they had got almost everything they needed, he moaned even more while Olly stirred marshmallow round and round into his hot chocolate and the rain went down the windows like a turbo-shower.

'And I'm worried about the roof and there's no way we can afford a new one. It'll have to be patches and Mum expects her studio to be state of the art by Christmas and I'm still working with cables and wires trailing where they shouldn't. I don't know, Olls . . . I think we bit off more than we can chew coming to Gullywith. Don't you ever long for the warmth and comfort of Number 58 Wigwell Avenue?'

'No!' Olly watched the last pool of marshmallow go down into a little chocolate whirlpool, which reminded him of the mere.

'I love it here. I don't ever want to move.'

'You're a funny chap.'

'Why am I?'

'What is it you like so much?'

The things that he could not possibly tell Pete Brown tumbled about inside Olly's head like clothes in the washing machine.

'Dunno. I just do.'

'Come on . . . what's to like so much?'

'Everything. I just do.'

'Well, if the house goes on falling apart at the seams and costing us a fortune, we'll be taking a hard look at things so you'd better not get attached.'

But I am attached, Olly thought furiously. I am part of Gullywith, I've come to save it.

He realised that that was exactly why he was there. Gullywith had to be saved and he had been chosen to do it. He didn't know how or who by but he knew it was true. Gullywith was relying on him. He had help, of course. He had KK, her brothers and Jinx, and Nonny Dreever and perhaps the small old round man in the bookshop and an army of tortoises. But he knew that was not many set against the enemies. He looked at Dad, who was staring into his half-empty coffee cup. His face was crumpled with worry and misery and Olly desperately wanted to tell him everything, where he had been, what he had seen, what had happened in the hill and the underground passages and Withern Castle. But how could he? Dad wouldn't believe him and even supposing he did he would probably say they had to move away tomorrow.

'Can I have an iced bun?'

'Better not. Mum will have lunch.'

'OK.'

'Listen, if it rains all day today and tonight and tomorrow morning, the fair –'

'It won't,' Olly said. 'It's not going to rain tomorrow and there will be the fair. There WILL.'

'Good man.' Dad finished his coffee and started to gather up the carrier bags. 'Better get this lot home so Mum can start on your costume, then.'

When they got back to Gullywith, Lula was waddling round the house wearing a bright yellow top and leggings painted with rays of the sun and a sunbeam bonnet and smiling a fat smile. The yard was a quagmire and there was another bucket under another hole in the roof.

'Olly assures me that it is going to stop raining,' Dad said, dumping all the bags on the kitchen table.

'Good,' Helen Brown said. 'He'd just better be right.'

He was. It poured for the rest of that day and when they went to bed it was still pouring. But something woke Olly in the middle of the night. At first he couldn't make out what it was but after lying there for a few moments, waiting for something to happen, as it so often did, he realised that what had made him wake was silence. It was *not raining*. He got out of bed and went to the window to check. He opened the window. Everything smelled wet but it was very very still and it was definitely, absolutely and completely not raining. He smiled with satisfaction and looked at his finished fancy-dress costume hanging up on the wardrobe door. That made him smile too.

He lay awake for a while waiting fearfully in case he heard the familiar rattle of rain on the window and down the roof. But there was only a wonderful country silence into which he fell wonderfully asleep.

CHAPTER THIRTY-NINE

Fiddleup Full Moon Fair

It was a warm and silky night with the Fiddleup Full Moon hanging like a pumpkin in the sky. Dozens and dozens of people were making their way in a long straggling file up the path to the top of Fiddleup Mount. Among them were Raindrops, Fluffy Clouds, Rainbows, Flashes of Lightning, Snowflakes, Icicles, Blue Skies, Jack Frosts, Mists and a very great many little Sunbeams. But so far at least there was only one Twister. Olly kept looking over his shoulder as more and more people joined the file but he was positively the only Tornado. It was extremely gratifying and Dad said he was the only one with a cast-iron certainty of winning the Best Fancy Dress on the theme of Weather.

At the top the mount flattened out into a wide field and in the middle of the field was the beacon, a huge pile of wood made into a wigwam shape by the Fiddleup firemen. There were also a couple of wagons selling hot chocolate and doughnuts and long queues to buy.

'Now don't go wandering off and getting lost, Olls. You easily could in this crowd.'

'Mum! I'm not three years old, you know.'

'All the same.'

But the argument was cut short as a great cheer arose and up the hill on to the field came first the procession of heralds, a double line of local men dressed in green tights and tabards with the Fiddleup town crest painted on and carrying bugles. At the back was one single man with a huge drum. They marched to the roped-off area in the middle of the field and stood in formation. The drummer did a tremendous flourish and then a great roll on his drum, the heralds lifted their bugles and played a fanfare and on to the field came the float pulled by the two tractors from Drinkwaters Farm. Mounted high on the float under a wide canopy was the Fiddleup Maid, her four attendant maidens and two pages, all wearing white and silver and with the Fiddleup Full Moon made of painted wood above them. There was a lot of cheering and clapping as they were all helped down and led by the drummer to the beacon.

'What's going to happen?'

'She lights it of course,' Dad said breathlessly – Lula was on his shoulders in her Sunbeam outfit, bouncing about with excitement.

The flame crept up the middle of the beacon and as it reached the top the drummer rolled another mighty roll and the sky burst open with fireworks, shooting stars and Catherine wheels, fountains of gold and silver, and red and green and blue flares roaring across the summer sky.

As Olly was gazing up at them, he got a bit of grit in his eye and turned his head while he rubbed it out. And as he did so, something caught his eye. In the crowd, to one side of him, face lit a strange electric-blue by the firework, he was certain he saw one of the stone soldiers, helmet down, lance in hand but pointing to the ground as if it were a walking stick. His eyes glinted for a second as the blue light faded. The bit of grit prickled Olly's eye again, and by the time he had got it out and looked back, the stone soldier had gone.

If it had been there at all. So many people in strange costumes, so many faces lit up briefly in the different-coloured light of the bursting fireworks, so many curious costumes. Maybe he was wrong.

He wasn't wrong about a particularly weird Rainbow though, which was colours splashed all over a white T-shirt and shorts and with a big cardboard arc balanced on top of its head. Beneath the wobbling bow of many colours was the unmistakable face of Mervyn Crust.

Oh no!

But the next minute, a rather beautiful Moonbeam and a Fork of Lightning had glided up on either side of him. The Moonbeam gave him a nudge.

'KK! Zed! Mum, look who are here!'

'Oh lovely, KK, you look beautiful and Zed you're pretty edgy too. Stay with us till they judge the fancy dress.'

They watched a magnificent Blazing Sun win first prize and cheered loudly when Zed came third, after a Hailstorm.

'KK, KK, KK, KK,' shouted Lula, bouncing even harder on poor Dad's shoulders.

'Be watchful,' KK whispered.

242

'I thought I saw –'

'They're here all right. A lot of them. Be really watchful, they'll be up to their tricks and you can't trust anybody.'

'Have you seen Mervyn Crust?' Zed nodded to the Rainbow, whose headdress was sliding down over one ear.

'Huh, there's another one you can't trust. But there are plenty of us, as well as them. Oh look, they're lighting the torches. Let's go and get ours before there's a queue . . . quick.'

To one side of the field, torches on the end of long canes were being lit and handed out, and KK slithered herself in between a Thundercloud and a Snowstorm to the front. She took one and then another, handing them back until they were all holding them up, apart from Dad, who had enough on his hands holding up Lula, and as everyone took their torches, the procession started down the hill following the heralds, the drummer and the float.

Halfway down Fiddleup Mount Olly looked back. It was a wonderful sight, with torches bobbing along in a long line burning brightly in the darkness. Ahead were more torches and as they came down and down towards the streets of Fiddleup, the full moon seemed to go ahead of them, lighting the way.

'Ouch!' Olly almost dropped his torch as a sharp pain went through his foot.

'What's the matter, Olly? You'll lose your place . . .'

'I've . . .' He looked at KK who was standing back with him as he hopped about in pain. 'I've got a stone in my shoe,' he said.

CHAPTER FORTY
The Mere is Rising

The fair took up the whole centre of Fiddleup. In the square at the bottom of the hill was the giant merry-go-round. At the top of the high street leading off it were the swing boats and the Ferris wheel and everywhere there were stalls with shooting ranges and coconut shies and hoopla, with small roundabouts and swings for tiny children in between. The night air smelled of burning sugar from the candyfloss stand and hot chips and doughnuts bubbling in oil, and in no time Olly and Mum were on the painted Jinny horses being whirled round and round faster and faster as the hurdy-gurdy played, while Dad sat with Lula on a roundabout of ladybirds. KK sat behind Olly, her hair streaming in the breeze.

But as they slowed down, he saw that a couple of horses in front of him was a strange figure dressed as a Thunderclap. As he got down, it turned towards him and he saw the glinting, flinty eyes behind a pale mask.

'Come on, let's go up to the helter-skelter.'

'I'll tell Mum.'

Helen Brown gave them two pounds each, they

arranged to meet back by the carousel and Mum went off to join Dad and Lula on the rocking caterpillar.

The helter-skelter was near the top of the town, by the Ferris wheel, and the main street going up was so thronged with people that KK dodged left down a side alley. 'I know a quick way. Come on, Zed, keep up.'

They wove in and out of the lanes. One or two other people had the same idea. Then Olly realised and pulled at KK's arm. 'Hailstones,' he hissed.

'Look . . . there are eight of them . . . all the same.'

They hung back and watched. The hailstones were white, gleaming and frosted, and as one turned the eyes flashed a sudden blue-white before going out again.

'Stay close behind.'

As they neared the top of the lane, they saw a mass of people again all making for the rides and every so often Olly caught sight of something small and quick, with gleaming eyes, darting here and there, behind a Sun or a Snowstorm. He and KK stood in a long queue for the helter-skelter.

'Look,' Zed whispered behind them. 'Over there.'

There was a hot chocolate and coffee wagon and in the shadows beside it, a Rainbow with a headdress that had slipped sideways was standing next to a tall, pale, strange figure in stiffly draped robes.

'He's taking something.'

Mervyn Crust was bending forward and holding out his hand.

'What's he up to?'

Olly remembered what Nonny Dreever had said – that

Mervyn Crust was weak and foolish but not bad. 'Easily led.'

He moved forward in the queue. They were only a couple of places from the kiosk now and the pile of mats for sitting on to slide down the helter-skelter.

At that moment there was a shout and the street was full of small pale shadowy figures running through the crowds, holding up torches and winding about, causing confusion.

'What are they doing?'

There was a noise no one recognised for a moment in the general noise of the games and the rides.

Olly looked up. The moon had gone in and the stars were no longer in sight and as he gazed over the top of the helter-skelter he saw a vivid fork of lightning zigzag down the sky.

A couple of people in front of him left the queue and he found himself standing at the kiosk. He held out his fifty pence.

'The mere is rising,' the man said, handing him his ticket.

'Oh . . .' The kiosk man was the small round man from the bookshop.

'Be watchful.'

But before he could ask any more, Olly was being handed his mat and hurried down towards the spiral staircase that led up through the middle of the helter-skelter to the top. It was dark. The stairs were steep and they wound so tightly round he could see nothing either ahead or behind. He lugged his mat and climbed on, longing to get out on to the platform and come whizzing down and down, round and round. But as he went round the next twist in the staircase, he saw small glinting eyes to one side and then to another, and he stepped on something hard and round and almost fell.

More eyes. More stones. The stairs became narrower and narrower and he seemed to be climbing for miles and the helter-skelter seemed far higher than he remembered.

Something tried to grab his elbow and something else pinched his leg. But as he tried to shake it off, he felt a quick gentle fluttering against his cheek and around his head and then he was out on to the platform, high above the lights and the music and the flares and torches and the bats were flying round and round his head, close to him, making their little friendly squeaks. Olly looked down. Far below, he could see a children's roundabout lit up with fairy lights but instead of teacups or ladybirds on which the little ones sat, they were riding on tortoises. He wanted to cheer. If the lanes had been full of mean, glinting-eyed stones and there were other enemies running around with torches knocking people over and causing mayhem, at least the bats and the tortoises were here too.

'The mere is rising.'

Olly looked away into the distance, over the top of the town towards the open country, and then he saw it. Far, far away but clear and getting clearer and wider, spreading even as he looked, he saw a great stretch of gleaming water.

The mere was rising.

'Hurry up, Olly, we've got to go, we have to get there.'

Behind him, KK got on to her mat and then Zed and the three of them shot down the slippery, twisting helter-skelter very fast, with the wind whistling in their ears. As they did so, thunder rolled, there was another zip of lightning over Fiddleup Mount and the first drops of rain came pelting down.

'The mere is rising, the mere is rising,' Olly muttered to himself as the three of them raced down through the storm towards the carousel. The lights had all gone out and as they ran the whole fair seemed to be dying as the rides went dark and still. Pete and Helen Brown were waiting with Lula, who had Dad's anorak over her head, and now everyone was running, pushing and jostling to get out of the rain, which was getting heavier and heavier. Water was washing down the narrow lanes, water and stones and sand and lumps of mud.

They caught a glimpse of Mervyn Crust, his rainbow headdress completely off now and the colours of the paint on his costume running together. Snowdrops and Sunbeams were being gathered up hastily, Thunder-clouds were being wrapped in mackintoshes and Olly's tornado outfit was clinging to his back.

They got soaked long before they reached the field which was being used as the car park and people were slipping in the mud and sinking into puddles.

'KK and Zed, you'd better come home with us and get dry. You can phone your mum when you get there. Olly, what's wrong with you? Why are you limping?'

KK shot him a look.

'I know,' he said, 'there are two of them in my shoes now, really sharp ones.'

The bats had long since disappeared and now the thunder was crashing right overhead and the lightning sizzled on to the path not far away, making people shriek.

'The mere is rising.' The words ran through Olly's head over and over again. 'The mere is rising.'

They ran the last few metres to the car through streams of muddy water that came pouring down the steep streets. Pete Brown had the engine turning before Olly had properly fastened his seat belt. There were puddles on the floor.

It was slow getting out of Fiddleup because everyone was leaving at once and they could hardly see out of the windows, which were misting up inside and running with water outside.

'I can't believe it changed so much so quickly,' Helen Brown said, feeling her soaking wet hair. 'To think we were all up on top of the hill watching the beacon, and now look. Scary.'

It was scary, Olly thought. Something was not right. Weather changed, rain and storms came on quickly, but . . .

'The mere is rising.'

He remembered the running figures down shadowy lanes, the whispering voices, the glinting eyes, the dark at the top of the spiral staircase inside the helter-skelter. Scary.

'Hurry up, Dad, we've got to get home and see if

everything's all right.'

'I'm not speeding on a night like this. Anyway, we know what will have happened – a few more leaks in the roof. Good job I bought another couple of buckets the other day.'

'We have to get the Polish builders back, we can't go through winter like this.'

'I'm going to ring them again in the morning – not that they can do anything until it stops raining.'

'I wonder how much longer I can put up with it,' Helen Brown muttered, not for the first time. 'If I'd known . . .'

'Chin up, old girl. Where's your fighting spirit?'

'Running out. And *don't* call me old girl.'

They bickered on cheerfully. Lula reached out to Olly and began to twist a bit of his hair between her fingers, a sure sign she was about to go to sleep, so he leaned nearer to her and sang 'Ten Green Bottles' quietly until he felt her hand relax and let go of his hair. There was a flash of lightning ahead and he could hear the water slooshing under the car tyres as they drove on.

'Cripes!' Pete Brown said.

They had reached the top of the lane that led down to Gullywith and it was no longer a lane but a fast-flowing river. Water went up in sheets on either side of the car as they drove very slowly down, bumping over stones and boulders that were being carried along in the flood. They rocked from side to side and Lula came awake with a wail. It was pitch-black.

The yard was under half a metre of water in places. Dad managed to get the car to the front door and they piled out, trying not to plunge into deep puddles, Lula now wide awake and shouting.

The water had got in under the front door and the flags of the hall could not be seen. It was also starting to seep into the kitchen.

'Put the light on, Olly, I'll get Lula straight upstairs. I suppose it might be dry up there.'

But the lights were not working. Everything had gone off. Olly plodded through the water to find the torches which were always left on the kitchen dresser. But the dresser was wet too and as he stood there Olly felt a drip-drip on his head.

The torches worked though. They had three and he left one on the dresser and switched on another to light his way up the stairs. But as he went, his foot crunched on something, first on one of the bottom stairs, then the next, then a few up. He shone the torch down. The stones were small and piled up in the corner of each stair but one or two had rolled towards the edge and were perched there dangerously, waiting to trip someone up. He kicked out at them angrily and a few rolled down, ping, ping, ping, ping, and landed with a small splash in the hall below.

He made his way to Lula's bedroom and put the torch on the chest of drawers.

'Can Dad manage, getting KK and Zed out of the car?' Helen Brown said.

There was a terrible, dreadful, awful total silence.

The lights went back on half an hour later. Lula was fast asleep and Mum had made hot chocolate and cheese and tomato toasties and Dad kept saying, 'Well, I didn't see them . . . well, they should have got into the car . . . well, it's not my fault . . . well, what do you expect me to do, go back to Fiddleup in all this? Well, why don't you just ring and find out if they've arrived home?'

'Do shut up, Pete. And I can't just ring them, we haven't got a number. Why haven't we got a number for them, Olly?'

Olly bent his head into his mug. He couldn't say what he was thinking, which was that KK and Zed were not the sort of people whose mum had normal things like a phone. He couldn't say he'd never even been to their house.

'Where exactly do they live anyway?'

But at that moment there was a strange noise. The rain had eased slightly so that it was no longer drumming on the roof and in any case this noise had not come from the roof, it had come from the opposite direction, sounding like a low rumbling beneath their feet.

'I suppose that's the next thing,' Pete Brown said cheerfully, helping himself to the last toastie, 'an earthquake.'

The noise went on. Stopped. They listened. It came again but more faintly. Stopped.

'Just leave it,' Mum said. 'Investigate in the morning. So long as it isn't another waterfall and the roof isn't about to collapse, I'm going to bed. Olly, don't you be long. Pete, make sure the lights are all out and you've bolted the front door.'

'Like someone is going to wade through this lot to break in.'

'Well, if they do, I hope they wipe their feet properly before they start traipsing all over the house.'

Dad and Olly sat on in the kitchen in gloomy silence. The rain went on and the thunder thundered on and occasionally there was lightning. After a bit, Dad got up and made some more toasties.

'I feel bad,' Olly said. ' I feel really really bad.'

'Not as bad as I feel.'

'I probably feel badder. They're my friends and I abandoned them.'

'I was in charge and abandoned them.'

'They're probably walking home by themselves in all this rain.'

'Soaked to the skin.'

'Shivering.'

'Their shoes letting in water.'

'Actually, I don't think it was our fault. I think they just . . . went.'

'What, disappeared you mean? Spooky.'

'I'm not worried about them, honestly.'

'Nor am I, Olls. They're streetwise those two.'

Olly burst out laughing. Streetwise was the last word he would have used in connection with KK and Zed. But he knew what Dad meant.

'You looking forward to going to school?'

'Sort of. Yes. No. Yes, I am.'

'Kind of mixed, then.'

Olly was about to say yes when they both leaped to their feet. From under the house came a tremendous roaring noise.

'The cellar,' Pete Brown said, 'it came from the cellar. Quick.'

They dashed out into the hall and down the passageway to the cellar door. The noise had stopped now and it didn't seem to have disturbed Mum and Lula.

The door was closed and bolted. Pete Brown put his head to it and listened.

'Odd . . .' he said. 'I can hear something but I'm not sure what. I think I'd better go down and have a look.'

'I'll come.'

'You stand right behind me and hold the torch on the steps.'

He unbolted the door, which creaked as he opened it. Olly aimed the torch beam down carefully in front of Dad but after only two or three steps, Pete Brown said, 'Cripes. Look at that!'

Olly swung the torch.

The whole cellar was full of dark, gleaming water and it was lapping up as high as the fourth step.

'The mere is rising.'

'What did you say?'

'Nothing. You'd better not go any further, Dad.'

'I don't intend to.'

Pete Brown retreated and then closed and bolted the door again.

'We'd better find something to put under here to keep

it out. The thing is, what?'

'Sandbags?'

'Oh yes, right, I think Mum keeps those next to the bread bin.'

'I'm only trying to help.'

'I know. Sorry. Only we don't have the bags or the sand.'

In the end, they got some old rugs and mats from one of the empty rooms and dragged them up to the door. Fortunately, it fitted quite tightly to the floor, so the water would only be able to trickle out slowly, even if it did reach to the top of the steps behind.

'Right, Olly, bed. No point in sitting up watching to see if this works. We'll find out in the morning and if the hall is under a foot of water, we'll worry about it then. What a night!'

Olly lay awake for a very long time. The fact that the cellar was filling up with water worried him a lot more than it seemed to be worrying Dad, but that was almost certainly because Dad did not know that the mere was rising. And it was rising not because of the rain, though that wouldn't have helped, but because if the stones could not get their hands on Gullywith one way they would do it another. They had failed so far in their terror tactics. No matter how many small stones they sent over to get into shoes and trip people up on stairs, to make holes in the roof and fill up the corners of rooms, it had only made the Browns all the more determined to stay. But if the mere rose higher and higher they would eventually be flooded out. Gullywith would disappear underwater, just as the castle had disappeared.

Was that what they wanted? And what about Nonny Dreever's house? If that was flooded, they would never get what they wanted most of all, even more than Gullywith – the Great Book. Olly did not know exactly where Nonny Dreever kept the Great Book but the stones probably did.

He tossed and turned, he got up and looked out of the window at the black wet night and he went back to bed again and tossed and turned more, and all the time, the mere was rising and he could not help worrying about KK and Zed and about Nonny Dreever on his own and what would happen if the cellar water got through the barrier of old rugs and . . .

His room was lit up by the most astonishing and vivid bolt of lightning there had yet been and it went on being lit for ages as the lightning flashed and flashed and zigzagged back and forth across the sky.

And then something pinged on to his window.

CHAPTER FORTY-ONE

Journey by Torboat

As he scrambled into his clothes, Olly wondered what was going to happen this time. It didn't occur to him that the stone thrown up on to the window could have come from anyone other than KK and Zed, and a couple of minutes later, he was leaning out, shining the torch down to let them know he was awake and on his way.

But as soon as he looked down he realised that he would not be leaving by the front door. The water had now risen up to the first floor of Gullywith and it was hard to see where the yard and the fields normally were because the whole area was one great black shining lake. Then he made out KK and Zed and gave a big grin. Whatever they wanted, they always found a great way of arriving. The tortoises they were riding – shaped just like the ones that had made up the little children's merry-go-round at the fair – were small boats with a hollow for them to sit in. Olly waved out of the window and then he saw that a rope ladder of some shining material was hooked to the wall just beneath him. KK and Zed watched as he put one leg cautiously over the ledge and took hold of the ladder. It swayed slightly but held firm, and a minute later he was at the bottom and climbing into KK's boat.

'Hey, this is great!' But KK's face was serious.

'We haven't long. The mere is rising and this is only the start but Gullywith's safe for now because this isn't what they want first. We've got to get to Nonny Dreever's – the stones are on the move, they've got a whole fleet and they'll try to surround him.'

'How did you find out?'

'We've known for a while that they were planning something on the night of the fair. Then one of the bats overheard something and hung about in a dark corner, listening to everything and passing it on to us. I just hope we won't be too late. Now sit down and hold on, we've got to move.'

There was a high-pitched whirring noise beneath them and they shot forwards across the water at tremendous speed, sending a low wave out at either side. Zed was alongside them, the wind was rushing through Olly's hair and then, as they reached the end of the water, with the hill in front of them, they rose into the air and flew forwards fast over the top and down again at a breathtaking pace.

'Wow!' Olly said. But his voice flew off like a scrap of paper into the swirling darkness.

He could see nothing ahead and hear nothing but the rushing air. They came down on to the water again and carried on and for one moment a couple of the bats were flying alongside, wings like outstretched sails.

And then he heard Zed, who was riding close to them,

give a low cry. At once KK slowed down.

Some way ahead, they could see a flotilla of tiny gleaming lights bobbing about in formation and moving slowly forwards across the dark water as they watched.

'They're ahead of us,' KK said. 'We can't go this way now.'

'Where? Where are we going?'

'To Nonny's of course. Don't you ever listen, Olly?'

'Don't waste time arguing,' whispered Zed, 'but you're right, we'll have to try and get in through the caves.'

Olly was about to ask what caves but bit the question back.

'Right. From seven or from nine?'

'Nine, it's further away. Turn round, I'll go in front.'

Seven what? Nine what? Zed leaned across from his boat and said, 'Whirlpools. They're numbered.'

'How many are there?'

'Thirteen.'

Now they were turning their boats carefully, trying not to make a splash. Olly looked over his shoulder and saw that the flotilla of lights was moving steadily further away.

'Right, hold on. Olly, when I say duck down, you duck down into the bottom. It'll only be for a few seconds.'

They started forward across the great stretch of water at a steady pace and with the engine making no noise at all. It had stopped raining but the sky was still cloudy. Their path ahead was lit by the boat lamps, which glowed topaz like the tortoise eyes. Olly saw the water swirling round at one point but KK steered past and when he looked back he could no longer see the bobbing lights from the stone ships.

'OK, duck!' KK said. The craft hit the whirlpool and was spun round extremely fast but then they were plunging down and down, the waters closing over their heads. Olly crouched in the bottom of the boat, terrified that he would drown, holding his nose and closing his eyes tightly. But, to his amazement, he lay dry and safe in a still pocket of air and when he opened his eyes they were dropping down as if they were in a lift, steadily but without turning. It went on for a very long time and he did not feel a drop of water on him or in the bottom of the boat, though there were gleaming black walls of water streaming down on either side.

He was wondering when they would ever reach the ground, or come out into the air again, when they stopped and the engine revved slightly as they began to go forward through a tunnel, a passageway between rock walls with water cascading down them. Some way on the water became a thin stream, then just a trickle in the rock, and Olly saw a light ahead of them.

'OK, you can sit up now.'

'Oh my gosh. Where are we?'

'The Crystal Caves. When we get through the first two, we're deep under the mere – the water is actually right above us. We can travel through the caves into the heart of Withern Hill going one way, but we'll turn off – it's very narrow but if we can find the way we can be underneath Nonny Dreever's house. It's quite difficult, though, because there are so many caves leading in and out of one another in all directions. The bats will help us. I've only been down here a couple of times before but it's our best chance. We can't go fast here either – we have to move as quietly as we possibly can or the sound waves reverberate upwards and they can shatter the crystal.'

They glided forwards almost silently while Olly stared around him.

The walls of the cave and the high roof were formed from crystal in astonishing colours and the colours kept changing, fading down and fading up, glistering and shining. They were violet and a deep deep blue, emerald and sea green fading to a silvery blue as pale as the sky at the top, and then they were flushed rose pink and deep crimson, then pearl white and silver, then sparkling gold. They were made of huge chunks of roughly cut stones, sapphire, ruby, diamond, turquoise, aquamarine, amethyst, topaz, rose quartz, tiger's eye. The colours reflected into the still water below so that as they glided forwards in their boats they seemed to be gliding over the surface of rainbows. They made almost no sound so that the only thing that could be heard at all was a soft, silky lapping of the water on either side of the little boats.

'Duck,' Zed whispered just in time as they moved out of the first cave under a low arch and into the next, whose walls were darker, made of smoother stones coloured dark silver and pewter.

There were so many caves leading out of one another that Olly lost count and every one was differently coloured. But they gradually became smaller, and the last two were connected by short passageways which were only just wide enough for the boats to pass through.

'This is the last,' KK said over her shoulder. 'Now we're right underneath and we'll have to be as quiet as we can.'

The last cave was very small and the walls were a dull gold. Here, the bats were hanging upside down from the roof and perching on ledges high up in the walls.

'Now what do we do?'

KK shook her head and pointed. Cut into the golden rock on their left was a flight of shallow steps. There seemed to be no way anyone could climb up it because there were no handholds and the last steps vanished out of sight into the darkness of the high roof.

And then they heard a faint sound. They waited, absolutely still. Olly looked up at the bats, whose small beady eyes pulsed on and off, on and off. The sound came again. It was like something rattling round in a tin can, far away.

The next sound came so suddenly that they almost leaped up in the boats and overturned them. It was like the crack of a rifle against the walls of the cave and it echoed round and round, a hard, unpleasant noise and so loud that it hurt their ears in the small space.

Olly had ducked down into the bottom of the boat but the horrible noise went on, hurting his ears even down there. KK gave him a push. He sat up slowly, feeling slightly ashamed of himself. The noise was fading.

'It's them.' Zed had a grim face.

'Yes but they may be further away than they're

pretending. You know what tricks they play. I vote we just go.'

'What if –'

'What if spot-if!'

'How do we get up there?'

KK looked scornful and did not reply, merely steered the boat carefully to the side, unwound a short length of rope from a coil at her feet and threw it neatly and expertly over an outcrop of rock. It held fast and the boat rocked slightly before settling against the wall. Zed hopped out and held on to one of the ledges. There was enough room for them if they pressed close and did not lose their footing.

It seemed to Olly that he was getting such a lot of practice climbing difficult flights of steps and stairs and ladders that he could take it up for a living. This one looked even harder than the rest but he had managed to get up safely every time before this.

Zed went first and Olly was about to follow when there was an almighty crash and the roof seemed to split open, letting a strong beam of light directly on to them. After the light came some shouting and the next moment stones began to cascade down and hit them, before bouncing off the walls and into the water with hundreds of sharp, fierce splashes.

'Jump,' KK shouted, 'jump back quick.'

They jumped, hitting the bottom of the boats so hard that they rocked perilously on the water and Olly thought theirs would turn right over. But KK had started the engine and was turning away, weaving in and out of the stones which were still hurtling down on to them. They heard Zed give a yelp of pain but he managed to follow and then they were darting under the arch and through the caves, forgetting that they had to be silent in their anxiety to get away. The colours on the walls seemed to sway and shimmer with the noise, making Olly feel slightly sick. Behind them, they heard a thunderous roar but KK speeded up and then they were spinning upwards very fast, rising on the whirlpool higher and higher, the water streaming past. They surfaced and flew up into the air a little way, before crashing back down and sending sheets of spray over them. It was dark and cool and the rain was still falling.

'We didn't get to him, we didn't rescue Nonny Dreever,' Olly shouted. 'We've got to go back.'

'We can't, not that way. They'll be swarming all over, we'd never get through.'

They were slowing down and heading across the water towards a low earth bank. KK pulled the boat in so that its nose went into the soft ground. Zed stopped beside them and the engines fell silent.

No one spoke for a long time. They sat miserably, looking at the black water, the rain trickling down their necks, not knowing what they could do, anxious, cold and frustrated. Olly could not imagine what might be happening in the house on stilts but the stone men were desperate to get hold of the Great Book and if Nonny Dreever had no one there to protect him and fight for him . . . he had said that his powers were no longer very strong.

'We have to help him,' he said aloud, 'we *have* to.'

'We just tried.'

'Shut up,' KK said, 'I'm thinking, aren't I? You don't think we're giving up, do you?'

They waited. She sat with arms wrapped round her bent head and no one spoke for a very long time. One of the bats flew past, dipped down and flew on.

Otherwise it was still.

Olly went off into something that was a mixture of a dream and a daydream. He was trying to picture where KK and Zed lived and what the rest of their family must be like, trying to work out things he had not yet got to the bottom of, trying to get explanations for things that would never be explained in the way that sums could be explained or how you made biscuits or why it was dark at night. He imagined various houses – a cottage, a big farm, an ancient ruin – tried to see KK and Zed in them, tried . . .

'It's no good,' KK said despondently, raising her head. 'However I try to work out a way, I can't.'

Olly sat up.

'But you always can.'

'Well, this time I can't.' He could tell that she was close to tears.

'Why don't we just go the normal way? Along the path and up the steps and in at the door? They won't be expecting that so we'd surprise them.'

KK shook her head. 'They'll be guarding everywhere. They're not fools, Olly. They'll have every entrance covered.'

'No,' Zed said, ' I think Olly's right. What have we got

to lose? They know we were trying the cave way and they'll expect us to get on the bats next and land on the roof. Or even go down into the Earth Tunnels and burrow our way up. I think it's worth a try.'

'Hang on . . . let me think, let me think,' Olly said. Something, something was in his mind, at the very back, like the bit of a puzzle you had lost and it had rolled away under the furniture. Like . . .

'If you don't hurry up . . .'

'Shhhh.'

His brain felt like a dark place with a tiny chink of light which kept moving around. He was chasing the chink but every time he almost grabbed it, it slithered away like a ball across an ice rink and twirled out of his reach. There was something, a clue, a hint, an idea . . . something he knew could help them.

'Oh no!'

He looked up, hearing the alarm in Zed's voice. They all looked.

Some distance away but moving steadily towards them came a flotilla of small, fierce, burning lights. And after a few seconds, they heard the sound of drumming.

'Quick!' KK kicked at the starter of the boat and spun it round. Olly hung on and they shot away across the black water. But something was wrong. Olly glanced round. Zed was not beside them or behind them. His boat was trapped, the engine was silent and he was helpless by himself and right in the path of the stone army.

CHAPTER FORTY-TWO

Tortoises to the Rescue

It was clear that they could do nothing for Zed by hanging around and that they were better going back, making sure they themselves were safe and then working out how best to get help both for him and for Nonny Dreever.

It was still getting light when they arrived back at Gullywith and everything looked totally different. When they had left, the rising waters had been halfway up to the bedroom windows. Now, the house seemed to be sailing serenely above the water, its windows gazing down on them and reflected on the water in the light of the moon. It had stopped raining but all around had been a waterland. The sight of the house now was confusing to say the least.

KK pulled the boat up to the front door. There were no lights on and no sounds from within.

'What's happened?' Olly said. 'I don't understand.'

'I think I might.' KK got out and walked round to one side, then the other, peering down.

'The water must have started to go down here somehow,' Olly said, following her. 'Maybe there are some ditches and it flowed into them. Or . . .'

Or what, he asked himself.

'Look.'

They bent down and at that moment the house moved very very slightly and it moved upwards. It was barely noticeable but the whole thing raised a fraction higher above the water. They waited. Nothing. Then it came again – the tiny upwards movement. It was so smooth and so small that no one inside could possibly have noticed anything.

'What's happening?'

KK had got down and now she was scrabbling with a bit of broken pot into the earth at the corner of the house. Olly knelt and watched closely. She scratched and scrabbled away until she had made a hollow, and then she put her hand inside it. A huge smile spread over her face.

'You feel,' she said.

Olly put his hand inside the cold, damp hollow of earth and felt around carefully. After a moment, his fingers touched a hard, ridged shell.

'The tortoises! But what are they doing, KK?'

'I think – I'm not sure but I think they've climbed on one another's backs higher and higher until they've lifted the house – like Nonny's house on stilts. That's holding it above the water.'

'But they can't stay there for ever.'

'No but the water's bound to start going down before long. It's stopped raining and the drains and dykes will eventually filter it back to Withern. The mere can't just go on rising for ever, can it?'

They were still staring down, but the house only shifted once more before everything seemed to settle and go still.

'You've got to go in now, Oll.'

'What about you?'

'Stuff to do. I'll see if Zed . . .'

But at that moment there was a swoosh of water and Zed steered his torboat up to them, turned it and came to a rest neatly alongside.

'I'm hungry,' he said. 'When will your mum be getting breakfast?'

'But you were trapped, your boat would't work, you . . .'

Zed put his hand in his pocket and pulled something out. In the palm of his hand lay a small brass tortoise.

'But . . .'

'Never,' KK said to Olly, her face serious, 'never go anywhere without yours. They can't always help, sometimes a situation is beyond even their powers, but they will always, always try.' She turned to Zed. 'What's happening?'

'They've got the house on stilts surrounded but I could hear voices above me. I think I heard Nonny – can't be sure. When the boat started up, I scooted. I wasn't going to be much use there by myself. Nothing can happen for now. If they're in there, they'll be looking for the Great Book.'

'Listen,' said Zed, 'there's something more important. Is your mum getting breakfast or what?'

But it was KK who did that. By the time Pete Brown came downstairs in his pyjama trousers and an old T-shirt, rubbing his hair and carrying Lula, the kitchen was rich with the smell of frying bacon and eggs, tomatoes and mushrooms, and Olly was stuffing the third round of bread into the toaster. Zed had his eye on the kettle as he dodged about for plates and mugs and knives and forks to lay the table.

'Where did you two spring from?' asked Pete Brown, dumping Lula in her highchair. 'I'm amazed you even got here, I thought we were going to wake up and find ourselves marooned. I dreamed the water had come up to the bedroom windows.'

Lula began banging her spoon.

Olly and KK exchanged glances. But Pete Brown often jabbered on without waiting for any reply and now he was pouring the tea and wondering whether the post would get through and reminding himself to check all the wiring in case water had got into it.

'Doesn't seem too bad,' he said, coming back from the fuse boxes in the lobby. 'I'm amazed actually. But it does seem to be going down now. I should think you had to row here in a boat, KK – is that for me? Where did you find those sausages? Brilliant. OK, Lula . . .'

But KK was already cutting up sausages into tiny pieces and turning Lula's egg over to make it crunchy. Pete Brown filled his mouth with bacon, sausage, tomato and mushroom and sat munching with a delighted smile.

Olly glanced out of the window. The water had gone down enough for him to see a bit of grass and gravel in the yard, though the fields beyond were still flooded. He wondered about Nonny Dreever and how Zed had escaped, whether the stone army was still on the march, how the tortoises would manage to climb down without the house collapsing, what . . .

'What on earth are those green things outside?' Helen Brown said, coming into the kitchen in her wellingtons and mac. 'Oh, hello, you two. You didn't paddle here, did you?'

They looked at each other in alarm.

'Dinghies,' Olly said quickly.

'Don't speak with your mouth full. Right. Well, if you've brought dinghies to play about in that's fine but you can't go outside the yard, not without life jackets and you'll have to wear waterproofs and . . . Lula, what are you *doing* with that?'

Lula shrieked with laughter as she put up her hand to squash half an egg further into her hair.

After breakfast, Zed and Olly went upstairs while KK headed round to the side of the house to check on the torboats.

'It's fine,' she said when she came back. 'They've deflated themselves and folded themselves up and they're tucked into a corner by the barn. Right . . .'

'I've got it!' Olly yelled, leaping up. 'I've got it, I've got it, I've got it. Sorry, I didn't mean to interrupt like that but I've remembered.'

'What?'

'I was trying and trying to think of something and I

couldn't . . . and I have.'

He went to the wardrobe and reached into the back.

'The game,' he said, bringing out the box. 'It's in the game. I couldn't work it out when I got it, but it just went click. Look. I just know that if we find out how to play it, if we can just work out the key, it tells us everything we need to know. That's why he gave it to me – the shop man, that's what it's for.'

At first, the game and its pieces spread out on the floor did not make any sense. They tried different ways of playing it, throwing the dice, moving the pieces to and fro. Nothing. They could make up half a game but without a key or any instructions, they got stuck each time. It seemed to have pictures and clues but no pattern.

Suddenly, Zed jumped up and down, waving his arms. 'It's the lines,' he shouted. 'It's all in the lines. The pieces don't matter. Look at the lines. Do you recognise them?'

They looked. Olly even turned the board round and round.

'Nope,' KK said, shifting her left leg, which had gone to sleep.

'I don't know what they are . . . they sort of wander about.'

'Yes. From where?'

'Er . . . anywhere.'

'Did you say you had a map, Olly?'

'Maps. Of course . . . the maps!'

They spread those out carefully on the floor next to the game – the map of Withern with its elaborate decorations and details and the patterned border, and the bare, skeletal map of Gullywith, with its thin lines and white spaces.

Zed bent over them, muttering to himself. He traced his finger across first one, then the next, then dodged back to the game and peered closely at the board.

'He's on to it,' KK said. 'He gets like this.' She stood up and went to the window. 'Only trouble is, it could take ages.'

Olly joined her. A weak and sickly sun was trying to get out between the grey clouds and failing but it was not raining any longer and there were stronger patches of green showing here and there.

At one point, Olly thought he felt an odd sensation as if he were in a lift going down.

'It's the tortoises,' KK said. 'I suppose they can only do it very gradually.'

'Olly!' Helen Brown shouted. 'Olly!'

He went to the door.

'Olly, that was Mervyn Crust's father on the phone. Mrs Crust has been taken into hospital.'

'Oh.'

'What?'

'I said, oh. I mean, oh, I'm sorry about that.'

'Yes. Well, Mervyn's coming here.'

'What?'

'His dad has to go on a business trip and he can't take Mervyn so he's coming here. He's being dropped off in about half an hour.'

Olly turned back into the room just as Zed leaped to his feet, waving his arms about again.

'Got it,' he said, 'got it, got it, got it. Look.'

They bent over the maps and the game.

'These lines . . . they're not any paths we know about already. They're not the track. They're not the underground tunnels. Not any of the ones we've been through anyway. They don't go in the right direction. But look . . .' He turned the Gullywith map round and placed it edge to edge with the game on one side and the map of Withern on the other. At once, they saw that some of the faintest lines joined together. 'These are either tracks or tunnels or passageways and they lead from here –' he put his finger on the Gullywith map, 'which is this house. Somewhere in it or under it.' He leaned over and put another hand on a green blob on the map of Withern. 'And here. This is Nonny Dreever's house on stilts. This is the wood behind it. Here's the forest. Here's Withern Hill. Now . . . if you follow them, the lines go in a bit of a roundabout route, from here to Nonny Dreever's house, actually crossing the game board. Without that, it doesn't join up. It's just two separate maps. The game is the missing piece. And I guess that if you knew exactly how to play it, you'd find the tracks and get the pieces from here to here in the shortest route . . . and there would be all sorts of obstacles . . . the mere . . . the hill . . . the caves . . . and they'd be divided into teams and . . . but the point is, now we know there's a way from Gullywith to Nonny Dreever's house. A direct way.'

'So all we have to do now,' KK said, 'is find the beginning in this house. Any bright ideas?'

CHAPTER FORTY-THREE

The Secret Runes

Zed went back to the game and began to trace his finger over and over the lines, before picking up each piece and looking at it carefully, then moving them over the lines in their turn.

'I wonder . . . the runes. Are there any in this house, Olly? Any markings, anything like this?'

'In the cellar. There are some stones there with markings.'

They raced down the stairs.

But when they opened the door leading to the cellar, and started down the first couple of steps, the water was there to meet them. There was no way of getting further and none of the stones on the walls or steps was marked in any way.

'We'll have to wait till the water goes down, then,' Zed said.

'But that could be days and days.'

'The barn? What about the stones in the barn? Where we came through the trapdoor.'

'We can't get to the barn. It's still underwater at that end. Besides, we know where those passages lead,' KK said 'and it isn't to Nonny Dreever's house.'

They were heading back for the stairs when there was shouting outside and Helen Brown shot out of the kitchen.

'Oh good, you three – I think that's Mervyn arriving. They probably don't want to drive down through the water in case they get stuck. Go and meet him, will you?'

They had no choice. There was more shouting. Olly pulled on his wellingtons. 'Go upstairs,' he whispered. 'I'll get him into the kitchen, give him food. He likes food. I'll come back up as soon as I can.'

Mervyn Crust and his father were standing by the gate looking pathetic. Mervyn had a long beige mackintosh, a yellow rain hat, and huge wellington boots. His father was carrying a suitcase. Mervyn had a rucksack and a carrier bag. It looked as if he had come to stay for a month.

'Come on, then,' Olly shouted. 'You can get down here. Just keep to the side. It's fine.'

But Mervyn stood looking so helpless that in the end Olly had to splash through the muddy water to the gate.

'Please make sure he gets dry as soon as he's in the house, won't you? He gets bad colds easily. Mervyn, take off your wet things before you do anything else and don't for—'

'Come on,' Olly said cheerfully, 'you're fine,' and was about to set off towards the house when Mervyn dumped his rucksack and carrier bag on to him.

'I can't carry *everything*.'

'Now are you sure your mother's there, Oliver. I wouldn't want to think you were being le—'

'Mum and Dad are both here and they never leave us.'

'Yes, bu—'

'Byeee. Come on, Mervyn. It's only water.'

'Muddy water.'

'Yeah, the colour of your mac so that's not going to hurt, is it?'

'Daddy . . .'

'Oh dear, I think I might drop your bags into the water, they're so heavy.'

'No, those have got my cars and my . . .'

'Well, come on, then.'

At last Mervyn Crust did.

The next fifteen minutes or so were a nightmare of getting Mervyn settled. He fussed about his boots, his mac, his bags, and then about his bed, the fact that the room felt damp and that he always had sheets and blankets not a duvet.

'I can't sleep with a duvet. It makes me sneeze and have nightmares.'

Helen Brown's patience lasted longer than Olly's and she kept on telling Olly that if she had to go into hospital he would be worried and upset and feel strange.

'I would if I had to go and stay at his house.'

'Well, there you are, then, now you know how he feels. What would you like to do, Mervyn dear?'

'He can watch my new DVD, he likes watching stuff. Come on, I'll put it on for you.'

* * *

When Mervyn was settled in front of the television with a milky drink, a plate of biscuits and *Shrek 2*, Olly raced back up the stairs. In his room, Zed and KK were lying on the floor poring over the game board.

'We've got it,' Zed said with a thumbs up as Olly went in.

'Look. See this?'

Olly looked where KK pointed.

'Er – what?'

'Come down here and look closely. You really have to practically have your nose on the map and then follow the thread.'

'What thread?'

'Do you need glasses? Look.'

Olly looked. And then he saw it. A very fine red dotted line, so fine he would never have seen it if KK hadn't been pointing.

'What is it?'

'The track. But look – see where it starts?'

'In this house. But we know that already.'

'We have to find the runes and where the right one is will be the entrance to the passage and we'll know that because there will be the scarlet thread.'

'What scarlet thread? What passage? What are you talking about?

Mervyn Crust stood in the doorway, his mouth smeared with milky biscuit crumbs.

'Hey, what's that?'

But KK had moved like a lightning flash and the game was in its box and the maps folded before Olly could see how she'd managed it.

'Just a game.'

'Boring game.'

'What are you here for anyway?' Mervyn Crust turned to Olly. 'I'm not supposed to have anything to do with them, my mum –'

'You won't have to,' Zed said. 'We're off. See you, Oll.'

They had vanished before Olly could stop them. He ran out of his room but they had already got to the bottom of the stairs, and were away, out of the front door and . . .

Olly went to the window. There was a furrow in the surface of the water, leading from the yard to the flooded fields. As he looked, the furrow folded back on to itself and the water was still.

A shaft of sunlight lanced through the misty clouds, and then disappeared again.

He remembered Nonny Dreever sitting in his house, telling him about the Stone King and the castle, saying 'Mervyn Crust is a low-grade spy. He works for them but they don't treat him well . . . he is not a bad boy.'

He had told Nonny that he would remember it and he had. He would. He definitely would.

He turned round to find Mervyn lying on the floor looking intently at the maps.

'Do you want to go outside? We can skim stones . . .'

He realised as the words came out of his mouth that they were not best chosen but Mervyn did not seem to have heard him. He was tracing his finger over the lines on the map.

'It's just an old map I found in a cupboard. I don't know what it's for. Come on, I don't want to mug up here all day.'

Mervyn Crust looked up at him. 'I know what's going on,' he said, 'I know what you're trying to do.'

'Not trying to do anything.'

'Where did she put that game?'

'What game? Oh, come on, I'm off outside anyway. You do what you want.'

He started for the stairs. But Mervyn Crust did not follow him and Olly was not about to leave him in the room to poke about until he found the game – or anything else. He stood on the landing, kicking one foot against the other, not sure what to do.

It was then that he saw it. On the floor, in the corner, by the door that led to the room they still did not use, the room with the cold patches and the damp and the fungus growing out of the wall. There was also a small stone and he picked it up. It had the strange markings on it. He turned it over in his hand but then decided he'd better put it back exactly where he had found it.

Olly moved quietly. The light wasn't very good. He bent down and reached out his hand.

'What's that?'

Olly stood up quickly.

'Mouse pooh,' he said quickly. 'We've got millions of mice here.'

'Why are you bothered about their pooh, then?'

'I'm not. Come on.'

'I can't see any mouse pooh.'

If Helen Brown had not shouted that she wanted them both downstairs, Olly was sure Mervyn would have seen what he had seen. Whether he knew what it meant he had no idea but it wasn't a risk he wanted to have to take.

'What happened to KK and Zed?' Helen Brown asked as they went into the kitchen.

'They had to go.'

'Those two appear and disappear like magic. I don't know. Mervyn, would you like tea, hot chocolate or Ribena?'

'Milk.'

'Fine. Milk. Oll?'

'Chocolate, please.'

'Good.' She glared at Mervyn. 'I've got a lot of work to do, Olly. Dad has too but he's going to have Lula this morning. I'll try and sort things to have her this afternoon but I may need you two to look after her for an hour so please don't you do a disappearing act as well. What are you going to do?'

'Play a game,' Mervyn said quickly, smiling at her, a sweet, sickly smile.

'Great. Here you are, then, and there's a bowl of fruit pieces and some biscuits. Take them upstairs and try not to spill anything.'

'We can play an I-spy game I got for Christmas,' Olly said desperately, when they got back upstairs. 'It's quite good.'

'Bo-ring.'

'Or Colditz. That's a good game.'

'I don't like it.'

'Well, we've got to do something.'

Olly bit into an apple slice so hard he bit his tongue as well.

'Yes and I know what.' Before Olly could do anything, Mervyn had slid off the bed and shot out on to the landing.

'Where are you going?'

But he was already in the corner, bending down.

'Oh.'

'What?'

'It was here. I saw it. I definitely saw it.'

'What – the mouse pooh?'

'No.'

Olly looked over his shoulder, his heart in his mouth.

But what he was sure he had seen, and what Mervyn Crust had probably seen as well, was no longer there.

CHAPTER FORTY-FOUR
The Scarlet Thread

Gradually the house went quiet as the night settled in. He heard Dad come down from his workroom and Lula call out in her sleep. He heard Mum go to her and then come out again and close the bedroom door. He heard the stairs creak as they always did. The lights went out. He heard an owl.

He waited and waited, lying in the dark, his eyes open. He counted one thousand. Then two thousand. Then three thousand. He almost fell asleep halfway through the last thousand and had to make himself sit up.

'four thousand nine hundred and ninety-one . . . four thousand nine hundred and ninety-five . . . four thousand nine hundred and ninety-eight . . . four thousand nine hundred and ninety-nine . . . FIVE THOUSAND. Yessss.'

He was an expert by now at getting up without making a sound. He took off his pyjamas, put on his shoes and clothes, got the torch and crept out on to the landing. The house made its little ticking and creaking sounds but otherwise everything was still and everyone slept. He waited a long time, listening intently in the direction of

Mervyn Crust's room but Mervyn, too, was silent.

He shone the torch along the skirting board slowly. Nothing. He went along peering down, along and along and along, until he reached the door to the unused room. Then he pointed the beam at the corner of the door jamb. He bent down.

It was there again.

Olly got down on to his hands and knees. The floor-board creaked twice, the second time quite loudly, and he froze, waiting for someone to call out, switch on a light, for his dad to come plunging out, shouting 'Who's there?'. But he didn't. No one came. The creaking stopped.

Olly held the torch with his left hand and with his right felt carefully along until he touched it.

It was quite definitely a scarlet thread, just a centimetre of it, a scarlet thread exactly like the one drawn on the map in a faint dotted line. Olly gave the thread a very gentle tug. Nothing happened. It did not come away in his hand, it did not start to unravel from somewhere inside the room; it simply stayed where it was. He turned the door knob and opened the door. It creaked and squeaked slightly but that was all and in a second Olly had slipped into the room and shut the door behind him.

Then he switched on the light. There was no lamp-shade just the bare, low-watt bulb hanging from the ceiling. The room was what Helen Brown called 'my despair' and Pete called 'my next challenge'. It was as dismal as on the day when Olly first saw it, still with its damp patch, still with its cold bits, still with its fungus.

But now, it had a line of scarlet thread which he saw led from the door jamb along the skirting board to the far corner, where it disappeared into a crack. The crack ran in a straight line all the way from the top of the wall to the bottom and the thread was about halfway down. Olly pulled it. Nothing. He shivered. He was standing right in the middle of one of the cold patches. If KK and Zed were here . . .

He went to the window and looked down, expecting, hoping, to find them below, waiting, throwing a stone at the window, in a torboat, on skis, even in a helicopter. He smiled. But it was dark and there was no moon and no sound. He supposed that this time he was on his own.

He returned to the crack and felt it with his finger, wondering what he was supposed to be doing and what the scarlet thread was telling him, if anything, when something happened which made him leap backwards, his heart thumping.

The wall began to open. A whole section of it opened like a door. But it opened out so that Olly nearly lost his balance and crashed forwards into a gaping black hole. It opened silently, as if its hinges were oiled. But there were no hinges, there was only the scarlet thread.

Olly shone the torch and saw that the thread ran down to the ground and then disappeared into the darkness at his feet. He moved the beam. He could just make out the first bit of scarlet as it dangled away but there did not seem to be any steps. Olly lay down and edged forwards. Then he reached out his hand and felt carefully round.

What he thought he felt was something cold and

smooth. He beamed the torch down on to it. Something gleamed. It seemed to be fixed into a beam which formed the underside of one of the floorboards and from there to drop down out of sight into the black hole. Olly felt it again. He knew it reminded him of something but he couldn't think what. It wasn't something he had seen often. He felt it again. Smooth. Slippery.

The helter-skelter! And hanging from a hook beside it was a mat.

He was supposed to sit on the mat and slide down. But where to? At the Full Moon Fair he knew he would come out at the bottom on to a soft mattress. But he couldn't see how far down the slide went or what it ended in. It could be hard ground. It could be deep water.

He stood alone looking down into the blackness for a very long time, clicking the torch beam on and off. Half of him wanted to go straight back to bed, get into his pyjamas, burrow under the duvet and go to sleep. Maybe when he woke the next morning, it would be gone; the door in the wall would have swung shut and the scarlet thread would have disappeared again.

Maybe.

The rest of him knew he had to go, by himself, to climb on the helter-skelter slide and follow the scarlet thread, which would lead him to Nonny Dreever.

He had to go. He just had to.

Something tickled the back of his hand. Olly looked down and saw a tiny money spider. For a second he and the spider looked at one another. Then Olly saw that it had gleaming, golden eyes, tiny as pin heads. After a moment, the spider winked at him.

He winked back.

'Hold on,' he whispered. Then he unhooked the mat, climbed carefully on to the slide, closed his eyes and let himself go.

CHAPTER FORTY-FIVE

Olly is on His Own

The helter-skelter at Full Moon Fair had been very fast so Olly was surprised because he felt himself sliding down quite slowly. He opened his eyes and discovered that it was not pitch-black, as it had looked to him when he had peered down. He could see a little, as if there were a dim light bulb somewhere above him. At first, though, there was nothing to see. There were the usual stone walls but these did not have ledges or niches like the other tunnels and passages, nor were there any eyes gleaming out of them. But sliding slowly round and round and down and down was quite pleasant and it was not cold. It seemed to go on for miles and miles and after a time Olly felt sleepy. But just as he was closing his eyes, he felt the slide give a final sharp few twists, down which he went very fast indeed, to land on something firm but not hard enough to give him an uncomfortable landing. He sat for a moment, getting his bearings. Although the light was still dim, it was enough for him to see that his right hand had come to rest beside a thin line of scarlet thread.

He looked around him. It was a small cave-like space

but it had nothing in it at all. He shone the torch slowly up and down and all round until he saw a tunnel leading away. Just one tunnel. The scarlet thread was running along the ground and disappearing into it, so he was pretty sure that he should follow. But he sat for a while without going anywhere. It was very quiet and he was entirely alone. The money spider seemed to have vanished as he came down the slide. There were no tortoises or bats, let alone people. But neither were there any stones. He looked on the ground, shining the torch close to the walls of the cave, but he decided that if any stone was there it was too small to be seen.

This was the first time he had set off alone in the night like this, uncertain of his destination, not knowing what he might come upon on the way and he was scared – but not so scared that he wanted to go back. He looked at the slide. If he did want to go back, it would be pretty difficult. How did you climb back up a slippery helter-skelter?

It seemed to Olly that this was some sort of test. If he got there, if he found Nonny Dreever, if, if, if . . .

He stood up, brushed the dirt off the knees of his jeans, beamed the torch ahead of him and set off into the tunnel.

It wound a little and then went straight on, curved and bent and went straight on again and the scarlet thread went with it all the way, running along the ground close to the wall. There was nothing else. It was a very long and boring walk but Olly plodded along, no longer feeling worried or scared, but on the contrary becoming rather peaceful. He found that he didn't mind his own company and the uneventful nature of the walk meant that he could think a lot of thoughts without being interrupted.

The tunnel went on. And on. And on. Olly thought he had walked a hundred miles.

And then it stopped. He came up against a wall. A stone wall. It appeared to have no door in it, no window, nothing. The scarlet thread stopped too, at the foot of the wall. And that seemed to be that.

But it was not.

There was a very small hole close to the wall and, as he looked, it began to increase in size as the tortoises on the other side of the wall dug and dug. Olly waited and watched as the hole grew. At one point he tried to help by scrabbling at the ground but all he got was dirt in his nails and a sore finger. The tortoises' sharp sets of claws were far more efficient.

He knew now that all he had to do was wait until the hole was big enough for him to get through. When he had, he would discover where the scarlet thread had led him.

There was not long to wait. The tortoises worked steadily and before long he was clambering through the hole. He had expected to be either somewhere in or beneath Nonny Dreever's house. Instead, as soon as he was beyond the hole, he felt mild air on his face and realised that he was outside, standing on a hill with a copse of tall trees at his back.

'You're here.'

'You did it, Olly. You did it on your own.'

Zed, Xylo and KK came out of the soft summer darkness, smiling, with Jinx running beside them.

'You found the scarlet thread.'

'What's happening?' Olly asked anxiously. 'Where's Nonny Dreever? And where are we?'

'You've come up on the far side of the mere, that's why you don't recognise it. But the stone army can't get to this side, their powers start to fade because of the scarlet thread. It's the only way we have a chance of getting to Nonny's house.'

'Does the thread stop now then?'

'No, we'll pick it up over there. But we don't need it now,' said KK. 'We can find our own way. It's good to know we can keep close to it though. Come on.'

Olly was glad to be with them and, to his surprise, it was quite a short time before he thought he recognised where they were. A few minutes later, the back of Nonny Dreever's house was just ahead of them.

It was very quiet apart from the occasional slight rustle of the leaves as the night breeze riffled through. There were thin clouds floating in front of the moon and little patches of starry sky in between.

Nonny Dreever's house was in darkness.

'We'll creep up. Olly, look in the left window. Zed and Xylo, go round the back. I'll look into the kitchen window at the side. But be quiet and be very very careful. If anything happens, whistle.' She slipped off into the darkness, with Jinx after her, and Zed and Xylo went round the back. Olly edged his way along until he got to the steps, then climbed them carefully, keeping himself close to the rail and stopping on every step to listen. But there was no sound at all. Even the breeze seemed to have died down now.

He reached the top. Waited. Then he crouched down and moved until he was right under the left-hand window. But as he was about to stand upright and peer in he heard a low whistle from behind the house. He froze. It came again.

The next minute, Zed and Xylo were beside him, pushing him down.

'Someone's there. I can't see but I heard something move.'

'What sort of move?'

'Shhh.'

Olly could feel Zed breathing in his ear and his own heart bumping. An owl hooted in the trees behind them.

They waited a long time but there was no further sound, no light, and KK eventually appeared out of the darkness below them and waved her arms to show she had found nothing.

'I think we should go in,' Olly said.

'Too dangerous.'

'Well, there isn't much point in standing out here all night. There are five of us and you've got your tortoise – haven't you?'

He glanced round. Zed's face was panic-stricken.

'Oh no! Ze-ed.'

'Never mind, we've got the scarlet thread.'

'Fat lot of use that'll be.'

'How do you know?'

'Look, shut up. You're hopeless, Zed, this is twice you've forgotten it or lost it. I'm going inside and I'll whistle if I need to. You stay there,' KK said.

But as she was about to start inching her way to the door there was a noise below them. A moment later, KK was shining her torch into the undergrowth.

'Right, come out here where we can see you. Now!'

There was a pause. They all looked at the patch of light. And after a moment, a figure emerged, blinking in the direct beam.

'Mervyn Crust!' Olly said.

Quick as a flash, KK had leaped forward, grabbed Mervyn Crust and pulled him towards the others. He stared round them all, trying to look bold and defiant.

'I suppose,' Olly said wearily, 'that you followed me.'

'So what if I did? I knew where you were going anyway.'

'Yeah, right.'

('Mervyn Crust is a low-grade spy,' Olly remembered. 'But he isn't a bad boy.')

'What are you doing anyway?'

'Mind your own business,' KK said. 'Zed, tie him to the bottom of the steps here.'

'You're not tying me up. Why do you want to tie me up? I haven't done anything, I don't have to be tied up.'

'We can't trust you,' KK said.

Zed took off his belt and hitched it on to Mervyn and round the wooden rail.

'And if you try to get away we'll hear you and if you do get away you'll be on your own and it is very very dark.'

They left Mervyn Crust looking red and angry but not struggling, and went back up the steps. Olly looked down. He didn't think Mervyn was going anywhere.

'Right,' KK said, 'we'll go in a little way. Then I'll shine the torch.'

She put her hand on the knob and turned it very quietly and then eased open the door. There was no sound from inside. Once she had the door open enough, she switched on the torch again and shone it into the room.

There was no one there. The small red lamp which was always lit and glimmering in one corner of the kitchen end was dark. The torch beam moved over the furniture, the models, the toys and dolls and small carvings, the musical boxes, the model theatre, the glass snow storms, the chunks of pink and blue and green crystals, the pictures, the little Gypsy caravan . . . It slipped down, to the table and chairs, the stove, the crockery on the shelves, the drawers, the floor. Then KK moved it up again to the armchair.

Nonny must have been there. His slippers were on the mat in front of the chair and his glasses on the table beside it.

KK reached out her hand and switched on the light.

'Look,' Zed said at once and went quickly to the chair and bent down. On the floor was a scattering of very small stones.

And then, coming through the front door which they had left ajar, they heard it. Steady. Slow. A little distance away.

'Drumming,' Olly said. 'It's the drumming.'

They went outside and stood on the top of the steps and then they could hear it more clearly.

Drrrmm drrmmm drrm . . . Drrrmm drrmmm drrm.

'Look over there,' KK said and pointed to the west, over the tops of the trees.

'What? I can't see anything.'

'I can,' Olly said. 'Like a fire. Something orangey red and glowing in the sky.'

'It's coming from over there,' KK repeated.

'Withern Mere,' Xylo said quietly. 'Whatever it is, it's happening there.'

They left Nonny Dreever's house and KK led them ahead, along the track that skirted the wood, down the slope, across the field, and up the steep hill that had the crown of trees on top. The glow had deepened to a dull red and spread higher into the sky.

The night was clearer now and the stars had brightened to sharp, dazzling points. There was a moon but there were still a few ribbons of wispy cloud floating in front of it to dull the light.

They had to walk in single file and Olly was at the back, Jinx following behind. They had been going for some way along the track when he stumbled slightly and as he recovered himself, glanced round.

'Wait,' he said. 'KK, look.'

Behind them, in a line that stretched back for a long

way, came the tortoises, their small eyes gleaming topaz and lighting the path as they went along.

Olly and the others stopped. The tortoises stopped.

'They're following us!'

'I don't think they're here because of us,' Zed said. 'I think they're going somewhere and they just happened to be behind us.'

'What, you mean we're all going the same way?'

'We'll soon find out.'

Something had been at the back of Olly's mind all the time. He had felt it nudging and niggling since they'd left Nonny Dreever's house, but every time he tried to bring it to the front of his mind where he could see it properly, it slithered out of his grasp.

Now he said, 'Oh help!' as it was there, staring at him, like a sign written in huge letters.

'What?'

'*Mervyn Crust!*'

CHAPTER FORTY-SIX

The End of the Battle

Mervyn Crust had escaped and there was nothing they could do about him now. KK didn't speak to her brother for some way but Olly knew Mervyn would have had help to get away and they had more important things to worry about. The tortoises were still following them steadily and the red glow in the sky was growing stronger as they climbed to the top of the last hill.

Olly was tired and dispirited and the sound of the drums getting louder and louder made his stomach churn round. He began to wish that things would settle down to normal, that Gullywith would become an ordinary house and Fiddleup a town without strange bookshops. He wished he could sleep without wondering how many night-time adventures he was going to go through and that KK and Zed would be ordinary, dull friends. He had had enough of climbing through holes and up steps and trudging through narrow tunnels and warrens of passageways and emerging in strange places, being pursued by tortoises and bats, however friendly and well-meaning, and finding stones with strange markings hidden around his house or inside his shoes. Some of it, like the Midwinter Revel, had been wonderful, some of it, like being shut in the chamber in Withern Castle, had been frightening, all of it had been weird or fantastic or magical. But in total it made his head buzz. He had almost forgotten what it was like to be calm and quiet and do normal things, like go on holiday to Spain or play with his *Star Trek* model or read about polar exploration or watch DVDs of the *Teletubbies* with Lula.

All of which was nagging away at him as he followed KK, Xylo and Zed the last few metres of the steep hill and came out slightly breathless, at the top. Jinx ran alongside.

'Oh!'

The scene below them was the most extraordinary Olly had ever seen and as he looked he knew that it was printing itself on his memory so deeply that it would come into his dreams as the ice caves of the Midwinter Revel had already done.

The flood waters had drained away. They stood together in a row above the great space formed by the mere and its surrounds and by the hills close behind it which turned it into a huge bowl like a theatre.

Flares lit the scene, flares which were scarlet and poppy red, and which had made the sky glow from so far away. They glowed like coals, reflected in the mere, and lit the castle in a weird, flaming light that ran up the walls. The castle itself was lit from within too. The slits and the arches shone gold and the gold rayed out to mingle with the red from the flares.

The drawbridge was down and extended right from

the castle across the mere to the land. Drawn up in front of it and lining the bridge itself, the stone army stood to attention, wearing helmets with black and white plumes which streamed behind them in the night breeze. More soldiers were three deep on the path round the water.

The tortoises were now descending the hill and taking their places behind the stone army in an orderly manner, their glowing eyes adding to the rich light in which everything was bathed.

The drummers were within the castle and on the ramparts, heard but unseen.

Then, as Olly, Zed, Xylo and KK watched, half a dozen trumpeters and buglers appeared on the ramparts and lifted their golden instruments. Only then did the drums cease. There was a moment of absolute, expectant silence. KK grabbed at Olly's hand and clutched it.

And then the trumpets sounded out with a strong, piercing, golden fanfare that rang across the mere towards them.

'Look, oh look!' KK whispered.

The whirlpool had begun to form in the mere, swirling round and round, faster and faster, deepening and widening, and from its heart the stone locks and then the head and shoulders, the spear and the robes and the outstretched hand of the Stone King emerged, rising up until he was standing huge and magnificent in the light of the flares. The trumpets flourished and stopped. The drums rolled a single long and mighty roll. The Stone King stepped on to the drawbridge and lifted his arm. And then, slowly down the slope of the opposite hill, preceded by a double file of the largest tortoises with the most brilliant eyes, came a figure, dressed in a plain long black cloak. He walked steadily, purposefully, boldly down nearer and nearer to the castle and the mere until he reached the end of the drawbridge. At that point, he looked round and up directly to the high point on which Olly, Zed, Xylo and KK were standing and then he raised his hand.

'Nonny. It's Nonny Dreever.'

'What's happening? What is he going to do?'

'And look – look behind him . . . carrying something.'

A small, white-faced boy was walking flanked by the tortoise guard and had now stopped immediately behind Nonny Dreever. He was carrying what looked like a thin cushion and on the cushion was a huge leather-bound book.

'So he didn't escape, he was taken,' KK said, as they watched Mervyn Crust, shaking a little under the weight of the book, standing dumbly, waiting.

'He seems to have changed sides,' Zed said with a smile.

There was a tremendous drum roll, which grew so loud the ground seemed to shake beneath their feet and then Nonny Dreever began to walk slowly towards the Stone King, followed by a worried-looking Mervyn Crust still carrying the book.

'Like a pageboy,' KK said.

Zed snorted.

'He should have white satin trousers.'

'Shh. But what's Nonny doing? He can't just . . .'

'Looks as if he is though.'

Nonny Dreever had taken the Great Book and, holding it in both hands, he held it out towards the Stone King. The drums were silent again. Everyone seemed to have frozen where they stood, the stone army, the tortoises, the buglers and drummers. The whirlpool had disappeared and the whole mere was like glass, reflecting the light, which shimmered faintly, the only thing that was moving.

There was a long moment. Olly wondered what would happen if Nonny Dreever dropped the Great Book. Or if the Stone King snatched it. Or if . . .

But none of those things happened. Nonny Dreever stood, holding the Great Book, and the Stone King took a step or two towards him, paused, and then bowed his head and held out his own hands. Nonny Dreever handed the book to him, laying it down carefully. They stood together in silence, looking down at the book.

What happened next made Olly jump so hard he thought he had actually lifted up off the ground and he felt the others do the same. Jinx gave a small yelp.

There was the most tremendous volley of gun salute from the castle and, at the same time, a roll on the drums and a fanfare which blew out across the night sky before reverberating back to earth.

A split second later, fireworks burst upwards, rockets shooting heavenwards trailing gold and silver stars, great cascades of scarlet and emerald and brilliant blue, pink and purple showers and a comet with a long, fiery dragon's tail. They stared up and watched and the fire-works went on and on, coming from the castle and even apparently from the depths of the mere itself.

It was a long time before the last one died down but as it did so, Olly saw that the Stone King and Nonny Dreever had moved away from the drawbridge and gone to sit at the water's edge on two identical thrones. The stone army and the tortoises formed up around them.

'Let's go down,' KK said.

'No, something else is going to happen and we can see better from here.'

Zed was right. Olly sat down on the grass. From up here, they were looking down on the whole scene, the illuminated castle, the mere, the armies, the lights and now, the beginning of what might be called a pageant, a tournament or a play. Whatever it was, he had seen nothing like it and, as they watched, knew that he almost certainly never would again. Things like this surely did not happen more than once to anybody.

The whole area exploded with sound and light and colour. Tumblers, jugglers, fire-eaters, dancers, acrobats, stilt-walkers poured out of the castle, the forest, the darkness, as lights played around the hills. Curtains of scarlet and shimmering gold and silver descended and rose again, flares changed colour. Fireflies flitted above their heads and, suddenly, sprites and goblins were sprinting and leaping out of the air and down to Olly, Zed, Xylo and KK, taking them by the hand and racing with them down into the arena. Before they knew what was happening, they were part of the throng of colour and music, dancing, leaping higher than they knew they could, leaping as high as the castle and down again as if their feet were on springs. They were twirled in the air by acrobats, fizzing coloured balls were juggled round their heads, and they were whirled off their feet and chased by tiny creatures dressed in strange, fiery costumes, stars swirling round their bodies as they moved. The whole drawbridge and the ground stretching out in front of the mere was filled with people dancing as their costumes of all colours flew out around them and wove together in patterns, flickering with light.

Olly found himself being spun round by a couple of sprites in vivid green, then dancing up and down a line of stone soldiers clapping in time to the sound of the drums. Zed was walking on stilts high above their heads, KK was twirling on a high wire stretched across between the trees, holding a parasol in rainbow colours.

And in the midst of it all, Nonny Dreever stood holding out his arms as the red and golden light played over him, so that now his face was on fire, now as bright as the eyes of the tortoises that gleamed from every side.

As he was whirled by in a frantic dance, Olly detached himself and stopped, flushed and out of breath. KK and Zed were there too, beside Nonny Dreever, who seemed to have grown taller so that he looked down on them from a commanding height.

'What happened?' KK asked breathlessly. 'We went to the house but you'd gone. We thought you'd been taken prisoner.'

Nonny Dreever laughed a great roaring laugh. 'What

makes you think they could ever do that?'

'You said your powers were weakening, you seemed so worried about what they might do.'

'I was worried. But then it came to me in a flash. Literally. It lit up my room. They had been trying to take the Great Book because they believe it belongs to them. Well, perhaps it does, perhaps it does not, but I have no use for it now.'

'But if they use it to do harm . . .'

'That is the risk. As a matter of fact, I doubt that they will. They want to own it, to put it in a great glass case in the room in the castle they have set aside for a thousand years. They want to gloat over it. They want to set a guard on it night and day. The Stone King has never felt safe so long as it was elsewhere. He has never felt powerful enough. So, I decided enough was enough. Enough of all the trouble it has caused. Enough of battles and quarrels and plots and fury. I decided I would hand it over. And as you saw just now, that is what I have done.'

'Will they give you anything in exchange? What have they promised? You can't trust them.' KK's eyes flashed in anger.

'I asked for nothing. They have promised nothing. And we have to trust them.'

KK snorted.

'Yes,' Nonny Dreever said. He turned to Olly. 'But I have something for you, Oliver Mackenzie Brown.' He reached into the folds of his shining black cloak and then held out his hand.

'Take it.'

It was a stone, a small, grey stone. Olly turned it over and over. On one side it was smooth. On the other, it had a single scratched marking. It was like so many others he had seen but those had had more than one mark. Otherwise, it was just another stone.

'You must take this back to Gullywith,' Nonny Dreever said. 'It belongs there. Not only that – it was the first stone ever to be found there, the first stone that marked the building of the house. Put it back in its place. That is all you need to do.'

'For what?'

'For the battle to be over.'

'You mean we've won?'

'I didn't say that. I said the battle for Gullywith would be over. Gullywith is yours and it will remain yours.'

'Are you sure?' Olly was remembering everything that had happened – the holes in the skirting boards and the collapsing barn, the leaks in the roof, the water-filled cellar . . .

'Take it home. Put it back in place. Wait and see.'

'Where is the place?'

'That you must find for yourself. Now, enjoy the revels. But when the last fanfare sounds and the waters close, be ready.'

Olly put the stone in the bottom of his pocket, and when he looked up, Nonny Dreever had gone.

'What did he mean?' he asked, turning to KK, but she had gone too, and was running towards the edge of the mere with Zed.

The person at Olly's side said, 'I suppose we'd better

do as he says or anything might happen.' It was Mervyn Crust. He looked so miserable and pathetic that Olly felt sorry for him. He had been used as nothing better than a messenger and a lookout by the stone army, then he had been taken over and turned into a page-boy carrying a cushion. He had had no revels and now he did not seem to know how to join in the fun at all.

Olly gave him a shove. 'Race you to the water's edge.'

Mervyn Crust looked puzzled.

'Well, come on . . . I want to join in before it all stops and we have to go back. Come *on*.'

For a split second, Mervyn still stood looking doubtful but then, as Olly set off, so did he, racing down the slope very fast and almost beating him to it, as he plunged into the crowd of revellers.

They had the most wonderful hour, dancing, leaping, enjoying the sweets and fizzing drinks that tasted of honey and raspberry and the silver foam that came in tall cones and exploded into a wonderful mixture of sweetness and sourness on their tongues. There were hot chocolate muffins dipped in white chocolate, ice cream, and bacon and egg and sausage pancakes cooked on griddles next to the chestnut-roasters and the blue and green and gold and pink candyfloss sticks.

Fireworks went up into the night sky every now and again and the flares from the castle changed colour, sending waves of purple and shimmering pink over the throng. There were musicians everywhere and strolling players, masked dancers and clowns. The tortoises danced reels, the bats performed a flying ballet, swooping down from the castle ramparts, the stones tap-danced up and down the drawbridge. It grew noisier and busier and more and more hectic. From time to time, Olly and Mervyn bumped into KK, Xylo and Zed and they all changed partners. KK jived with a stone soldier. Xylo flew on a bat's back to the highest castle turret and shot down again, laughing in delight, and as they landed, disappeared for a moment in a huge puff of silver smoke that exploded round him before it rose floating away into the darkness.

'Oh, don't let it stop,' Olly shouted to KK as they passed, and he felt the stone in his pocket to be sure he had not dropped it. Once he would have worried about it being stolen. Now, he thought, nothing like that could happen. The battle was over.

He paused for breath and to look round him, choosing what to do and where to go next, but as he did so, the music, which had been coming from all around, tunes and instruments mixing up with others in one great happy muddle, began to sort itself out and to become quieter. One by one, the musicians stopped playing – first the bands, then the fiddles and the drums, the accordions and the flutes and the guitars and the pipes fell silent. It took a little while. But as everything became quiet, so everyone became still. The dancers stopped dancing, the jigs ceased, no one swung anyone else round and round. It was as if the whole world had been spinning and now it was slowing down.

The fireworks no longer exploded into the air and

above them the sky was dark and pricked with stars and the moon shone out, at last unobscured by the faintest wisp of cloud.

The lights stopped changing colour and now the whole area was bathed in soft silver which darkened at the edges to dull gold.

Everyone waited. Everyone watched.

There was the most enormous, waiting, watching silence.

Then the Stone King separated himself from the crowd and began to walk towards the drawbridge, and behind him the stone soldiers formed up to follow him, two by two. Nonny Dreever was there waiting and, as the Stone King reached him, he bowed deeply. The Stone King inclined his head.

Then Nonny Dreever moved slowly away. The drawbridge started to rise, hauled on its chains, until it was completely closed.

As it did so, there was a magnificent fanfare from the buglers on the ramparts and a single great roll of drums. The lights which had been brilliant began to fade little by little.

Olly held his breath. Everyone stood absolutely still and silent.

And then the castle began to sink down, down into the waters of Withern Mere as they watched. It sank steadily and the dark waters rose around it and after a few moments, only the turrets were visible, with the flares blazing out from them and a single trumpeter sounding a faint, melancholy note.

And then it was gone. The waters closed, fell back and were still and the last silver brightness faded away, leaving nothing but the cool, pale moonlight and darkness all around.

Olly shivered, not with cold but with a strange sort of sadness. Beside him, KK, Xylo and Zed and Mervyn Crust stood quietly. Everyone else had faded away. Who they had been, where they had come from, where they went, none of them knew.

'It's over,' Olly said.

'Yes. We have to go.'

Olly waited for Mervyn Crust to wail 'I want to go home. How are we going to get back to Gullywith?'.

But he didn't. He just shrugged. 'Come on,' he said to Olly. 'It's quite a long way.'

CHAPTER FORTY-SEVEN

Home

They trudged home quietly together in the silky night and the moon sailed just ahead of them to light their path. Olly felt strange – tired, sad, and confused by turns. He hoped that it had all been true, that the stones would leave Gullywith now, and that his own family could settle down in it at last without any more disasters. He hoped that he could find the right place to set the stone that was in his pocket.

But he wondered if he would ever see Nonny Dreever again, if KK and Zed would come to school like anybody else, if, if, if . . .

He was afraid that the magical happenings were over as well as the battle and he didn't want them to be. Life had to settle down but he didn't want it to settle into a boring rut. There ought to be some surprises.

Mervyn Crust walked steadily along beside him. That was strange too. Mervyn Crust seemed to have changed overnight – or maybe he, Olly, had changed. At any rate, Mervyn no longer seemed so tiresome and Olly was quite glad of his company as they wended their long way home, up the steep hill and down the other side and then on to the track.

When they neared the last gate, leading to the Gullywith field, Olly glanced round as he climbed over it. Behind them was a small trail of light, moving steadily. He waited. Seven tortoises had followed them and were clearly going with them all the way home, their eyes gleaming. Olly smiled.

The house was in darkness and everyone was sleeping as usual. They crept in and up the stairs.

'You've got to find where the stone goes,' Mervyn Crust whispered.

'I can't do it now. It could be anywhere.'

'It won't be far. Look out of your window.'

Olly glanced at him. 'Why?'

'Just do it.'

Mervyn seemed strangely sure.

'OK.'

Olly took the stone from his pocket and held it in the palm of his hand. It was quite small and there might be a space for it anywhere but he went to his bedroom window, opened it and looked out.

The moonlight was shining on the stone ledge just below and on a very small gap in the silvery-grey stones.

'It fits exactly,' he said. 'You wouldn't know there'd been a gap, look.'

'I know,' Mervyn Crust said, yawning. 'Told you. I'm going to bed . . .'

'Night, then.'

'Night.'

The door closed softly. Olly stayed for a while, leaning

out of the window, looking at the fields and the hill beyond in the moonlight. Down below, he saw that the tortoises had gathered and their topaz eyes formed a little gleaming cluster but, as he watched, they dimmed and flickered and one by one went out as the tortoises went to sleep.

Olly felt a great drowsiness come over him. He got into his pyjamas and sank down into his deep mattress, pulling the duvet over his head. He was too tired to worry, too tired to think or wonder, too tired to do anything.

He slept and the rosy lights from the flares and the gleams of topaz played gently around his dreams and he heard from far away the faint sound of the bugles from the castle deep, deep under the waters of Withern Mere.

Afterwards

The last weeks of the holidays were good. The sun shone almost every day and the fields and yard dried out, the water in the cellar went down and down, and one morning the Polish builders simply reappeared and set to work. The barn roof was mended, the walls rebuilt, and then they turned their attention to the house, putting in a damp course, repointing, replastering and decorating. Pete Brown's new computer room and Helen Brown's studio were completely ready and up and running, putting permanent smiles on their faces. The small attic room no longer had cold places and the builders got rid of the fungus, the holes and the damp patches, and painted the walls sunshine yellow.

The windows and doors were all left open to the sun and summer warmth. Gullywith was flooded with light. And the small stone on Olly's windowledge stayed firmly in place.

On a bright September morning, Olly was arriving for his first day at Fiddleup School. The entrance was teeming with pupils wearing the scarlet sweatshirts, grey trousers and skirts, and purple and scarlet ties of the school uniform, carrying bags and satchels and sports kit and making a noise Olly thought he would never get used to. His London school had been small. This one seemed vast and he was certain he would never find his way around.

But the first person he saw was Mervyn Crust, who gave him a thumbs up.

'It's OK,' he said. 'It's always like this but when the bell goes it'll be quieter. Stay with me and you'll be fine.'

Sure enough, when an electric bell drilled out loudly, everyone stopped talking and began to move into the building, filing off to left and right. As he was following Mervyn to the left, Olly felt a nudge in his back.

'Hey.'

KK was immediately behind him, grinning away, and Zed over to her right, going in the other direction with a couple of friends. Xylo was a few metres away.

KK looked like any of the others, Olly thought, with a neat new sweatshirt and white collar, grey skirt, leather bag and hockey stick. She had her hair tied back neatly with a red band and slides. It was hard to believe that . . . no, not hard, it was impossible. Pictures flashed through Olly's mind, of KK on the torboat, whooshing across the water, KK climbing up the iron ladder in the dark, KK swirling in the dance on the ice at the Midwinter Revel. KK.

'See you,' she said.

But as she turned her head, Olly saw something bright. He looked. Nothing. Looked again. The slides in her hair had tiny tortoises on the clip and as he looked two tiny golden eyes winked brightly before KK turned away.